REMATCH

STINGRAYS HOCKEY
BOOK 3

MARI CARR

REMATCH

One night, one kiss, and a spark hot enough to melt the ice.

Preston's all in on his hockey career as a Stingray, and Chelsea's just about to start a new adventure in Paris—until an unforgettable night at an Ugly Christmas Sweater party changes everything. A few drinks, some dirty jokes, and a kiss under the mistletoe leads to a night of toe-curling, name-forgetting, no-strings-attached fun.

They part ways in the morning, no regrets—just a sizzling memory they both assume will fade.

A year later, Chelsea's in Baltimore, launching her dream bakery—and navigating life with a baby she never saw coming. The father? Mystery man from that one unforgettable night. What she really didn't expect? Him walking through her door, very real, very sexy… and very much still capable of making her forget how to breathe.

Preston hasn't been able to get her out of his head. Now that he knows the truth, he's not going anywhere. The question is—can they turn one accidental night into a real shot at forever?

AUTHOR'S NOTE

Rematch was originally published a couple of years ago as a short story, Fun and Flirty, in a limited-run hockey anthology. The story has been greatly revised and expanded.

It's been revised so much it's probably more accurate to say I scrapped the short story for parts because man…this story is completely different!

CHAPTER ONE

"THIS IS MADNESS. How many tickets did they sell to this party?"

Allyson laughed, then yelled over the throng. "Hell if I know! Ours were free, so who gives a shit."

Chelsea Murphy rolled her eyes but didn't have time to respond because the music changed to a popular line dance, and a mass of people cheered at the same time they rushed to claim a spot on the makeshift dance floor—aka, a massive dining room that had literally been stripped of all furniture.

Allyson was at the head of the crowd, jockeying for position. Chelsea considered joining her, then decided to sit—stand—this one out. She'd only just returned to the social scene as a single lady six months ago, when she'd had the rug pulled out from under her, her future completely and cruelly rewritten in a few horrible minutes.

Six. Months.

She couldn't quite believe how half a year could simultaneously feel like an eternity and the blink of an eye.

Chelsea fought her way through the crowd standing just

outside the dining room, watching the crazy dancers shake their asses in unison, so that she could seek a quieter—ha ha—spot.

"Nice sweater." A guy wiggled his eyebrows at her suggestively.

Chelsea laughed but kept walking, cursing Allyson for goading her into making matching sweaters. One of Chelsea's two besties in the whole world, Allyson had spent the better part of yesterday poring over Ugly Christmas sweater sites before landing on this design, proclaiming they'd win the contest for sure. Then she had dragged Chelsea to Walmart for all the supplies, and they'd spent nearly three hours last night armed with a glue gun—and two bottles of wine—creating these so-called masterpieces.

It spoke to how distracted Chelsea had been of late that she'd gone along with the design without thinking it through all the way to the end, because their sweaters had oversized mittens covering their breasts, the words "Feel the Joy" emblazoned in green and red underneath. They had even added tinsel around the neck and wrists to "festive" it up.

Chelsea, with the help of the wine, found the concept funny, but within five minutes of arriving here, she realized she'd basically plastered a "grope me" billboard on her chest. Not that anyone had gone that far yet, but the night was still young, the keg far from floating.

Luckily, she had a T-shirt on beneath the sweater, so at some point, she'd simply proclaim herself too hot and rip the thing off before too many drunk guys accepted her stupid, unwitting offer.

God.

How the hell had she wound up in Philadelphia a week before Christmas?

Well...she knew how. She just couldn't believe she'd agreed to the impulsive road trip, because she had way too much other shit to do.

Some friend of a friend of Allyson's had purchased tickets, planning to attend this Ugly Christmas Sweater party with her boyfriend, because she'd heard the inn where it was being held was haunted. Then, said friend of a friend got whisked away for a surprise holiday vacation by her boyfriend—now fiancé—and started looking for someone who might want to use the two tickets.

Allyson wound up somewhere down the line on that phone chain and, of course, despite the fact it was a two-hour drive from Baltimore to Philadelphia, and it meant they'd be sleeping on a blow-up mattress in the tiny living room of Allyson's cousin's apartment, her bestie had snatched them right up, proclaiming this was one of their last chances to party before Chelsea's big move to Paris.

In. A. Week.

Which was why she *really* shouldn't be here.

However, Allyson was a professional when it came to living life to the fullest while not spending a dime. Somehow, her best friend always came into free shit. If the radio was holding a contest, nine times out of ten, Allyson was the lucky caller. It was how the two of them—plus their other bestie, Ethan—had scored tickets to no less than five rock concerts, two murder mystery dinner theaters, and even a midnight dance cruise around the Inner Harbor.

Tonight was no different. The second Allyson heard "two free tickets," she'd decided this was going to be their last hurrah. And while Chelsea would miss her friends dearly, she was not going to miss all the nightclubs, bars, and parties Ethan and Allyson had dragged her to over the past six months, in an attempt to help mend her broken heart.

Finding a quieter corner, Chelsea took a sip of her Chardonnay, considering how different this holiday was going to be from the one prior.

Last year, she'd spent Christmas with her fiancé, Rick, the

two of them celebrating with their families. They were fortunate to both be from Baltimore, so they didn't have to add hours of travel to the already hectic season. There was also the added benefit of Rick's mother and hers being best friends since high school. It meant their families' holiday festivities had been combined...for most of Chelsea's life.

Their mothers—who'd been more excited about the upcoming nuptials than the bride and groom—had spent most of the last holiday season planning their June wedding, conversations consumed with flowers, color schemes, caterers' menus, and decorations. It had been thrilling and slightly overwhelming, and Chelsea had loved every second of it.

The day of the wedding had been absolutely perfect—bright blue sky, seventy degrees, warm breeze, not a single cloud to give even the tiniest threat that a drop of rain might fall. She'd spent the morning getting her hair and makeup done, donning her white wedding dress, then trying not to cry, as her mom, Allyson, and Ethan helped her put on her veil, all of them moved by the moment and the special time together.

When her dad knocked on the door, she'd been so ready to walk down that aisle with him.

However, the second he'd stepped into the room, Chelsea knew something was wrong. She wasn't sure how or why—because she certainly hadn't suspected or had the slightest feeling something was amiss—but when Dad looked at her, she'd blurted, "Rick's not here."

Dad had held out his arms, and she'd fallen into them, trying hard not to cry because she didn't want to ruin her makeup, still hopeful the asshole would show.

He hadn't. Worse than that, he hadn't even called or sent her a note or...anything.

Nope.

Instead, he'd sent his best man a text.

Tell her I'm sorry. I can't do it.

He didn't offer an explanation.

She'd tried to call him but was sent immediately to voicemail. Her texts went unread, as did the best man's and Rick's parents'. Minutes ticked by, and after two long hours passed, she had to accept he truly wasn't coming.

That was when she'd let the tears fall. She'd stripped off the dress and returned to the apartment she and Rick shared, only to discover he'd packed all his shit and moved out.

That was where she'd found the note.

He'd met someone at work, and while he hadn't physically cheated on her, he'd begun an emotional affair with this other woman. Then he went on to say he would always love her, but— and this was the part that had truly shattered her—for the first time in his life, he understood what it meant to truly be *in* love with someone else.

He'd managed to successfully ghost her for months. Which was no small feat, considering how tight their families were. He'd blocked her on his phone and on social media, and, while their mothers both remained hopeful that he would "come around," he knew her schedule well enough to avoid her. He'd been too busy to attend their families' Fourth of July and Labor Day picnics, and he'd been out of town on business over Thanksgiving.

Suuuuure, he had.

Chelsea had wanted to confront him, go to his office and force him to face her, but Allyson and Ethan had been managing her pride at the time. They barred the door whenever she had a serious moment of weakness, assuring her that her "confrontation" would devolve from anger to tears to begging on her part, and Rick wasn't worth it.

She hated that they were right, but they were. For too many

months after that almost wedding, she'd hoped he would come back to her.

She'd discovered from her mom—via *his* mom—that the new woman was another lawyer in the firm where Rick worked. She'd been transferred from their New York office to Baltimore at the beginning of the year. So while Chelsea had been planning what she'd thought was their dream wedding, he'd been falling in love with someone else.

Then, two months ago, she ran into them on the street. Like, *literally*. No doubt if Rick had seen her, he would have crossed the street to avoid her. Instead, he'd nearly plowed right into her, his eyes plastered on the tall, willowy, not-a-hair-out-of-place, power-suited woman he was holding hands with.

Meanwhile, Chelsea had been wearing yoga pants and an "Every Thelma needs a Louise" T-shirt, with her hair pulled up haphazardly in a messy top bun, looking just as short and fluffy —she really needed to lay off the sweets—as ever.

When he saw Chelsea, Rick offered the most awkward introduction in the history of introductions. Especially when he looked at Vanessa—of course, her fucking name was Vaaaanesssa—and said, "This is Chelsea."

Vanessa's eyes widened in surprise before quickly morphing into something much worse.

Pity.

Rick attempted approximately twenty-two seconds of strained conversation that consisted of, "Well, it was great to see you again. Hope you're doing okay. Say hello to your parents for me."

They'd walked away, and that was when Chelsea realized she hadn't said one damn word, her throat completely closed during the interaction.

It was another five minutes before all those things she wished she'd said started firing off like rockets in her brain.

After that, she'd stopped at the convenience store on the

corner, bought two bottles of wine, then spent the rest of the night getting shit-faced drunk with Ethan and Allyson, the three of them reimagining the run-in a hundred different ways, most ending with Chelsea either karate-slamming two-timing Rick to the sidewalk or throat-punching runway-worthy Vanessa before completely wrecking that perfect blonde updo of hers.

Since then, she'd been saying "good riddance" to the asshole, trying to believe she was well and truly over him.

And for the most part, she was.

Probably.

Sort of.

Chelsea had been asked out a few times, but none of those dates had led to a second. Her ability to trust was in the gutter, and her heart simply wasn't into giving romance another try.

She took a sip of wine and pushed the negative thoughts away.

They served nothing.

Ethan and Allyson had been her godsends since June, swooping in and basically taking over her life. They'd convinced Chelsea to move out of the apartment she'd shared with Rick and in with Ethan, who had an extra room. They had consumed gallon after gallon of ice cream with her, drunk enough wine to float a boat, and comforted her as she cried and raged.

Her best friends had done everything right.

Given her time to grieve.

Practiced patience after every backslide.

Dragged her out of the house and back into the social scene—mostly kicking and screaming.

And then last week, the two of them sat her down over salted caramel cold brews at Starbucks and helped her plan the next chapter in her life—Paris—even though they were devastated she was leaving.

Best. Friends. Ever.

Chelsea was starting a new life in a new country, and Ethan

was convinced some hot French guy was going to sweep her off her feet.

While she was bummed Allyson had only scored two tickets, which meant Ethan couldn't come tonight as well—the event had been sold out for months—she did what she'd been doing for months and allowed Allyson to take the wheel, dragging her two hours north on a frigid December night. She'd much rather be sacked out on the sectional in her living room, wrapped up in a fleece blanket, watching Hallmark Christmas movies with Ethan and enjoying his hilarious running commentary about how different the movies would be if both leads were gay men.

Chelsea drained the rest of her wine, then tried to decide if she wanted to fight her way through the crowd to the kitchen for a refill. It felt like a long walk through a shit-ton of people.

But the need to remain alone was overridden by her desire for more alcohol. Only wine was going to get her through this night, because she didn't doubt for a second Allyson would be one of the last men standing. It was her friend's M.O. First to arrive, last to leave. The FOMO ran strong in Allyson.

Chelsea started to make her way across the living room, but she had to stop short when a burly guy, who'd clearly already over-imbibed, stumbled in front of her. It was a back-up-or-get-crushed situation.

"Oof!"

She twisted quickly, intent on apologizing to whoever she'd just bumped into.

"Ouch!" she cried, her scalp stinging. Her head didn't manage to make the full circle, jerking back hard enough to pull a large section of her hair roughly.

"Shit." A strong arm wrapped around her shoulders, holding her still. "Hang on. Don't move. Your hair got wrapped around my Christmas lights."

Chelsea turned her head more slowly this time, then looked up and up and up until she saw—holy fuck—the hottest, largest guy she'd ever met, grinning down at her. His eyes landed on her face for a moment before sliding down to check out her sweater.

That was when his sexy grin got even bigger.

She reached up to unwind her hair from the holiday lights, but too much of it was tangled close enough to her scalp that she was basically plastered to his chest, his sweater tickling her cheek.

The guy tightened his grip on her shoulder, then tugged her hand away with the other. "Let me do that."

She lowered her hand and waited, then narrowed her eyes when he made no move to free her.

"Well?" she asked.

The big, friendly giant with the world's greatest smile gave her a shameless shrug. "I'm thinking."

"This isn't rocket science," she mused. His smile was so infectious, she found herself returning it. "You just unwind the hair from the lights," she added.

"Oh, it's not the process I'm pondering. It's the wisdom of letting the gorgeous girl I just trapped escape too quickly. When you catch a fish, you admire it, maybe even take a picture with it, before you toss it back."

"Are you comparing me to a fish?" Chelsea pretended to be annoyed, though she loved that he'd called her gorgeous. She was a curvy girl, thanks to her love for dessert…and wine. God, she loved wine. No matter how many times she tried to lose weight, she ultimately failed because of macarons, baklava, glazed croissants—sweet Jesus, she adored glazed croissants. As well as Cabernet, Malbec, Shiraz, and…well, the list went on and on.

Once again, she reached up, determined to free herself. And once again, he brushed her hand away.

"Bad analogy." He had an amazing laugh to match that smile. "So, what brings a nice girl like you to a place like this?"

"Seriously? You're going to drop bad pickup lines on me while I'm stuck to your chest?"

The guy used his grip on her shoulder to tug her closer. "Didn't like that one? How about this? What's your sign, baby?"

She sighed, then realized she didn't really mind this close proximity. The BFG smelled good, his cologne not too potent or overpowering, just the faint scent of Armani.

"I'm a Virgo. Um…the lights are sort of hot." The sudden heat she felt probably had fuck-all to do with the Christmas lights wrapped around his chest, but she wasn't going to say that aloud.

"Oh shit." He reached into the pocket of his jeans and turned them off. "Sorry about that. Better?"

Nope.

Not even a little. Which confirmed what she thought.

It wasn't the lights making her hot. It was the man.

True to his word, he began to unwrap her hair, taking care not to pull it as he did so. "Damn, when you get stuck, you get stuck."

Chelsea giggled, aware he probably had his work cut out for him. "I have ridiculously thick, curly hair. I'm also long overdue for a haircut."

"Seems a shame to cut it off, but I've always been a sucker for a pretty woman with long hair. What do you do for a living, Joy?"

"Joy?"

He pointed to her sweater.

Ah. Two could play that game. "Very funny, BFG."

Now it was *his* turn to be confused, until she said, "Big friendly giant. Roald Dahl. It was one of my favorite books when I was younger."

He laughed loudly. "BFG. Hey, I like that. So, seriously, what brings you to the party?" he asked again. "Please tell me you're not here with a guy. My heart couldn't take it."

"You're incorrigible," she said, though his playful flirting amused, and even flattered her.

He continued to free her hair from the lights as they talked. She didn't think that much had gotten wrapped up, which meant he was taking his time, untangling it a strand at a time to keep her close. Not that she was complaining.

"That's not an answer," he murmured, reminding her of his question. "Put me out of my misery."

"I came with my friend, Al…lyson."

He chuckled at her well-placed pause.

"She scored a couple of free tickets from a friend of a friend. How about you? Here with a girlfriend?"

"Oh, sweetheart. You have no idea how much I love the jealous type."

She narrowed her eyes. "I'm not jealous. Just making sure no one is waiting in the wings to kick my ass for…" She waved her hand toward where she was still plastered to his chest.

"I'm here stag, so I'm all yours for the night."

"I wasn't looking for a date. Just freedom." She tried to tug her head loose, though she wasn't exactly hoping he would hurry.

BFG raised his hands, palms up. "If that's true, then I'm going to have to stop here in case you run away the second you're free."

"Keep working," she said, trying to infuse some level of warning in her tone. She failed completely. Since when did she sound so breathy and flirty and feminine?

"Let me buy you a drink and I will."

"It's an open bar," she joked, as he unwrapped another strand. "Wine and beer were included in the ticket price."

He bopped the tip of her nose. "Even better."

She rolled her eyes, but mercifully, he kept unwinding her hair.

"Alright, I think I'm just about…there."

She felt her head give way, free at last. And suddenly, she regretted that he'd let her go so quickly. It had been a long time since she'd been this close to a man, felt someone's arm wrapped around her, holding her.

Well, that wasn't entirely true. Ethan was a big hugger from way back, but given the fact he preferred guys and considered her a sister, he didn't count in the way she needed.

She sighed, overwhelmed by the all-too-familiar loneliness she'd struggled with since being left at the altar.

"You okay? Does it hurt?" BFG clearly misunderstood her sigh, running his hand through her hair, strong fingers stroking her scalp in what she knew was meant to be comforting. He missed the mark by a mile, however, as her girl parts perked up and paid attention.

"I'm fine." Then her gaze slid down, able to take in his sweater for the first time, and she laughed. Then she laughed even louder when he put his finger under her chin, drawing her eyes back to his face.

"Up here, Joy," he joked.

Chelsea shook her head. "That sweater is…wow."

He was wearing a festive green and red sweater, adorned with the lights that had trapped her. If it had just been that, it would have been cute, if boring, but he'd gone the extra mile. A huge stocking was safety-pinned to the bottom hem, covering the crotch of his jeans, drawing her attention exactly where he wanted it.

Emblazoned beneath the lights on the sweater were the words, "My eyes are up here."

"I'm an in-it-to-win-it guy," he explained. "So when I heard there was a prize for best sweater, I did some serious shopping looking for the best one. And since arriving tonight, I've done some recon, and I think you're my biggest competition."

She agreed that of all the sweaters she'd seen, hers and his were probably the most creative and funny. "I made the sweater myself," she admitted. "I'm sure that's gotta be worth extra credit."

"Handmade was not a requirement of the contest," he said. "Might have to point that out to the judges."

"Where did you get yours?" she asked.

"Where I get everything. Ordered it online. Amazon Prime for the win. Although I did add the lights."

"You used shipping tape," she pointed out. "Pretty lazy, if you ask me. I'm definitely working the handmade, crafty, mad-glue-gun-skills angle. There's no way that won't sway the vote in my favor."

He considered that, then gave her a wicked grin. "Tell you what. Let's put a little wager on this. If I win, you have to dance with me—a slow dance."

"And if I win?" she asked, in a voice that was too fun and flirty to come from her.

"You have to slow dance with me," he replied, without a moment's hesitation.

"That's a prize for *me*?"

"Of course it is," he replied shamelessly. "And, in the unlikely event that neither of us win, you still have to slow dance with me. Consolation prize. I take my losses pretty hard."

Chelsea considered requesting a different prize if she won, then realized she wanted exactly what he was offering. It had been a long time since she'd slow danced with a man.

A vision of her and Rick sharing their first dance at their wedding reception drifted through her mind. She had dreamed of that dance for years, and it never happened.

BFG studied her face, and she realized she was wearing her damn heart on her sleeve, letting her sadness creep out.

"Well." The moment turned slightly awkward when she couldn't think of anything else to say. Probably best to cut and run before she made a jackass of herself. "Um...I, uh...I guess I should..."

He cupped her chin, studying her face more closely than she was accustomed to. "Is it a bet?"

Shit. She really needed to get out of her own head sometimes. Chelsea nodded, then smiled. "Sure."

With one fingertip, he stroked her cheek. "Those dimples of yours are going to be the death of me. Fucking adorable."

She felt herself blush, aware she was falling for his charm too easily. While she'd gone out with her besties more times than she could count since June, she'd taken the term wallflower to new levels, constantly hovering in the background. The few guys who'd asked her out hadn't captured her interest like BFG. His attention felt nice and—for lack of a better word—sincere. She didn't get creepy, only-in-it-for-sex vibes from him, which had been the problem with more than a few of the guys she'd dated the past couple of months.

"Now, what about that drink I owe you?" he asked.

She raised her empty wineglass. "I'm going to take you up on that. I was just headed to the kitchen for another glass of Chardonnay when I bumped into you and your sweater."

He tilted his beer cup to show her he was empty as well. "I need a refill too."

Chelsea turned toward the kitchen, but the living room was still packed with people. Funny how she forgot about them while she'd been talking to him. One conversation and the rest of the room had vanished, becoming nothing more than white noise in the background.

She probably should ask him his name, but for some reason, she was enjoying the anonymity.

BFG stepped around her. "Grab hold of the back of my sweater. I'll clear a path for us."

She did as he said, impressed by how quickly they managed to cut a swath across the room. He didn't even have to zigzag. Instead, he just plowed straight ahead, everyone wisely stepping out of his path. Which made sense. *She* would have stepped back to make way for the large man as well, if she saw him barreling toward her.

When they entered the large kitchen—which was, mercifully, less crowded—he took her glass from her. There was a bartender manning the makeshift bar. BFG requested Chardonnay for her and another beer for himself. They both thanked the bartender when he gave them their drinks.

"So, what should we do now?" He gave her a cocky grin that told her he had no plans to let her out of his sight soon. The best and most surprising part was, *she* didn't want their conversation to end, either. She'd expected to spend the majority of the party hovering on the fringes of the crowd, since Allyson, the dancing queen, would spend ninety-five percent of the night shaking her ass in the dining room, the other five percent refilling her wineglass.

Hanging out with him was infinitely more fun than holding up a wall by herself. He was seriously attractive, with a ruggedness she wouldn't have thought a turn-on for her.

Rick had been the epitome of clean-cut, while BFG was sporting a five-o'clock shadow she was tempted to run her fingers over, curious if it was scratchy or soft. Then she let herself imagine how it would tickle if they kissed.

Down, girl.

His hair was a shade too long, but not shaggy. He had laugh lines by his eyes—which were the lightest, most striking shade of gray she'd ever seen—and an incredible smile.

He shifted closer, and she resisted the urge to take a step back. Not because she minded him in her personal space but because her libido—after a long, looooong hibernation—had just now woken up, well rested and ready to play.

She was grateful her sweater was thick enough to hide the fact her nipples were budding, her body reacting to him in a very visceral way.

"I think you mean, what should *I* do now," she corrected,

practically daring him to come closer. "Drink level achieved," she joked.

He wasn't deterred. "*We*," he stressed. "We're just starting to get to know each other. So do you want to dance or spend a few minutes under that mistletoe?" He pointed to the doorway they just walked through, wiggling his eyebrows playfully. Hanging above it was mistletoe that she hadn't seen on the way in.

"A few minutes?" She seriously considered taking him up on that option.

His gaze slid to her lips for a second. "Or an hour or so. I have a feeling you're the kind a girl a guy could kiss for days without ever coming up for air."

She had to hand it to the man. He was the king of flirts, quick with the smooth lines. She'd never considered herself susceptible to that kind of thing. God knew, Rick was the opposite, serious, introspective, and self-important, something she hadn't recognized until after he'd dumped her. Because she and Rick had been high school sweethearts, and he'd been her only boyfriend —her only anything—she'd made his intelligent, staid, well-groomed style "her type," but ten minutes with her sexy, funny, brawny BFG had her rethinking that.

She considered his invitation to visit the mistletoe, flushing not with embarrassment but with a need she hadn't felt in so long, she feared it was gone forever. Her sex drive had vanished along with her fiancé.

Her libido had always been bigger than Rick's. So she'd been no stranger to taking care of business herself with her battery-operated toys whenever Rick gave her the "I'm too tired tonight" excuse. She hadn't pulled any of them out since June, her desire completely dried up.

"Where do you keep going?" BFG asked, and she frowned.

"What?"

"Every now and again, I feel like I lose you."

Wow. She'd dated Rick for way too many years, and he'd *never* noticed when she was upset or preoccupied.

"Sorry. It's not you. I'm easily distracted," she lied.

He didn't appear satisfied with that answer, but he didn't call her on it. Instead, he placed his hand on the small of her back, guiding her out of the kitchen, through the living room. The mansion had previously been someone's home, though she couldn't imagine one family living in a house this large. The ticket taker at the front door confirmed that it really was haunted when she and Allyson asked, though she assured them the ghosts were friendly.

"What about the mistletoe?" Chelsea was sorry she'd stupidly lost her chance for a kiss because she couldn't stop thinking about stupid Rick. "Maybe we should go back and top these up?" Her glass was filled nearly to the brim, but she would have no problem chugging wine, considering what was on the line.

BFG chuckled but he didn't turn around, leading her farther away from the music and dancing. "Don't worry. We're going to revisit that mistletoe later, maybe a few times. I thought we could find ourselves a quiet corner and get to know each other first."

"Okay."

Apparently, this Ugly Sweater party had started when the inn first opened as a fun way to draw people in to tour the property. According to the chatty ticket taker, the turnout the first year had been so good, the owners decided to do it again the second year. This was year three, and given the size of the crowd, it was a safe bet a tradition had been established. The tickets—as well as every room in the inn—had been sold out for months. This party had become this inn's equivalent to the New Year's Eve packages so many other hotels offered.

The inn had a huge screened-in back porch furnished with oversized cushioned couches and chairs at the rear of the first floor. It was probably a wonderful spot to hang out during the warmer months. However, because it was December and cold as shit, the summer screens had been replaced with thicker plastic, and there were several heaters scattered around. The space was surprisingly warm and cozy, despite the low temperature outside.

There were fewer people out here, most just standing around, talking. Like her and BFG, it appeared these partygoers had been seeking a quieter place.

He led her to one of the large couches. She claimed one end, expecting him to take the other, so she was surprised—pleasantly—when he plopped down next to her, his leg pressed against hers. Then he went one step further, resting his arm along the back of the couch, his fingers toying with her hair.

The feeling of his fingers there was innocuous enough, but damn if it didn't send her thoughts straight to the gutter. Because it was on the tip of her tongue to tell BFG to stop messing around and pull it…hard.

Jesus.

Maybe she should slow down on the wine.

"Favorite musician?" Chelsea blurted, trying to distract herself enough that she didn't give in to the urge to straddle his lap and get to know him in a far more physical way.

Yeah, maybe she should just skip the wine and switch to water.

BFG smirked, and for a moment, it felt as if he knew her thoughts had taken a dirty direction. Mercifully, he went along with her game. "John Lennon."

"Oh my God. I love him, too." She lifted the right leg of her jeans and tugged down her sock, revealing a tattoo of the word "Imagine" on her ankle.

He bent down, running his finger over it in disbelief. "Holy shit. That's an awesome tat."

"That song never fails to move me."

He nodded in complete agreement. "My mother used to sing 'Beautiful Boy' to me when I was little. It was our lullaby."

Chelsea smiled at his sweet memory, then they spent a few minutes discussing their favorite John Lennon and Beatles songs.

"Okay. Your turn. Favorite movie," he said, continuing their game.

"Have you ever seen *Serendipity*?" she asked.

"With John Cusack?"

She nodded. "I absolutely love it."

He grinned. "Would you laugh at me if I told you that was one of my all-time favorite movies too? Watch it every year around the holidays, along with *Love Actually* and *Die Hard*. Also thanks to my mom. She forced me to watch them with her when I was younger, but now, I find myself pushing play on those old movies every December all on my own. Watched *Serendipity* a few nights ago."

Her eyes widened. "Shut up. No way!"

He lifted one shoulder casually. "Kate Beckinsale is fucking hot."

"I should have known that was reason. And by the way…*Die Hard* is not a Christmas movie."

One tiny push, and suddenly they'd launched into the age-old debate. This one lasted for several minutes because apparently BFG had strong feelings about *Die Hard*, which only made her want to fight harder—not because she cared so much but because his passionate arguments were hilarious. So the more he said yes, it *was* a holiday movie, the more she said no, until they finally agreed to disagree.

"I need to confess," he said. "Kate Beckinsale's not the real reason I love *Serendipity*. It's totally the love story. I've got a bit of a reputation among my friends for being a romantic."

"Really?" She thought that was both hysterical and adorable, because it was kind of hard to think of the large, almost rough-looking man as a romantic. He was a big dude who dwarfed her five-foot-five frame. He struck her as more caveman than Casanova, the type of guy who would fling a girl over his shoulder and fireman-carry her all the way to the bedroom. Which, now that she thought about it, was pretty dreamy. "A romantic, huh?"

"Yep. That's me. A regular Romeo."

She laughed, amused by his self-deprecating grimace that told her he didn't hate that nickname as much as he pretended. She was enjoying their game, so she hit him with another question. "Do you have any pets?"

BFG nodded. "Sure do. I have a big-ass aquarium at my place with a couple of fish."

"Just a couple?"

"Yeah. Clownfish. They can be tricky to place with other fish, as they're somewhat aggressive. Did you know clownfish pair for life, and they actually thrive with a partner?"

"What did you name your fish?" she asked, enthralled by everything this guy said.

"My dynamic duo are Johnny and June."

"Perfect names, Romeo."

He shook his head. "Uh, uh, uh. That's BFG to you."

Chelsea tried to restrain a shiver as he drew the tip of one finger along the side of her neck. "You know, now that you mentioned it, I have to admit, *Walk the Line* is another favorite movie."

"A great flick," he agreed, and they spent a good twenty minutes listing their top five movies each, debating their merits. He had great taste in films.

"I think it's cool that you're romantic," she said. "Not many men would admit that."

He chuckled, even as he shrugged. "Never really seen much use in hiding who I am from others or pretending to be something I'm not. I have no problem confessing to my romantic nature, though lately, I'm wondering if I should throw the word 'hopeless' in front of it."

Chelsea tilted her head. "Why hopeless?"

"Because I'm thirty-five years old and haven't met the woman of my dreams yet. Starting to feel like I'm never going to manage to make that magical trip down the aisle."

"That's not a bad thing." Even Chelsea could hear the outright bitterness in her tone.

BFG frowned, confused. "It's not?"

"Oh my God. Ignore me. I didn't mean to sound so jaded. It's just…" She shut up because this conversation was hard enough to have with people who'd been there and witnessed her mortification.

"It's just what?" he prodded.

Chelsea bit her lip, then surprised herself when she replied. "I was supposed to get married last June."

She saw the faint look of confusion on his face. "But you didn't?"

She shook her head. "No. My fiancé…well, my *ex* is the more accurate term now…didn't show up."

BFG scowled. "What do you mean, he didn't show up? To the *wedding*?"

Chelsea grinned at his vehemence, wondering what it was about this man that made him so easy to talk to.

Perhaps it was because she didn't know him—not even his name.

Or because she didn't live in Philadelphia, so the chances they'd run into each other again were practically nil.

Or maybe it was because of this undeniable, unexpected connection she felt to him.

Despite the fact they were strangers, she couldn't shake the feeling that she knew him on some instinctual level.

"He sent a text to his best man a few minutes before the ceremony was supposed to start and said he couldn't do it. He'd fallen in love with someone else."

"What the fuck? Are you kidding me?! Who does something like that to someone? He couldn't tell you that *before* the wedding day?"

Chelsea was touched by his anger on her behalf. "It was a dick move," she agreed.

"Jesus, Joy. I'm sorry. That must have been so rough on you."

She tried to brush it off with a casual shrug and self-effacing grin. "I've had better years."

"Yeah, well, anyone who would do that…" He shook his head, still fired up. "He's a fucking douchebag. You're better off without him."

Chelsea had heard that comment no less than a million times from countless well-meaning friends, but she'd never really felt like she was. Not really. She'd been in love with Rick since ninth grade, and when she saw her future, it was always with him. It probably didn't help that his mother and hers had joked from the time they were kids right up until that failed wedding that they'd been "betrothed" since birth. Trying to reconfigure her life without him had been one of the hardest things she'd ever done, even after the hurt he caused.

Now, though…there was something in BFG's tone that resonated and rang true. God, maybe she'd finally turned a corner—because suddenly she knew all the way to the depths of her soul that she was better off without Rick in her life.

"That fucker didn't deserve you, and he's in for a rude awakening when he realizes just how big a mistake he made letting you go."

"You barely know me," she felt compelled to point out.

He paused, considering that, then he gave her a bemused grin. "I guess I don't," he admitted. "But…" He leaned toward her, bumping his shoulder against hers. "Well, strange as it may sound, I feel like I do."

His comment took her aback, warming every cold, lonely corner inside her. Because…he felt it too. This connection.

He reached down, taking her hand in his, shifting toward her. Their faces were inches from each other, and she was so tempted to lean forward. He glanced at her lips again, but he didn't move, didn't take what she was beginning to sense they both wanted.

"Are you ever going to tell me your name?" he whispered.

She shook her head. "Not yet. I like being your Joy."

Chelsea wondered if he might insist, but instead he gave her that affable grin. "I like being your BFG. Wouldn't mind that nickname sticking for a while."

"Well, then that's your name. All night."

"And maybe longer," he murmured.

"No. No longer." Chelsea shook her head, even as she shifted closer. She wasn't sure what her end game was here, because she was going back to Baltimore in the morning, and then on to Paris in a week. As much as she was enjoying this time with him, nothing could come from this night.

Well…not *nothing*, she reconsidered, shocked by the direction her thoughts had traveled.

She'd never had a one-night stand in her life. However, she would definitely consider it with him.

BFG kept the distance between them, his grin fading at her negative response. "Why don't we see where tonight leads us. There's no reason to put a time limit on this. I feel like…I'd really like to see you again, take you out to dinner or to a movie or a hockey game."

God, every word he said was perfect, amazing…heartbreaking.

"The truth is, I can't give you more than tonight. Right after the holidays, I'm moving out of the country. I'm going to live in Paris."

He cursed under his breath. "What's in Paris?"

"A fresh start."

He didn't like her answer. "You don't need to move for a fresh start. You realize some people just opt for a new wardrobe or a haircut or something less life-altering after a relationship ends."

She grimaced, because he made a good point, but she hadn't been in a great headspace for a long time, and after that run-in with Rick on the street, she'd decided the only way to dig herself out of her depression was to reboot her life. Like, *majorly* reboot it.

Chelsea had earned an associate's degree in culinary arts, while working full-time in a donut shop in Baltimore. Her dream had been to open her own bakery someday with Ethan, who'd majored in marketing with a minor in business administration. That future had now been traded for one that would happen across the Atlantic.

She'd become close to one of her culinary professors, so it had felt like fate opening a door when Dr. Nally emailed her about a job opening in a Parisian patisserie the very same day she'd seen Rick with Vanessa.

She had applied for the position that night, and because the owner of the patisserie was a good friend of Dr. Nally, her glowing reference had basically assured the job was Chelsea's.

When she accepted it, her first and primary thought had been that she wouldn't have to worry about running into Rick if she was in another country. That *really* shouldn't have been the driving force, but she'd been so desperate to escape—the hurt and embarrassment and anger—that she'd jumped at the chance. Because seeing him with that beautiful woman had reopened the wound she stupidly thought had healed.

Of course, she hadn't admitted that avoiding Rick was her main impetus for leaving to her best friends, who were distraught that she was breaking up the Three Musketeers. She,

Ethan, and Allyson had been inseparable since elementary school.

Somehow, she managed to convince them that moving to Paris was an amazing opportunity, because Chelsea knew they would try to talk her out of going if they suspected she wasn't running *toward* something, so much as she was just flat-out running away.

Paris had become her escape hatch, her way of fleeing all the shit that had been swimming around in her head since Rick kicked her in the teeth.

"You leave after the holidays?" BFG asked.

"Like right after Boxing Day."

His long sigh took her off guard, as did his next words. "Well, that figures."

"What does?" she asked.

"Looks like I'm destined to remain a hopeless romantic."

She tilted her head, confused. "Why's that?"

"Because I finally meet the girl of my dreams and she's about to move four thousand miles away."

CHAPTER TWO

JOY LAUGHED. "Oooo. That might be your best line yet."

Preston grinned, even though he wasn't entirely sure it had been a pickup line.

Just like the two of them running into each other hadn't been random. He'd spotted the beauty the second he walked into the party tonight, his gaze drawn to her time and time again as he socialized with his buddies.

His opportunities to attend parties like this during the hockey season were always hit and miss, depending on whether he had a home game, late practice, or was on the road. Today, the Baltimore Stingrays had played a one p.m. game in Philadelphia, so he and a couple of his teammates stuck around to attend tonight's party with Elio Moretti. Elio had played for the Stingrays before retiring a few years earlier to run this inn with his wife, Gianna.

To make things even better, Preston had tomorrow off—he needed the recovery time—before flying to Florida with the team the day after. So he'd decided to take advantage of the opportunity to chill with his friends for a couple hours. His original intention had been to drink a beer and rehash the glory days with Elio and the guys, and then drive back to Baltimore because he preferred sleeping in his own bed versus staying in a hotel.

Sleeping in hotels got old quick, and considering he'd been doing it for fifteen hockey seasons, it was safe to say he was well over it.

That plan changed when he saw *her*. Suddenly, one beer became two as he watched her, captivated by her pretty face, her gentle demeanor, and something else he hadn't been able to put his finger on. There was a vulnerability about her that he'd initially attributed to shyness…but now he knew it had been put there by an asshole ex.

He'd been approaching her, trying to figure out what to say, when she'd stumbled into him, her hair getting caught in his Christmas lights.

"What makes you think it's a line?" He attempted to keep his tone light and fun.

"If it's not, then you really should get to know me better before you go making a wild, sweeping claim like that," she said, grinning.

"I think that's a great idea. So tell me. Why Paris?" While it was a crazy thought, he couldn't help but wonder how married she was to the idea of skipping off across the pond.

"The opportunity was too good to turn down. I landed a dream job and, well, it's Paris," she said, as if that should explain it all.

"Dream job, huh?"

"Yeah. But I'm not going to lie," she confessed. "It's going to be difficult leaving my hometown, my parents, and my friends. It's just…the offer presented itself at the perfect time, and I realized there was nothing holding me here."

She turned slightly on the couch so that she was facing him more fully. Preston couldn't resist the desire to cut the distance between them, so he shifted forward until their faces were closer, his arm still resting on the back of the couch, allowing him to stroke the side of her neck once more.

She glanced over her shoulder, back in the direction of the dancing, and he wondered—okay, worried—that she was uncomfortable with his touch or thinking about ending the conversation here.

"Tell me one of your childhood dreams," he said quickly, unwilling to let her walk away.

Her attention returned to him, and she was clearly pleased he wanted to continue their get-to-know-you game. "Let's see," she said, tapping her lower lip with her finger playfully. "Oh, I know. For one whole year, I wanted to be a meter maid. I used to ride my bike up and down our street, putting tickets on all the neighbors' cars."

"Bet they loved that," he said sardonically.

She shrugged. "Luckily, it was a great neighborhood, so they were mostly entertained, and a couple even played along, paying my quarter fine."

Preston chuckled. "So I have to ask. Did that dream come true? Are you off to Paris to ticket the French for double-parking by the Eiffel Tower?"

She snorted. "Not even close. After a year as a 'meter maid,'" she air-quoted the last two words, "I moved on to bus driver. Stopping my bike outside every house to pick up imaginary students for school."

"Did you have better luck making that dream come true?"

She leaned closer, lowering her voice as if sharing a deep dark secret. "Not even close. I'm a terrible driver."

"Good information to have. I'll be careful never to let you get behind the steering wheel of my Audi R8."

"Way to work in a brag about your badass car."

Preston chuckled. "You're only giving me one night here. I have to take my shots where I can."

She rolled her eyes good-naturedly.

"So your big childhood dreams were meter maid and bus driver?"

She lifted one shoulder. "Not really. Those dreams were short-lived. I guess what I always wanted to be when I grew up was a baker. I used to spend every Sunday in my grandma's kitchen when I was younger, learning how to bake cookies and cakes and her world-famous apple pie."

"World famous, huh?"

Joy nodded. "It won first place in a local apple pie baking contest ten years in a row."

Preston whistled appreciatively. "That's quite the record."

"One day, I'd love to open my own bakery. I even know the name of it." She held her hands out as if imagining the sign. "Sugar and Spice."

"I like it," Preston said.

"What about you? What did you dream of growing up to be?"

Preston answered honestly, aware that in addition to not sharing his name, he hadn't told her about his profession, either, though he wasn't sure why. "I suppose my dream is a popular one with most young boys. I wanted to become a professional athlete."

"What sport?" she asked.

"The best sport ever. Hockey."

Joy crinkled her nose. "Hockey, really?"

"What the hell is wrong with hockey?"

She considered his question, then shrugged. "Nothing, I guess. To be honest, I've never watched an entire hockey game. Just seen clips here and there."

Preston clearly spent too much of his time around people who were all hockey mad. His family, his teammates, the fans. Then he realized the reason he'd probably held back about his career was because she wasn't looking at him like every other woman he'd spent time with over the past decade and a half. To them, he was a rich professional athlete, and he knew their desire to be with him was based on *that*, rather than who he was as a person.

"You're kidding," he said. "You've never watched a whole game?"

She flipped her hair over her shoulder. "My dad is a Ravens fan, so we were a football house."

"Fucking football," Preston grumbled. "Crap sport. Trust me when I say, real men play hockey."

She laughed. "I'll have to take your word for it."

For the next half hour, Preston filled her in on the finer points of hockey, while she interjected her own misguided opinions on why football was better. The lively debate was fun and funny, and Preston found himself wishing this night would never end.

Mercifully, Joy didn't ask if he managed to achieve his hockey player dream, because he wasn't quite ready to reveal who he was to her just yet. "Do you have any siblings?"

She nodded. "Two sisters, much older. I was a late-in-life kid, and while I'm pretty sure I was an oopsie, my mom swears I wasn't. Both my sisters are married with kids. One lives in Dallas, the other in Sacramento. How about you?"

"I have a younger brother. He moved to Denver a few years ago, married a nice woman, has a couple of daughters. He sells real estate, something he loves way too much. Whenever he calls, I get a full rundown of all his sales, as well as the deals that fell through. Boring as shit."

"So he didn't have that same dream of becoming a hockey player?"

"Nope. Guy doesn't have an athletic bone in his body. We tease each other all the time about one of us being switched at birth. I say it's him. He swears it's me. We're opposites right down the line, but I couldn't imagine my life without the guy."

"I feel that way about Allyson and Ethan."

"Allyson is the friend you came with?" he asked, recalling her mentioning that name earlier.

She nodded.

"And Ethan?" Preston had never suffered a day of jealousy in his life, but he didn't like knowing there was an Ethan that she couldn't live without.

"They are my two best friends. Because of the age difference, I've never been particularly close to my sisters. So, Ethan and Allyson have become the siblings of my heart. I honestly couldn't have survived the past six months without them."

Preston still couldn't understand how anyone could date someone as cool as Joy and walk away. More than that, there was a special place in hell for the kind of man who would jilt a woman at the altar. The fact he didn't even show up to offer an explanation or apology proved the guy was a loser with a capital L.

"They've been dragging me out since June, trying to help me get my head back in the game. Rick really did a number on me," she confessed, though he could see it was hard for her to admit.

"How long did you date the asshole?" Preston asked.

"Forever."

He tilted his head, waiting for her to give the correct answer.

"Seriously," she said. "We grew up together. We were high school sweethearts. He was my first kiss, my first boyfriend, my first everything."

And that just catapulted Rick the Dick from merely a loser, to the world's biggest prick. "That's a long time."

She nodded. "Our mothers were—*are*—best friends, so we've always known each other. I think that's why I was so blindsided when he..." She paused. "Jesus. I'm sorry. You don't want to hear all of this."

Actually, he did. He wanted to know everything about her. "I don't mind...if it doesn't bother you to talk about it."

"It doesn't," she replied, and he could see she was telling the truth. He could also see she was surprised by it.

Preston sank deeper into the cushions, pleased when she followed suit, the two of them quite cozy on their couch. "Why did he let things go so far? I mean, it was your fucking wedding day."

"He met someone else at work. He swears he never cheated on me—physically—but I guess it turned into an emotional affair. We didn't speak for months after the..." She blew out a long, sad sigh. "Jilting."

Preston frowned. "Months?"

"He ghosted me. Blocked me completely on everything."

"Fucking coward," Preston muttered.

"Totally," she agreed. "While I was at the church, waiting around in my white dress, he was packing all his shit and moving out of our apartment and in with Ms. Emotional Affair. I probably could have tracked him down at work or at his parents' house, but Ethan and Allyson insisted seeing him would only drive the knife deeper."

"What's Rick's last name and where does he live now?"

She laughed at his questions, but Preston wasn't fucking joking.

"Turned out, my best friends were right. I bumped into Rick on the street a couple months ago. He was with *Vanessa*."

Preston was amused by the way she said Vanessa, pursing her lips like the name was made out of shit.

"It was a quick conversation, where I failed to say one single fucking word. Why is it you can only come up with zinger lines afterward? I mean, I had a ton to say to that asshole and none of it came out."

"It was the first time you'd seen the guy, and as you said, it wasn't a planned meeting. You had no time to prepare yourself. I suspect the next time you run into the prick, you'll find your voice."

"I hope that's true. It feels like I've gone through every stage of grief since the almost-wedding—angry, depressed, sad. For a while, I was stuck in the bargaining stage, trying to figure out how to win him back. Thankfully, that stage was a short one because Ethan and Allyson were NOT having it, telling me they would never let the shithead back into my life."

"They're good friends. So how do you feel now?" he asked.

She didn't respond right away, and he liked that she was taking time to consider the question. "I've finally hit acceptance."

"Oh yeah?"

She nodded. "Yeah. Lately, I've even started to think he was right."

Preston frowned. "To leave you standing at the altar?"

"No. Not that part. That made him a total asshat, but…" She shrugged. "I've spent most of the last six months in a fetal position…when I wasn't devouring pints of Ben and Jerry's New York Super Fudge Chunk. It turns out, that position gave me a lot of time to think."

He chuckled. "And what did you discover?"

"With distance comes perspective, and once the pain faded, logic kicked in. I can see now that it wasn't the perfect relationship I'd convinced myself it was."

"Lot of fighting?" he asked.

She shook her head. "Not at all, which is probably what blinded me to the truth. The *lack* of fighting was the problem."

Preston stroked one finger up and down her arm. "You *want* knock-down drag-out battles?"

She laughed. "Maybe not that extreme, but *some* emotion is better than none. At least it would have told me he cared enough about me to have a feeling, *any* feeling, even if it was just me pissing him off over something stupid. Rick never got mad, and I believed that was because he was so stable and steady, but it occurs to me now…it was less about his nature and more about the fact that he simply wasn't plugged into me or anything I did. I mean, we'd known each other our whole lives, and we'd hit a level of comfortable that was boring and predictable. Maybe we were both just phoning it in."

Preston heard a hitch in her voice that told him *she* hadn't been phoning it in. "We? Or him?"

She shrugged. "I want to say him, but the fact that he went looking and found someone else makes me wonder if I hadn't done enough, either."

"Stop. Stop right there. Don't lump yourself in with that asshole."

Joy grimaced. "Maybe I overstated it when I said I've accepted everything."

"I think you're closer than you think. It's natural to seek answers when shit goes sideways. And it doesn't sound like Rick's been very forthcoming with the whys."

"Wow. Everything you say makes me feel so much better. I've been a mess for months, and now, just a couple hours with you, and it's like you've helped me make sense of all the chaos swirling in my head. How do you do that?"

"I've got all kinds of mad skills."

She laughed, but Preston wasn't finished. "Rick wasn't right for you, Joy. You deserve a relationship filled with excitement and passion and fun, and the occasional fight even."

She shifted closer, and he could feel the heat of her breath against his cheek a moment before she kissed it. "You're good for the soul, BFG."

He was tempted to turn his head, claiming that kiss of hers on his lips rather than his face. "Preston," he whispered.

"Preston," she repeated. He waited for her to share her name, narrowing his eyes when she gave him a mischievous grin that told him she was still holding out.

"We've talked too much about me. What's your story?" she asked.

"My story?"

"You're a super-nice and apparently romantic guy, Preston. So why don't you have a girlfriend?"

She'd been completely open with him tonight, and he wanted to give her the same, even though he wasn't quite ready to let go of his anonymity. He liked this opportunity to get to know a woman without his career getting in the way.

Puck bunnies were a dime a dozen, and during the times when he had been between girlfriends, he'd taken advantage of their advances. He was far from a saint, but as he got older—and wiser—he'd become more discerning about choosing lovers. His preferred status was boyfriend, and he'd had several long-term relationships, but, sadly, none of them had gone the distance.

"No one's ever wanted to play the permanent role of Preston's girlfriend. I go out on dates, always with women I'm not just attracted to but who I genuinely like. I love to be in a relationship. It's just, every time I meet a woman I start to fall for…she leaves."

Joy frowned. "Seriously?"

Preston's relationship history was a source of great amusement for his teammates, because while most of those guys were true hound dogs—looking to get laid and nothing more—he didn't mind having a girlfriend. He actually preferred it, which was why he'd become known as the team romantic, his buddies teasingly calling him Romeo.

A couple of his *former* teammates had met women and fallen in love, Alex Stone and Elio Moretti, both now married with kids. The last time they'd gone out for drinks, he'd spent the entire evening listening to his friends talk about their wives and showing off pictures of their kids, while Preston sat there, aware to the depths of his soul that he wanted exactly what they had.

"I had a serious girlfriend in high school, but that ended after graduation. Then I dated a woman for a year or so when I was in my early twenties, but Julie got a job offer in New York and left.

We both had," he paused, then brushed over the real reason with a vague term, "careers that added an extra wrinkle to the long-distance relationship, because our schedules were busy enough and opposite enough that we'd known right from the start it wasn't going to work."

"Were there more than those two?"

Preston linked his fingers, cracking his knuckles. "I'm just getting started. My next girlfriend, Becca, came along a couple years after Julie. We dated for ten months, until her ex came back on the scene, and she realized she was still in love with him."

"Oh no. That sucks."

He lifted one shoulder casually. He'd been equal parts pissed and hurt at the time, but he was over it now. "After Becca, I dated a great girl, Jenn, for a year. We had a ton in common and I really thought she was the one…right up until she came out of the closet."

Her eyes widened. "No way!"

"My friends *still* give me shit about that one. Say I should have known, even though none of *them* did."

She grimaced. "Anyone else?"

"A few short-term deals that never jumped the line from casual to serious. It's been a pretty long, painful dry spell since Jenn. Which sucks, because the dating game is fucking brutal."

"You can say that again." She reached out to take his hand, giving it a squeeze. "I respect your resilience because that's quite a history."

Preston lifted her hand, kissing it. "I'm starting to think it's not so bad, because if any of those relationships had worked out, I wouldn't be sitting here with you." He wiggled his eyebrows, laying on the charm.

She snorted—actually snorted. Goddamn, she was adorable. "Again with the smooth lines. You should write a book since you're such an expert. You can call it *Love Lines from a Hopeless Romantic*."

He laughed. "Maybe I will."

"But I guess I understand the hopeless romantic description better now."

Preston shrugged. "I haven't thrown in the towel yet."

"I admire your optimism. I wish I could be half as positive as you. I've spent the past six months in a complete downhill spiral. Allyson started calling me Eeyore after a couple months of listening to me bitch and moan about how I'd never meet anyone else and was destined to live the rest of my life alone."

Now it was Preston's turn to roll his eyes. "Never gonna happen. You're beautiful and funny, and despite the fact you're clumsy, I have no doubt you're going to meet a guy who's perfect for you."

"Clumsy?"

"I wasn't the one who tangled you in my Christmas lights," he teased.

She grumbled but didn't defend herself. Instead, she did something much better and sweeter. "Thank you for hanging out with me tonight," she whispered. "I can't tell you what the last couple of hours have meant to me. My confidence has been shaky at best since June. Tonight…with you…well…"

She didn't finish that thought with words.

Rather, she leaned toward him and let her lips tell him in a different, hotter way.

He pulled her toward him, wrapping her in his embrace, refusing to let this kiss end too soon.

Kissing her was a heady thing. She hummed against his mouth, the heat between them rising until he was tempted to rip off these damn sweaters—hers *and* his.

He wasn't sure how many minutes—or maybe hours—they sat there, simply kissing. As they'd talked, he'd been vaguely aware of the noise surrounding them outside this room…the music, the loud voices, the laughter. All of that vanished as they kissed, his entire universe whittled down to this tiny space, this woman, this kiss.

When they parted, she gave him a breathy, giddy laugh, and he couldn't resist pulling her into his arms, hugging her tightly.

Then, she gave him what he'd been wanting all night.

"Chelsea," she whispered in his ear.

He was overwhelmed by the desire to keep her in his arms. Then he realized the best way to accomplish that. "Dance with me, Chelsea."

He was pleased when she stood immediately.

When Preston first arrived, Elio had met him at the door, warning him that Gianna had lost her mind when it came to organizing and decorating for the evening. Then he proceeded to tell him how he and his brothers and cousins had spent the better part of the day moving furniture. Apparently, the entire dining room suite was in the garage for the evening because Gianna insisted they needed a proper dance floor.

Preston had thought that over-the-top and crazy a few hours earlier, but now he was glad Gianna had gone to the effort. Especially when the two of them fought their way through the crowd bumping and grinding on the dining room dance floor and claimed their own bit of space. There wasn't a lot of room, which was fine with him, because it meant he could pull her close. The upbeat number had a thumping rhythm, and they moved together. He wrapped his arms around her waist, his hands stroking up and down her sides.

While her sweater was cute and funny as shit, it was too bulky for him right now. What would he give to slip his hands underneath the thick material to feel her curves? Or better yet, to take her up on that offer to "feel the joy."

She was a great dancer, moving in time to the song, her legs split by one of his so that when he tugged her even closer, it felt as if she was riding his thigh.

Too much more of this and he'd never be able to keep his

erection at bay. He'd been sporting a half-chub ever since dragging her to the back porch and claiming a spot next to her on the couch.

Her hands slid along his thighs, moving upward until she fisted his sweater near his waist. She looked up at the same time he glanced down, their faces inches from each other.

He closed the distance, giving her a quick kiss. Chelsea returned it, then pressed the side of her face to his shoulder as he raised one hand, cupping the back of her neck, holding her there, against him.

God, she smelled good. Like cinnamon and apples. He bent his head, his cheek resting against the top of her head. She raised her hands to his back, caressing up and down—at least as much as the stupid Christmas lights he'd wrapped around the sweater would allow. He was ripping them off the second they took a break from dancing so he could feel more of her hands on him.

Unable to resist, he placed a knuckle under her chin, lifting it so that he could place a kiss on her cheek, then another. Chelsea nuzzled closer, like a kitten, purring, begging for more.

They'd spent the last couple of hours talking, getting to know one another, yet it felt as if they were saying more here...now... with this dance and these kisses.

He was thrilled this attraction wasn't one-sided, but there was something else more shocking than his sudden, intense sexual desire. It was the realization that if Chelsea didn't want to take things to the next level, he'd be just as happy to sit next to her for the rest of the night, merely talking.

Preston wasn't one of those love-at-first-sight guys, a firm believer that love took time. But damn if he didn't think this woman and tonight might convince him otherwise. The second she ran into him, he'd felt a connection—literally and figuratively. She was easy to talk to, smart, pretty, and funny. She ticked every single one of his boxes.

"Chels!" A woman next to them danced closer, her eyes

widening as she looked at him. "I wondered where you'd disappeared to."

Preston assumed this was the friend Allyson, given the fact she was wearing the exact same sweater as Chelsea. He laughed when she gave him a once-over, then a twice-over, before fist-bumping Chelsea.

"Damn, girl. Good job!"

A guy came up behind Allyson, wrapping his hand around her waist and drawing her into a bump and grind. "Thought I lost you, babe."

Allyson shimmied against her dance partner. "Best. Night. Ever. You two don't do anything I wouldn't do," she joked. Then added, "Which leaves your night wide open!"

Allyson disappeared back into the throng of dancers with her guy as Chelsea laughed. "She's kind of a lot, but I love her."

"She's cool. I'm glad she dragged you out tonight."

"Me too. Lucky she scored those tickets at the last minute."

"I was a late addition as well. Didn't plan to come until yesterday morning, when my buddy called to invite me."

"Incredible. It's like fate was drawing us here together." She blushed when she realized what she'd said. "God. Now you've got *me* delivering cheesy lines."

"There wasn't a damn thing cheesy about that. I think you're right. Us meeting. It was fate. Serendipity."

The song ended, a slow one starting. Chelsea shifted slightly, their bodies connecting in a different, more intimate way as she placed her head against his chest again. He tightened his grip, the two of them swaying in time.

Preston had danced with countless women in his life, but it felt different with Chelsea, and he wondered why.

Not that he'd have too long to ponder it. She was leaving for Paris in a week.

When he was younger, he wouldn't have had a problem initiating a no-strings-attached one-night stand with Chelsea.

But he hated the idea of it tonight. Because she was a woman he wanted to spend more time with, wanted to get to know on a much more personal level.

In truth, she was exactly his type. Which was funny, because before Chelsea, he didn't realize he *had* a type.

She lifted her head, looking up at him. "I haven't slow danced with anyone in ages. Most of my dancing lately has been shaking my ass with Ethan and Allyson in nightclubs. This is nice."

"It's *very* nice." He hated the idea of someone as sweet as Chelsea reeling for so long from a broken heart. He had the uncharacteristic desire to find her ex and punch the guy's lights out.

She must have read that intention, his poker face failing. "I let the pity party go into overtime. I shouldn't have done that. Tonight, with you…"

She paused, and when it felt like she wouldn't continue, he prodded, curious about what she'd planned to say.

"Tonight?"

She didn't reply immediately, but he got the feeling it wasn't because she didn't want to. More like, she wasn't sure how to. Finally, she said, "Everything feels right."

It felt more than right. It felt perfect.

The song ended and they stepped apart, even though letting her go was the last thing he wanted to do.

"Come with me." He took her hand and pulled her back toward the kitchen. He stopped as they stepped beneath the mistletoe, drawing her into his arms again.

"Finally." Her sexy whisper and dimpled grin were too adorable to resist. She lifted her face to his, a clear invitation, one he was not going to refuse. He took her in his arms, and when his lips touched hers, it was no quick peck. Her lips parted, their tongues finding each other. He tasted the wine she'd been drinking on her breath. Lifting his hand to the back of her head, he deepened the kiss, the two of them taking their time to explore, to discover.

She was one hell of a kisser, adventurous, daring, holding back nothing. He loved the feeling of her hands at his hips, his dick growing thicker when she slipped them beneath his sweater, stroking bare skin.

He ran his fingers through her hair, then closed his fist in it, tightening the grip slowly until she gave him what he wanted, a low, throaty moan that told him this woman would be a spitfire in bed.

He hadn't had a one-night stand in three years, determined the last one would be the *last*. He'd had too many shots, celebrating a big win that night, and he'd let the alcohol do his thinking. Preston had woken up the next morning in his own bed, hungover as hell, sleeping next to a naked woman whose name he didn't remember.

Not exactly his finest moment. Especially when it had taken him the better part of that day to get the woman out of his apartment. In his alcohol-laden stupor, he'd managed to pick up a stage-three clinger, one he'd stupidly given his cell number to while drunk off his ass. He'd had to block her number after two dozen voicemails and twice that many texts. Mercifully, she'd drawn the line at stopping by his apartment, but he'd made a vow, one that he stuck to, that one-night stands were off the table, and he wouldn't bring a woman to his bed if they weren't in a relationship.

That oath was on shaky ground tonight, because there was nothing he wanted to do more than take Chelsea to bed and expand on this fucking incredible kiss.

Chelsea was the first to break free, though her actions had less to do with desire and more to do with the fact they needed to come up for air.

"Preston." Her cheeks were flushed in a way that told him she was feeling the same heated desire he was.

The crowd had started to thin out, though there were still plenty of partygoers who looked ready to keep things going until dawn. His plan had been to stay a couple hours, then drive back to Baltimore, so he hadn't bothered booking a room here, or at any other hotel. No stranger to keeping late hours, he'd been fine with driving at night, intending to be home and in his own bed by one or two a.m. at the latest. That idea had flown out of the window the second Chelsea had come onto the scene.

"Wanna leave?" she asked.

"Together?" His response made it clear too much of the blood in his body had flowed away from his brain, occupying a place farther south. His dick was so hard right now, he was in pain, the zipper of his jeans likely to leave a permanent imprint.

She nodded, though hesitantly, and he saw the slightest bit of doubt begin to creep in. He hated it. Hated that her stupid ex had made her question her worth.

"Chelsea, I want you so much, it hurts. But I have to ask… there's been no one since Rick, has there?"

She sighed. "No one before, either."

Preston gave her a quick kiss, impressed by her honesty. He thought that might be a huge part of the appeal of this woman. He'd spent too much of the last decade and a half around women who would say anything—most of it lies—to catch his attention or impress him. He didn't doubt every word Chelsea said tonight had been the truth, and she hadn't shied away from telling him the uncomfortable stuff—like being jilted at the altar.

"Are you sure?" he forced himself to ask, praying to every single deity she said yes.

Once again, she took the time to consider his question, which reassured him way more than an immediate response would. Because she wasn't being impulsive.

Finally, after what felt like a hundred years, she gave him a smile that was pure seduction. "I've never been surer of anything in my life."

He took her hand in his, lifting it and kissing her palm. "Let's go."

CHAPTER THREE

CHELSEA STEPPED out of the passenger seat of Preston's badass Audi, staring up at the Rittenhouse Hotel, butterflies fluttering wildly in her stomach.

They weren't bad butterflies. Not based on nerves or second-guessing or fear or anything like that.

Nope, these butterflies were driven by pure excitement, anticipation, and hormones.

She bit her lower lip to hide her grin, not wanting Preston to think she was unhinged or anything.

This was so out of character for her, and yet, it felt perfectly natural to be following this sex-on-a-stick man whom she'd JUST met into a swanky five-star hotel.

It was hard for her to believe she'd only met Preston a few hours ago. Practical, play-it-safe Chelsea would never have left a party with a virtual stranger, going to a hotel with him, but the truth was, every single one of her instincts told her she could trust this man. Which was *also* shocking, considering she thought her trust meter was broken for good.

"This place looks nice," she murmured. He started to agree, but she shook her head. "No. Like, *too* nice. Too expensive."

Preston chuckled. "It's on me."

"That's not what I'm saying. It's just…"

"Chelsea. I'm not dragging you to some seedy motel. I wanted to take you somewhere nice, and this is one of the best hotels in Philly."

"Yeah, but we don't even have any luggage. It's going to be kind of obvious we're just here for a hookup."

"I'm pretty sure hotel hookups are a common thing, even in the ritzy places. Are you having second thoughts?" he asked.

"Good God, no."

Preston gave her a kiss on the cheek. "Good girl." He handed his keys to the valet, then placed his hand on the small of her back. "Don't forget, you promised to text Allyson the name of the hotel."

Since she and Preston had both gotten their tickets to the party secondhand and at the last minute, neither of them had been able to book a room in the inn, those spots filling months ago.

The fact Preston was reminding her to do the mature, self-protective thing proved just how far off the deep end she'd fallen. Because Chelsea, the never-stick-a-toe-out-of-line, so-predictable-you-could-set-a-clock-by-her girl had checked out of the building, replaced by this impulsive, wild, fly-by-the-seat-of-her-pants woman.

"Oh right." She quickly fired off the hotel name to Allyson, who had absolutely lost her mind when Chelsea told her she was heading out with Preston. Her bestie had squealed with delight, hugging her before high-fiving the man.

Completely mortifying, but one hundred percent Allyson.

Then, she and Allyson had done the unthinkable and switched friendship roles, Allyson demanding Chelsea text her where she was going and insisting she call her first thing in the morning, as well.

"Proof of life," her insane friend dead-panned.

Chelsea had promised, then left the inn with Preston.

He was the one who'd suggested a hotel, which made her curious, wondering why he wasn't inviting her back to his place, but she brushed it off, deciding it was no big deal. Maybe he was a slob or had annoying roommates or preferred to maintain his privacy. And it wasn't like she could invite him to share her blow-up mattress at Allyson's cousin's place.

It didn't really matter to her where they went, because she meant what she'd said to him.

This was just a one-night stand.

Her first ever.

And she realized the timing on it was right.

Tonight felt like a bridge from her old life to her new. She wanted to reboot her life, and by taking this step with Preston, it was as if she was shedding some of old Chelsea's inhibitions and embracing this new version of herself. This Chelsea emphatically shouted "Yes!" to amazing opportunities, like finding a dream job, moving to a new country, and spending the night with a sexy, sweet, romantic man.

Once they stepped into the foyer, her phone rang. Glancing at the screen, she rolled her eyes.

"Allyson has a big mouth." Chelsea flipped her phone around so Preston could see Ethan's name on her screen.

"Your friends are protective of you. That's not a bad thing, Chels. Why don't you talk to him while I go get us a room?"

She nodded, enjoying the view as Preston walked to the check-in desk. Sweet Jesus, she could bounce quarters off that tight ass.

"Hello," she said, distractedly.

"Giiiiiiirl. Ally just called."

"I figured that out," Chelsea said, grinning. "Considering you don't usually call—"

Ethan was too fired up to listen to her response because he started talking over her. "She said you left the party with some hottie. I'm worried someone roofied her or she's tripping balls, because I told her there is no way in hell our sweet little cupcake would go home with a man she just met in a strange town."

"Philly's not that strange," Chelsea joked.

"Cupcake." Ethan had been calling her cupcake since fourth grade and her grandma sent in the sweet treats for the entire class on her birthday.

"No one roofied Ally," Chelsea reassured him.

"Sweet Jesus. I'll tell you right now, you hooking up with a stranger was not on my bingo card for this year. Or next year, either."

Chelsea giggled. "That's funny, because *you* hooking up with a stranger is always on my bingo card in multiple squares."

"So you're with this guy right now?" He refused to be distracted by her attempt at humor.

"Yep. He's at the front desk getting us a room in a swanky hotel."

"Describe swanky," Ethan demanded.

"Well, it's no Super Eight, I can tell you that. Google the Rittenhouse Hotel. It's in the city center and it's bougie as hell."

She could tell from the way Ethan's voice became fainter he'd put her on speakerphone and was doing exactly what she suggested. Especially when he all but gasped. "I am so depressed."

"Why?" Chelsea asked.

"I should have insisted you stay home to pack for the move to Paris and taken that party ticket for myself because dayum, girl. This boy is treating you right. I wouldn't mind being on the receiving end of that."

Chelsea rolled her eyes, amused. "Right, Ethan. Because Preston would totally be with *you* right now if you'd come instead. Hate to break it to you, but he is extremely straight."

"Did he tell you that?"

"He didn't need to. He gives off alpha—*hetero*—male with a capital A vibes."

Ethan scoffed. "You underestimate my powers."

Chelsea didn't underestimate Ethan's charm or his good looks or his ability to pick up guys.

Gay guys.

Well…and bi guys.

Anytime she, Allyson, and Ethan went out, eight times out of ten, it was Ethan leaving the bar with a hot guy. And Allyson was the other two times out of ten.

Chelsea, prior to June, had always used the "I have a boyfriend/fiancé" line whenever someone tried to pick her up. In the six months since, she simply hadn't met anyone who captured her attention or got her motor revving. Not like Preston.

Looking across the foyer, she saw the front desk clerk hand Preston the key card. "Listen, I need to go. He has the room."

"Call me first thing in the morning," Ethan demanded.

"I'm already calling Allyson."

"And now you're calling me too," he insisted, undaunted. "What's the guy's name so I know what room to send the cops to if you don't call me?"

Chelsea hesitated. "Um…"

"Wait, you don't know the guy's name?"

"It's Preston. I didn't get his last name."

Ethan barked out a loud laugh. "Holy shit, girl. When you break bad, you break fucking bad. I'm starting to think I've been a bad influence on you. The problem is, I don't feel a bit guilty about that. Fine. I'll direct the cops and SWAT team to Preston No Last Name at the Rittenhouse Hotel if you don't call me by seven."

"Seven? It's midnight, and I have high hopes for Preston's stamina. I'll call you around nine. Or ten."

"Nine. And not a minute later. Now…go get laid, Cupcake,

and clear some time in your schedule for tomorrow afternoon when you get home because I'm going to want all the dirty details. I might buy a whiteboard and markers because I'm a visual learner."

"I'm not drawing pictures of sex acts for you, you perv."

"We'll see," Ethan drawled.

She and Ethan said goodbye and she tucked her phone in the back pocket of her jeans as Preston returned.

"All good?" he asked.

She nodded. "I'm experiencing some weird *Freaky Friday* kind of shit because usually I'm the friend on the other end of the phone, demanding Ethan and Allyson make smart decisions and be safe."

Preston wrapped his arm around her shoulders, the two walking toward the bank of elevators just beyond the front desk. "I promise you're perfectly safe with me. And as far as smart decisions go, I'm not sure where you stand, but this is the smartest thing I've ever done in my life."

"Me too," she said, aware of just how much she meant those words.

She'd been waiting for her common sense or whatever part of her brain that kept her from doing spontaneous stuff like this to kick in, ever since issuing her invitation to a one-night stand.

But it hadn't.

Not when he accepted.

Not when she found Allyson to say she was leaving with him.

Not on the ride here.

And not even now, as she stepped onto the elevator.

In fact, every step that led her closer to the bedroom only solidified how right this felt to her.

Preston placed a kiss on the top of her head as the doors slid closed.

She'd never been with such a large guy. Rick liked to tell

people he was six feet tall, but he was probably an inch or two shy of that. Plus, he was lanky, with a long-distance runner's frame. Preston, on the other hand, had close to a foot on her, and he was built like a brick house, all muscle.

"This is my first one-night stand, so I'm a little shaky on the protocols."

Preston chuckled, taking her hand and leading her off the elevator and down the hall. "No protocols. Tonight, we're just doing whatever comes naturally."

Opening the door, he allowed her to walk in first before following, then he threw the latch once it was closed, leaning against it and smiling at her.

"Alone at last." He reached out to pull her into his arms, resuming the kiss they'd started under the mistletoe.

His lips were warm, his breath hot, and his large, strong hands on her back equal parts comforting and tantalizing. It felt as if he was drugging her with his kisses and touches, and she was suddenly light-headed, giddy.

It had been too damn long since she'd had sex, and she didn't know when she'd have the chance to indulge again, considering she would be busy with the move, new job, adjusting to life in a new country, and trying to recall the three years of French she'd taken in high school, while adding to it with her Babbel app.

She was taking advantage of tonight because Preston seemed like the kind of man who knew his way around a bedroom.

She and Rick had both been virgins when they'd started dating, and while that had always felt like something special they shared, she was starting to see the benefit to playing the field because their sex life hadn't exactly set the world on fire. It had just been…pleasant.

God. Yet another place where she'd settled. Had she seriously thought a sex life that was *pleasant* was enough?

Sex with Rick was not passionate, not panty-soaking, not anywhere near what she was experiencing just *kissing* Preston right now. Her skin tingled, her pussy clenched, and her body temperature currently rivaled that of the sun.

Preston pulled away slightly, running his fingers through her hair. She jerked slightly when he drew one fingertip down the middle of her forehead and down along her nose.

"You disappeared again. Second thoughts?"

She shook her head before he even finished his question. "Hell no."

Her quick response provoked a loud laugh from him.

"You understand there's no point of no return. You say no and it's no."

"I'm not going to say no," she reassured him.

"God, you're gorgeous." Preston was so open with his actions and his compliments and his stories, even those that others might be too embarrassed to tell. She'd spent the entire evening fascinated by how easily he expressed his emotions, whether it was laughing at a joke or even scowling whenever she talked about Rick.

"Do you want a penny for your thoughts, or should I guess where your mind wandered?"

She thought about brushing him off, uncertain how he would feel if she confessed to thinking about her ex. Because she didn't want him to get the wrong idea, didn't want him to think she wasn't one thousand percent ready for this night with him.

In the end, her response wasn't necessary.

"Rick?" he asked.

She grimaced, then nodded. "It just occurred to me that the lack of passion in our relationship carried over to the bedroom. Another item in the boring category."

Chelsea wanted to kick her own ass for bringing up her ex yet again.

"Preston, I'm sorry. Rick is not what I want to talk—"

"Challenge accepted," he interjected.

"What?"

"Tonight. I have one goal. To show you exactly how you deserve to be treated in bed, so you never settle for less again."

Chelsea didn't realize her mouth had fallen open until Preston placed his finger under her chin to simultaneously close it as he leaned in to kiss her again. Then he twisted them, switching their positions, pressing her against the door at her back. He reached down, grasping one of her legs, lifting it around his waist so that he could press his denim-covered crotch against her.

There was no mistaking the thick bulge beneath his jeans, and her mouth watered at the idea of taking him in her hand, her body.

Preston rutted against her as they kissed, Chelsea tilting her hips as much as possible, trying to steal every bit of delicious friction she could.

She twisted her head when the kiss dragged on. She loved kissing him, but she needed so much more than that.

"Please," she murmured. "I need you. Need..." She let her fingers do the talking as she reached between them, drawing her fingers along his dick. She couldn't see it, but she could sure as shit feel it.

Preston was big everywhere.

He groaned, placing his forehead against hers, their hot, panting breaths mingling.

"You're driving me crazy," he admitted. "In the best fucking way, Chels."

He wasn't alone in his madness. She pressed harder against his cock, then reached for the top button of his jeans.

He captured her wrist, stopping her. "Not here. I want you under me, in bed. All night."

"Yes. God yes. I want that too."

He took her hand and led her to the bed as she took a moment to look around. It was a nice hotel room, the king-sized bed extremely inviting.

Preston had turned on the hallway light upon entering, but now, he switched it off before turning on one of the bedside lamps. The softer lighting, as well as the moon shining in through the window, cast the room is warm shadows, creating the perfect atmosphere for what came next.

"So..." she said, a tiny bit of uncertainty creeping in. She'd been with only one man her entire life, and they'd established a definite, boring routine of undressing themselves before crawling between the sheets.

She was flying blind here.

Preston, once again, seemed to be in tune with her thoughts and feelings. "I know we just met, but can you trust me to take the lead on this?"

She blew out a long, slow breath. "I was hoping you would."

"How adventurous are you feeling?"

His question should have sparked some concerns, but instead they felt more like a dare, a challenge, one she wanted to rise to.

"Refer back to my comment about getting out of a passionless relationship." And then, before she knew what was happening, a flirty, fun side she'd never fully embraced emerged. "Bring it on," she challenged, her tone pure sex kitten.

Preston reacted like a sprinter to the sound of a starting pistol. He cut the distance between them within seconds, his hands cupping her cheeks as he gave her a kiss a million times hotter than all the ones that came before.

This touch, this kiss, was one of utter possession. She was no stranger to romance novels, always drawn to the darker, steamier ones where the alpha hero claimed his woman. Clearly, she'd been seeking the passion that had been lacking between her and Rick through fiction.

Preston wasted no time taking what he wanted. His fingers brushed her sides as he lifted the hem of her sweater, removing it in one quick tug. He did the same with the T-shirt she wore beneath it, then her bra. The pile of clothes at their feet was growing. Unfortunately, it was all hers.

Preston reached out, squeezing her breasts, his gaze locked on her chest. She was tempted to use his sweater line on him, reminding him where her eyes were. But she didn't because the way he was looking at her—like she was Christmas and the Fourth of July personified—filled her well in a way she needed oh-so badly.

He bent forward slightly, drawing the tip of his tongue over one nipple, then the other, in a touch that was too light to be much more than a tease.

She was tempted to grasp the back of his neck, the same way he'd done to her a couple of times tonight, forcing him to suck her nipples harder.

Preston lifted his head, giving her a knowing look that made her wonder if he could read minds.

"If we hadn't just met, I'd tie you to that bed and play with those nipples for hours until you were begging me to fuck you."

It was on the tip of her tongue to beg him to do just that.

Unfortunately, Preston spoke first. "But you don't know me well enough for that. Bondage requires a much higher level of trust. So I'll have to find other ways to make you beg."

Her pussy clenched tighter, and her panties grew even damper. She'd never wanted Rick like this, her arousal off the charts.

However, one thing kept playing over and over in her head on repeat.

One night with Preston would never be enough.

Preston licked her nipples again, but this time, he punctuated that tender stroke with a much firmer pinch, his thumb and forefinger tightening until she cried out in pain and desire.

"God," she breathed, as he continued to play with her breasts, every touch, taste, bite, pinch, and suck making her dizzy with need. And then, she did indeed beg. "Please. Preston, please."

Finally, after several *years* passed, he lifted his head. She expected to see a self-satisfied smirk. Instead, she was met with a mirror image of her own face—one lined with a yearning that bordered on painful.

"I want you. Now." Chelsea started to divest Preston of his sweater as well, but he pushed her hands away.

"Might go faster if I do it." He'd pulled the stocking off and left it in the car. Now, he unwound the Christmas lights. "I wrapped them around me after I put the sweater on and I'm not sure I can get the thing off until they're gone."

"I love how you used shipping tape. Very classy." She couldn't help but make the same joke she'd made at the party, enjoying their easygoing, teasing banter.

He tugged the lights off, the slight ripping of the tape he'd used to hold them to the sweater, filling the room. "You don't want to see me try to thread a needle."

Finally free, he dropped the twinkle lights to the floor, then pulled the sweater over his head with one hand. Unlike her, he hadn't worn anything underneath.

Chelsea moved without thought, her hands sliding over his smooth skin. There was a light smattering of hair around his nipples and before she could consider her actions, her lips were there, offering his tight brown nipples the same sensual torture he'd given her.

Preston's hands closed in her hair, the firm grip causing her scalp to sting. This was her first taste of hair pulling, so she was shocked by the reverberations it sent through her body, drawing a throbbing line along her spine from her scalp to her pussy.

Overwhelmed by sensation, she sank her teeth into Preston's pec. He grunted, then growled.

"Bad girl," he drawled in that deep dark-chocolate voice of his, backing up those sexy words with a smack to her ass. It shocked more than stung, and she instantly tried to think of ways she could encourage him to expand on the spanking.

He pulled away from her, pushing gently on her shoulders until she was standing next to the bed. Sitting in front of her, he reached for her hips. "Take off your jeans, Joy."

She smiled at his nickname for her.

Chelsea unfastened the button, then slid the zipper down. She shimmied the tight denim over her hips as Preston watched from his front-row seat on the side of the mattress. The jeans fell to the floor, but Preston's grip on her hips didn't allow her to bend over to take them off. She tried to toe them and her shoes off, but skinny jeans were unforgiving.

She struggled for a few moments before Preston shifted off the bed, kneeling on the floor in front of her.

Chelsea leaned forward slightly, bracing her hands on his shoulders to steady herself when he lifted one foot, then the other, freeing her of her shoes, socks, and jeans.

All that was left between her and complete nudity was her panties. Not that they lasted long.

Preston didn't bother to rise. Instead, his fingers slipped beneath the elastic, sliding them over her hips and down.

"Preston," she whispered, his name ending on a sharp gasp when he leaned forward, stroking his fingers along her wet slit. Her heart began to race when he shifted even closer, pushing her thighs apart.

She shivered as his tongue traveled the same path his fingers had just taken.

Holy shit.

The way Preston devoured her, his low hums and moans, turning her on as much as his actions. She ran her fingers through his light brown hair.

He lifted his face to hers, and she couldn't help being disappointed, thinking he was done. He hadn't even touched her clit.

Then he said, "Lift one of your feet to the bed. I need more room to work."

She laughed breathlessly when he followed that demand with a wink and the world's most charming smile.

God, this man was dangerous. Not in a scary way but in an "I could fall so hard and fast" way.

She lifted her left foot, slightly afraid she wouldn't be able to maintain her balance.

Once again, Preston seemed to have an inside track to her thoughts. "I won't let you fall," he reassured her, just before he leaned forward. This time, he found her clit, his tongue homing in on it like it had its own GPS. He sucked it into his mouth so perfectly, she saw stars.

Chelsea regained her grip on his shoulders, needing the extra support as her knee went weak.

"Preston! I...God..."

He nipped at her clit with his teeth at the same time he drove two fingers inside her throbbing pussy.

She cried out loudly as she came, silently hoping no one was staying in the hotel rooms next to theirs. She'd never been a noisy lover, but there was no way she could control her volume.

Not when...

"Fuck!" she shouted in bliss as Preston eased a third finger in along with the second two, as her orgasm waned. He was stretching her just beyond her comfort level, but then she recalled the bulge in his jeans. Maybe that was intentional?

Allyson had nailed it earlier.

Because it was definitely the best. Night. Ever.

She was right there on the verge of coming again. Her breathing was so labored, begging wasn't an option at this point.

"Ahh," she cried, just about to go over again when Preston pulled his fingers out and backed away.

Her eyes had been closed, but they flew open, her hands

reaching out to grab whatever she could to bring him back. "No! I was—"

Her world went topsy-turvy as Preston rose from the floor, flipping her around and then back, pushing her onto the bed.

"I promised not to let you fall," he murmured, half lifting, half shoving her to the middle of the large mattress. He pushed her thighs apart, settling between them on his knees.

"You…you weren't finished?" She was aware it was a stupid question, given the fact he was definitely going back for seconds.

"Finished? Fuck no. I just realized one of those orgasms wasn't going to be enough, and you were already wobbly."

She heard his words, but she was struggling to get them to sink in because…

One orgasm wasn't enough for him?

Was that a thing?

Because if so, for the first time since Rick's departure, she was *glad* the fucker had jilted her.

Before she had too long to play with this new, ecstatic feeling, Preston bent his head, and she was lost for good.

It only took a matter of seconds before she was right where she'd started, his fingers, mouth, and tongue working their magic.

Her back arched, and for a moment, it felt as if she'd been struck by lightning, her second climax hitting harder than the first.

She called out his name, her hands flying upward, landing on the pillow beneath her head.

Preston didn't stop, didn't give way. Even when her orgasm started to wane, and she started to panic.

It was all too much, too fucking good.

"Preston." She reached down, intent on pushing him away.

"Put your hands back on the pillow," he growled. "You're not finished surrendering to me."

Surrendering…

Chelsea tried to wrap her head around that word, certain it was the sexiest threat she'd ever heard.

Before she could talk herself out of it, she lifted her hands, palms up, the position one of sheer submission.

Preston's gaze darkened.

She started to wonder if she was really here or if this was a dream. She wasn't this wanton, wild woman. And she'd certainly never been on the receiving end of such potent desire.

"Preston," she whispered.

She had grown accustomed to his easy smile and infectious laugh over the past few hours, but none of that was present here. That laid-back, affable man had been replaced by a dominant, sexy alpha. She hadn't read that wrong.

"That's right, Chelsea," he said. "Say my name. Remember it, and this night. Don't you ever forget it."

There was literally ZERO danger of that. She'd remember this night on her death bed.

He lowered his head again, but this time, Chelsea didn't fight, didn't attempt to deny herself what she didn't even know she needed.

Preston pushed her into a third orgasm, using just his lips and his fingers.

"Please," she said, her voice hoarse from her cries.

"Please?"

She lifted her heavy eyelids, her vision slightly fuzzy as the vestiges of the climax wavered. Preston had risen so that he was kneeling between her outstretched legs, looking down at her with a pleased, if slightly pained, grin.

That was when she realized he was still wearing his jeans.

"Please," she repeated. "I want you. Inside me."

Preston tilted his head, studied her, and she got the sense he was still giving her a chance to change her mind.

As if she freaking would.

Only a fool would walk away from this bed and this man. And her mother didn't raise a fool.

She lifted one spaghetti arm, her strength zapped from the abundance of orgasms. "I'm not going to say no. Now take those pants off and get inside me. Please."

One side of his mouth quirked up. "I do like the way you beg. Or should I say demand?" He gave her a brief glimpse of the fun charmer she'd enjoyed spending time with at the party. "Don't move."

She gave him an incredulous look. "You're kidding, right? I think I live here now. Couldn't move if I wanted to."

Her words provoked the chuckle she'd grown far too fond of, given their short acquaintance.

"I wouldn't complain if you wanted to set up camp here for a few nights or…"

He didn't fill in that last blank, but there was something in his eyes that told her he meant that. Then she recalled his past dating history. How he was genuinely interested in a true relationship. Why couldn't they have met a few months earlier?

Preston rose from the bed, facing her as he unzipped his jeans, shedding them and his boxer briefs at the same time.

Chelsea hadn't thought a second wind was in the cards, but apparently, she'd just been dealt a royal flush.

"Wow," she murmured.

Preston reached into the pocket of his jeans, pulling out his wallet and then a condom, slipping it on. "What was it you said earlier? Oh yeah. Good for the soul. Gonna have to say right back atcha on that."

She hadn't lied. She'd spent months wallowing in self-pity, self-doubt, and misery, constantly searching for some remedy, some way to pull herself together.

Preston had found the cure to all three of those things in one fell swoop—with his humor, his compliments, his compassion, and his off-the-chart abilities in the bedroom.

She'd hoped Paris would offer her the clean slate, but now, it looked like she would be traveling to France with her board already cleared. Preston had done that, given that to her.

He helped her find her confidence, but more than that, he'd shown her that she was ready to move on.

The mattress sank as Preston climbed back into bed. He crawled toward her, not stopping until she was caged beneath him.

"Ready for more?"

More?

Most people might have considered three orgasms more than enough, because she'd certainly lit up like the grand finale of the Fourth of July fireworks.

Preston clearly was not most people.

She nodded enthusiastically. "Hell yeah. Give me more."

CHAPTER FOUR

PRESTON STARED at Chelsea for a moment, committing her face to memory. Tonight had been one of the best of his life, which thrilled and depressed him at the same time.

He'd never felt such instant chemistry or connection with a woman, and the damned romantic fool inside him was convinced Chelsea had been made for him.

He'd met his soul mate—and in one week, she was flying to Paris. Possibly forever.

Karma hated him.

Preston gripped his dick, pressing the head of his cock to her opening before sliding home.

It was strange that *home* was the first word that popped into his head, but that was sure as hell what it felt like.

He pushed that thought away. There would be plenty of time to sulk over what might have been, later.

Tonight was all he was going to get with Chelsea, and by God, he was going to make it count.

He held still for a second, giving her time to adjust, when he saw her wince slightly once he was seated to the hilt.

"Okay?" he asked.

"How much would the words 'well-endowed' feed your ego?"

"Nom nom," he joked, pretending he was feasting on her compliment.

Chelsea giggled. "I was afraid of that." Then she reached up, one hand stroking the side of his face. "I'm better than okay."

He sent up a small prayer of thanks because, while he would have stopped if she'd complained about it being too much for her, blue balls hurt like a bitch.

Preston withdrew, then returned, starting slow and shallow at first, giving her time, stretching her out.

However, all ability to keep himself in check flew out the window when her pussy tightened around him like a vise as he found her G-spot, and she cried out his name. Her begging gave way to demands, and damn if his girl wasn't good at making her needs known.

"God, harder." She tilted her hips in such a way that he thrust in even deeper, the two of them groaning in unison.

She was fucking hot, and wet, and her pussy was gloving his dick so firmly, he feared he'd have bruises tomorrow. Chelsea's hips began moving in time with his downward thrusts, the impact powerful, overwhelming.

He wanted to make this last, determined to make up for all the lackluster sex her clueless asshole of an ex had subjected her to.

Chelsea deserved so much more. Fuck, she deserved everything.

When she lifted her legs, gripping her knees, changing the path and the sensations again, he was a goner.

Fuck it. He had three more condoms left in his wallet. He'd use every damn one, keep her in this bed as long as he could, build this memory big enough to last.

He began to piston in faster, driving deeper.

Chelsea went over fast, her climax hitting hard. She yelled his name loud enough he worried the folks in the next room might call the front desk to complain.

Still, Preston thrust, desperate to wring out every single drop of pleasure he could. Chelsea landed, but only briefly.

Tossing her head side to side on the bed, he would have thought she was gesturing "no," if not for her words.

"Yes! Oh my God. Preston. Fuck! Right there. Just. Like. That!"

He was there, too close. If they were embarking on something more than just tonight, if they weren't limited to only the here and now, he might have given in to his baser instincts, would have come now without her.

But this was it. All they had.

So he wanted to do it right. The first time. And every single time that came after.

He reached between them and found her clit. Chelsea's eyes had been closed, but they flew open on the initial stroke. Because he was fighting the very devil himself to stave off his climax, he couldn't draw enough air to laugh at the panic reflected on her face.

"One more will kill me," she said, with a seriousness that told him she really believed that.

"One more," he demanded, thrusting hard as he continued to stroke her clit.

He feared he'd fail, his balls growing tight. He couldn't hold off for another—

Chelsea's head flew back and she cried out, a steady stream of curse words with his name peppered in for good measure. "Jesus Christ! Fuck me. Preston!"

Her orgasm took him down like an avalanche, his own cries mingling with hers as jet after jet filled the condom. He'd never come this hard in his whole life.

"Chelsea. *Fuck*. Goddammit."

Her nails scored his back, the sting adding another layer to the pleasure. For a second, he swore to God he had an out-of-body experience, the edges of his vision fading to darkness, everything straight ahead nothing but a bright white light.

Only her voice, breathlessly calling out his name, kept him tethered to Earth.

They remained there for several minutes, him caging her beneath him, his weight resting on his elbows by her sides. He kissed her gently, over and over, obsessed with her lips, her tongue, her. All of her.

Resting his forehead against hers, he smiled, breathing in her scent, certain he'd never smelled anything sweeter.

Chelsea shifted slightly and he realized just how much he didn't want to leave her body.

Slowly, he withdrew, his dick still riding at half-mast despite the fact he'd just come. He paused when the condom slipped, and he quickly reached between them, his fingers dipping inside to grab it, pulling the condom out of her before it fell off completely.

"Slipped," he murmured. "I've got it."

Chelsea didn't say anything, her eyelids heavy with exhaustion, her cheeks flushed pink from all the pleasure.

He left the bed, heading to the bathroom to toss the condom before washing his hands and splashing some water on his face.

He studied his reflection in the mirror, his thoughts hazy as he tried to gather his wits. What a night! When regret that this was all they could have slipped in, he shut the feeling down and returned to the bedroom.

Walking to the bed, he dropped next to her on his back. The bed was damp from their exertions, the room actually steamy. He wondered if she had enough energy to join him in the shower.

Chelsea was the first to break the silence. "Preston?"

"Yeah?"

Please don't ask to leave, he thought. Preston would drive her home if she wanted, but he really hoped he could convince her to give him the whole night. And then maybe he'd talk her into staying for breakfast in the morning. He was ready to be greedy, to take as much as he could before saying goodbye.

She twisted on her side to face him, so he turned his head to look at her.

"Tonight was incredible," she said. "I don't think I can express what it's meant to me. What you've done for me."

He smiled, even though he hated the tone of finality in her voice. He'd gone into this knowing it couldn't be any more than one night, but apparently, the hopeless romantic had decided to move in for good.

"Tonight *was* incredible," he repeated, agreeing. "But it's not over. Spend the whole night with me."

She nodded. "Of course. I'd like that. I want to."

He was suffused with relief, even as he cursed himself for being a fool. For prolonging the inevitable. "Could I convince you to join me for a shower?"

She giggled. "A sexy shower?"

"The sexiest." Preston stood once more, reaching to help her out of bed. He let his eyes slide over her gorgeous curves. Too many of the puck bunnies who hovered around him and his teammates were super-thin women with Botoxed lips, boob jobs, dyed hair, extensions. Everything about them was more fake than real, as they spent big bucks trying to achieve what they thought men wanted. He couldn't speak for other guys, but all that money-generated beauty missed the mark by a mile when it came to what he found attractive in women.

Chelsea, with her curly chestnut hair, expressive dark brown eyes, and curvy figure with round hips and tits that filled his hands to perfection, was all real, and his exact idea of true beauty. She didn't wear much makeup because she didn't need to. She had a healthy complexion with her pink cheeks, full lips, long, thick lashes, and the cutest damn dimples he'd ever seen.

She blushed under his intense scrutiny of her body. "I, uh, I have a bit of a sweet tooth. While I love cupcakes, they don't exactly love me." As she spoke, she covered her rounded stomach with her hands.

Preston pulled them away, then ran the back of his fingers over her side before digging them into her waist softly so that he could pull her against him. "You're beautiful, Chelsea, and your body is banging."

She laughed. "I think we're going to have to agree to disagree on that because…" She drew her fingertips over his chest, lightly scratching him with one of her nails. "If anyone has a banging body in here, it's you. I swear to God, it's like you're chiseled from stone."

"Too much time spent in the gym." That time was a necessary part of his job, but he didn't add that tidbit.

"If that's the end result, I'd say it's the perfect amount."

Preston took her hand, leading her to the bathroom. She leaned against the sink while he reached into the shower, turning on the water and adjusting the temperature.

Once it was warm enough, he crooked his finger, allowing her to step inside first. There was a rain showerhead above them, in addition to the one at the side, so that both of them were submerged beneath the jets.

Chelsea tilted her head back, wetting her hair and slicking it back with her hands, as he pumped a few squirts of shampoo into his palm from the bottle provided by the hotel.

She looked surprised and pleased when he began to wash her hair, the citrus-scented suds filling the air. Chelsea moaned as he massaged her scalp, applying pressure meant to relax her.

"That feels incredible." She closed her eyes when he guided her under the showerhead, rinsing out the shampoo.

Opening her eyes, she gave him a mischievous grin. "I'd like to return the favor, but I think I need a step ladder to reach your hair."

Preston chuckled, then craned his head toward the corner behind him. "Lucky for us. There's a bench seat." He sank down on it, his firm hands on her hips, pulling her forward until she stood in front of him.

Chelsea reached for the shampoo, gasping softly when Preston put their new position to good use, sucking one of her nipples into his mouth.

She managed to work up a lather in his hair as he tormented her breasts with his teeth and fingers and tongue. He loved the way she forgot herself at times, her fists closing in his hair, tugging it roughly in response to his ministrations.

"So good," she whispered. "You make me feel so good."

Unable to hold back, Preston rose and quickly rinsed his own hair before twisting Chelsea away from him, pushing her chest against the tiled wall in front of her.

With his hand, he guided his cock between her legs, stroking it along her wet slit. Chelsea gripped him between her clenched thighs, adding her own motion to the thrust.

Preston continued to stroke, the head of his cock brushing her clit over and over. On one return thrust, Chelsea tilted her hips too much and his dick slipped inside her pussy. He clenched his teeth, gripping her hard to hold her still. He'd never taken a woman without a condom, and honestly, he could have gone a lifetime without knowing how fucking amazing it felt, because now…

Jesus.

He couldn't linger inside her, but pulling away was almost physically impossible.

Why the fuck hadn't he thought to grab a condom before leading her to the shower?

Probably because he'd just fucking come.

Chelsea squirmed as much as his tight grip would allow, her pussy clenching around him, seeking more, until she realized why he was holding back. He groaned as the two of them pulled away from each other, his dick mourning the loss of her hot cunt.

"Sorry," she murmured. "I didn't...I mean... It just feels..."

"Yeah," he agreed, pushing his cock back between her thighs, resuming the tantalizing, irresistible feeling of being tucked between the lips of her pussy. Reaching around her, he rubbed her clit, pinching it a couple of times, causing her to rise on her tiptoes as she moaned. The friction between her thighs was driving his arousal higher than he expected.

"God. I think I'm going to..." she gasped. "This isn't... normal."

It spoke to just what a loser her ex was that she seemed shocked to discover she could come more than one—five—times in a night.

"It's completely normal," he replied, increasing the pressure of his fingers on her clit as he continued to slide between her thighs, the motion pushing him to the brink again as well. While he wasn't a stranger to multiple orgasms in a single evening, his recovery time was usually longer. Something told him he could come right now, and only need a few minutes before he was ready to take her again.

Suddenly, three condoms didn't feel like anywhere near enough.

Chelsea used her forearms, pressed flat against the tile wall, to help propel herself back and forth in time with his movements.

Unable to resist, he gripped her ass cheek with his free hand while still working her clit with the other. Sliding his thumb through the crack, he wiggled it over her anus, loving the loud gasping burst of air that erupted from her lips.

"Preston!"

There was enough shock in the tone to let him know she was novice at anal play. If that was all he heard, he would have pulled back. However, there was just as much interest in those two syllables, so he wiggled his thumb again.

Her head bowed forward as her body began to tremble, a sign her climax was rapidly approaching. Not for the first time tonight, he cursed the fact she was leaving.

Fucking Paris.

"God," she cried out, her back arching as she came hard. While Preston would have killed to be inside her body, experiencing that orgasm in 4-D, it was just as potent this way because he was able to focus more on her response than his. He held her upright, her body too shaky to do the job. Her breathing was staggered, and he could feel her swollen clit pulsing between his fingers. She closed her hands into fists briefly before opening them again and splaying them on the tile, seeking purchase, support.

She didn't need it. He would never let her fall.

There was something truly beautiful about watching this woman come undone in his arms. Because in that moment, she wasn't just giving him her body.

No. Chelsea was giving him something so much better.

Her trust.

She'd been hurt this year, and he had gotten the sense from their conversations that her ex's cruel actions hadn't just broken her heart but wounded her ability to trust.

The knowledge that she was offering that trust to him tonight, warmed him all the way to the depths of his soul.

Only when the last vestiges of her climax had waned did Preston give in to his own needs. Gripping his cock in his fist, he pumped it roughly, rapidly, no more than a dozen strokes necessary before he came between her thighs, as well as on her lower back and ass.

"Fuck," he said through gritted teeth, shocked by how much come there was, considering he'd just filled a condom less than half an hour ago. "Jesus. Chelsea." Her name fell from his lips like a prayer. God knew that was what this night with her felt like. The answer to a prayer, something he'd never even thought to ask for.

The side of Chelsea's head rested on her hand against the wall, her gaze cast over her shoulder in his direction. "You are so sexy," she murmured.

He couldn't hold back his grin as he leaned forward and kissed her shoulder. "Can't hold a candle to you."

Chelsea pushed herself upright, and Preston spun her around until her back was directly under the stream of hot water. Pumping some body wash on his hand, he scrubbed away his come, then dragged his fingers through her slit, cleaning off her own arousal.

"It occurs to me I've been doing showers wrong my whole life," she said, her voice husky as she looked up at him through long lashes.

"Oh yeah?"

"I've always used them for getting clean. I see now, the best showers are the ones where you get very, very dirty."

Preston laughed, even though she made one hell of a point.

Turning off the water, he reached for a towel before helping her out of the shower. She giggled as he vigorously dried her off, then swatted his hands away as he started sluicing water from her long hair.

"I'm perfectly capable of drying myself off," she said, grinning widely.

"Well, I'm not, and this is definitely a tit-for-tat situation." Preston grabbed a dry towel and handed it to her, wiggling his eyebrows suggestively.

Chelsea took it without complaint. While his attempt at drying her off had been playful, hers was full-on seduction as she slowly drew the soft material over his skin.

His cock took notice—because of course it did—and within minutes, he was riding at half-mast again. She was going to be the death of him. And he didn't fucking mind a bit. He'd had a good life.

Once they were dry, they returned to the bedroom, crawling beneath the covers together. They hadn't even known each other six hours, and yet it felt completely natural to lay next to her, neither of them uncomfortable in their nudity.

"I've lost count of how many times I've come tonight," she whispered.

"You keep mentioning that."

"Because it's pretty fucking notable," she said, half joking, half serious.

"Am I to assume you've broken some sort of record? Tonight's your personal best or something?"

Chelsea's eyes widened. "Or something, for sure. My previous best was twice in one night, and that was because Rick was tipsy and riding high over a big promotion at work. It put him in a frisky, celebratory mood." Then she sighed. "Dammit. I'm sorry. I hate that I keep bringing him up."

Preston gripped the back of her neck, tilting her downturned face upward until her gaze connected with his. "Chelsea. I'm never going to bitch about comparisons between me and your ex when I come out sounding like a total stud."

His joke had the desired effect as she cracked up. "Oh my God. I can't remember the last time I've laughed this much. You are too much."

"Aaaaaand?" he prompted.

"A total stud."

"Good girl. Now, how would you feel about recreating that shower scene here in bed? Only this time, with a condom…and me buried deep inside your body?"

Chelsea didn't bother to respond with words. Instead, she did one better, flipping over onto her hands and knees, shaking her sexy ass at him.

"Only if you promise to spank me again," she said.

Preston, unable to resist, lifted his hand and smacked one of her gorgeous ass cheeks.

Chelsea glanced over her shoulder at him. "Do that again. But harder."

Preston didn't need to be asked twice. "I knew you were a kinky girl."

She laughed in delight. "Only with you."

Unable to resist, Preston lowered his head and gave her a light nip on her now-pink ass cheek, while she tried to wiggle away. "Good answer. I like the idea of keeping all your kinkiness to myself."

Preston spanked her again, and while the first few were light and silly, it quickly morphed into something hotter.

Especially when Chelsea lowered her head to the bed, lifting her ass higher. "So hot," she murmured.

Her flushed cheeks—both sets—proved that statement true.

Unable to resist testing her limits, Preston ran his finger through her ass crack once more. Ordinarily, with a new lover, he took his time, broaching new bedroom adventures over countless evenings rather than trying everything right out of the gate.

But with Chelsea, there was no time, and he was overcome by the need to claim as much as he could because he knew this was all there was.

Chelsea moaned softly when his thumb brushed her anus.

"New kink or familiar one?" he asked.

"New."

Dragging his hand lower, he dipped his fingers into her pussy, loving how she was wet and ready for him...again. He wasn't the only one experiencing some top-notch recovery times. Coating his fingers, he returned to her ass, pushing one inside, just to the first knuckle.

Chelsea stilled—her body, her breathing, everything.

"Okay?" he asked.

Her hands clenched into fists around the pillow beneath her head. "So okay."

He took that as permission to forge on, so he did, shallowly thrusting in and out, adding a bit more until one finger was locked tight in the grip of her ass.

"Holy shit," she whispered. "I never knew…expected…"

Preston slowly fucked her ass with just one finger, letting her get used to having that tight hole filled. He wouldn't go any further tonight. He couldn't. And while that realization practically killed him, he refused to do anything that Chelsea wasn't fully prepared for.

He wanted her memories of this night to be nothing but good.

When she tilted her hips toward him, moving in time with his finger, he decided to up the ante. Reaching around her with his free hand, he brought her clit into play. It hadn't taken him long to learn her clit was the key to her city.

She shivered when he stroked it, then began to writhe, begging him for more. He wanted to ask her to be more specific, not because he didn't know what she wanted but because hearing her describe what she wanted him to do to her was so fucking hot.

However, he didn't have a chance because Chelsea had been way more primed and ready than he'd expected. As he increased the speed and force of his stroking—both of her clit and ass—she came quickly.

The sound of shock that preceded it told him she hadn't been expecting it either. He didn't stop touching her, though he slowed his roll, drawing out her climax as long as he could.

Chelsea's knees gave out and she sank facedown into the mattress. "I…didn't even…know…" she said between gasps.

Preston withdrew his finger from her ass, gripping her butt in his hands. Still kneeling between her outstretched thighs, he took a moment to study the delicate curve of her back, the way her hips flared out, the soft slope of her ass.

She was utter perfection, and he tried to commit her body to memory. Hell, he was tempted to ask if he could take a picture of her, just like this, something he could look at during the long, lonely nights he was facing in the future. He'd spent his entire adult life looking for someone like her.

He didn't have to pretend with Chelsea, didn't have to guard his words or reactions, didn't have to shield parts of himself lest he come on too strong. God, she didn't even know what he did for a living, which made this so much more powerful. Because he knew all the way to the depths of his soul, she was here for him—the real him—not the professional athlete.

"Preston?" she said after a few minutes.

He'd gone quiet for too long. "I'm still here."

"I wish I'd met you sooner."

Fuck. Those words hit him like a freight train.

"I wish the same thing."

They let those confessions hover there, neither of them saying anything else.

Fortunately for him, Chelsea found a way to bring them out of that heaviness. Pushing back to her hands and knees, she captured his gaze.

"I want you to fuck me. Hard. I want to be able to still feel you next week when I'm in Paris."

Preston wasn't the type to shy away from a challenge, and goddamn, if he didn't want to leave that kind of a lasting mark on her. Because she was sure as shit leaving hers on him.

Putting on a condom, he gripped her hips, slammed inside, and then he took them both on one hell of a ride, fucking her until they were delirious, out of their minds. He no longer gave a fuck who heard them, and it was probably a sure bet everyone on this floor could.

Chelsea came twice more, and on the second orgasm, she pulled him into the sweet abyss with her.

Preston wasn't even sure how long they remained in place, connected, before he recovered his wits enough to withdraw and dispose of the condom.

When he returned to bed, she became the little spoon to his big one and they both drifted to sleep for an hour or so.

The rest of the night passed in a blur of sex interspersed with short naps and long heart-to-hearts, where they shared countless stories of their childhood and continued their "favorites" game, covering books, food, vacations, and more.

Neither of them was willing to waste the time sleeping, knowing this was all they could have. They were counting down the hours together, so they created a lifetime of memories in a single evening, sharing every secret, hope, dream, and fear.

At four a.m., their bodies and minds wore out and Preston fell into the deepest sleep of his life.

When he opened his eyes again, he blinked several times, a bright stream of sunlight from the curtain they'd forgotten to close last night nearly blinding him.

It took a second before he realized it wasn't the sun that woke him up but the sound of someone walking around the room.

Rising, his chest tightened when he spotted Chelsea, fully dressed, sitting on a chair and putting her shoes on.

She glanced at him, offering what he was sure she'd intended to be a cheerful smile. She wasn't selling it as well as she might have hoped because he could read every bit of the sadness he was currently feeling in her expression.

"I called for a rideshare," she said softly.

Preston shook his head, quickly climbing out of bed, reaching for his jeans. "No. I'll give you a ride."

She stood and crossed the room to him, putting her hand on his, stopping him from fastening his jeans.

"The car is already on its way, and I think this is better."

He scowled. "Better?"

"Rip the Band-Aid off."

"Give me your phone number, your address, your last name," he demanded. "This doesn't have to be it."

He knew by her utter stillness she wasn't going to give him any of it.

He huffed out a sigh. She'd told him it could only be one night. She wasn't the one trying to change the parameters. He was.

"Fine," he grumbled. Preston ran a hand through his hair, fighting back the rising rage. None of this was her fault. She'd been very honest with him about exactly how far this could go. She'd shown him the finish line and now they'd reached it.

While he wanted to fight her on this, wanted to demand more time, wanted to beg her to reconsider Paris, he wouldn't do any of that. Because he didn't want to ruin what had been the best night of his life with words he'd regret.

"I hate saying goodbye to you."

The glassy sheen in her eyes let him know the feeling was mutual. He wasn't sure why he took a modicum of comfort in the idea that she was as sad as he was. Maybe the old saying was true. Misery *did* love company.

"Preston, I can never thank you enough for last night or tell you just how much it meant to me."

Her hand still rested on his, so he turned his wrist, clasping their palms together. "I'm never going to forget you, Chelsea."

She smiled, blinking rapidly, beating back all but one tear that escaped, sliding down her cheek.

He reached out and brushed it away. "I hope you find happiness in Paris, my sweet Joy."

She smiled sadly, then leaned forward and kissed him on the cheek. "I hope you find your soul mate, my dear, wonderful, hopeful romantic." She'd changed the descriptor, and while he liked it, he knew his own was more accurate.

Because he'd never felt more hopeless.

They pressed their foreheads together, soaking in these precious last few moments before…

Chelsea stepped away first, squeezing his hand. "Goodbye, BFG."

He followed her to the door, holding it open as she gave him one last smile, then turned and walked away.

As the door closed, he leaned against it, closing his eyes as he whispered, "Goodbye, Chelsea."

CHAPTER FIVE

ONE YEAR LATER...

Preston tightened his jacket around him, cursing the cold wind that had kicked up since he'd decided to walk to the restaurant rather than drive. It was a pretty, if chilly morning, but it wasn't like he was a stranger to the cold. Hell, after spending a lifetime playing on ice, it was rare that he even *felt* cold. But today's biting wind—paired with his too-light jacket— was in danger of freezing his nuts off.

He should have driven, but he'd hoped a nice brisk walk outside might energize him. He'd been sluggish and...well, blue since Thanksgiving. For a few days, he wondered if he was coming down with something, but when the doldrums persisted, he realized his troubles were mental, not physical.

Preston was typically an upbeat guy, but this had been a tough year for him, starting with saying goodbye to Chelsea last December. While it had been hard to watch her walk away, he honestly thought he'd bounce back. That the memory of her would fade and he'd move on.

More the fool him.

The immediate attraction or infatuation or whatever the hell it was when he'd met her had only grown with each passing month, until he'd reached this point. This celibate, never-go-out-on-dates, lonely bachelor state that showed no signs of ending.

Possibly ever.

He crossed over a couple of blocks, hoping to find a side street that was less wind tunnel before continuing in the direction of the restaurant where he was meeting Victor for breakfast.

This new route was less familiar, the street one he never walked or drove down. After a few blocks, he slowed his pace, noticing several new businesses had sprung up in the area. They'd been gentrifying this street in stages over the past few years, but he'd missed the latest round of improvements to what was now a lovely tree-lined block. The storefronts advertised an array of shops and boutiques, offering everything from candles to Baltimore souvenirs to an Italian deli.

Halfway down the block, he paused when a sign across the street caught his eye.

"Sugar and Spice Bakery." There was a cardboard sign tucked in the corner of the window that said, "Coming Valentine's Day."

Sugar and Spice was Chelsea's dream bakery name. Just recalling it took him back to that night last year, the one he'd played over in his mind so many times, it was a wonder he hadn't gone mad. While he knew this couldn't be Chelsea's bakery, given the fact she lived in Paris, he still couldn't help but hope.

Then he shook himself. Even if Paris hadn't worked out, she would have moved back to her hometown, to Philadelphia. The chances of her opening a bakery twelve blocks from his condo in Baltimore were zero to nil.

Regardless, he stood there for a full minute, tempted to cross the street and peer in the window. It was a stupid whim but a powerful one. After all, what would it hurt to take a closer look?

It wasn't like he could obsess over the one who got away any more than he already did.

Given it was nearly nine on a weekday, there were a fair amount of people walking around, all of them with their heads down, dashing off to their nine-to-fives. There was quite a bit of traffic as well, as a steady stream of commuters drove to work, which meant that as he stepped to the end of the curb to cross, he was forced to wait.

Then he remained where he was when he saw a tall man in an expensive suit stop in front of the bakery window, waving to someone inside.

It wasn't until Preston saw *her* step outside that he realized he'd been holding his breath.

Chelsea.

It was *his* Chelsea.

His Joy.

Here in Baltimore.

Preston froze, blinking rapidly, convinced he was seeing things. Perhaps today was the day he finally went around the bend, losing his mind once and for all.

It didn't make sense for her to be here, and yet…

She smiled as she approached the man. Even from across the street, he could see the smile was somewhat forced, not the genuine, easygoing ones she'd given him.

Preston couldn't hear what Chelsea and the man were saying as he was too far away, and there was too much noise from the foot and vehicle traffic. He also couldn't beat back the sudden rush of jealousy as the man bent toward her, cutting the personal space between them in half. This didn't feel like a polite conversation between acquaintances. They were too familiar with each other, the man too friendly.

Preston had wished for an entire year that he could see Chelsea again, and now here she was, less than thirty feet from him, and he couldn't make himself move, too many questions holding him back.

Why wasn't she in Paris?

When had she moved to Baltimore from Philadelphia?

Who was this man?

Why was he standing so close to her?

Full-blown envy erupted when the man reached out, tucking one of Chelsea's curls behind her ear, the action too intimate for Preston's peace of mind.

Unfortunately, it was only the man's face Preston could see clearly, Chelsea turned at an angle so that he only caught the occasional glimpse of her profile. As such, he couldn't see how she was looking at the man.

Was she in love with him?

Were they a couple?

That idea hit hard, and as much as he hated to acknowledge it, it hurt. Bad.

Chelsea lifted one arm, pointing to something inside the bakery as she and the man continued to speak. Preston drank in the sight of her because, holy fuck, the past year had been good to her. Her hair was longer, her curves curvier, her hips wider, her breasts larger, and that ass. *Fuck*, he loved her ass.

She was a living, breathing goddess, and the woman who'd invaded every single one of his dreams since the night they'd met.

And here he stood, immobile, unable to make himself approach her.

Not just because of the other man.

What if Chelsea didn't remember who he was?

What if he'd been the only one to build that night up into something magical and unforgettable and perfect?

He mentally cursed at himself and took a step off the curb, refusing to be a goddamn coward.

However, he didn't take another when the man leaned forward and kissed Chelsea.

Preston turned away rapidly, his heart thudding too hard in his chest. There was no way he could watch another man kiss her.

Departing quickly—lest he lose his mind, cross the street, and punch the fucker out—he maintained a steady, relentless pace, refusing to look back.

When he arrived at the restaurant, he was out of breath and torn between pure rage and utter despair. Victor was already waiting for him in a booth, and the astute bastard read both expressions before Preston could even attempt to school his features. Not that he was trying too hard.

"That's a fucking brutal look," Victor grumbled as Preston joined him. "What the fuck happened? Did someone piss in your aquarium?"

Preston didn't—couldn't—fix his face, so the scowl remained. "I'm fine," he replied, too shortly to sell the words.

Victor snorted in disbelief. "Yeah, right."

Before his friend could continue to question him, the waitress, Yvonne, approached them. "Hey, Preston, Victor. You guys want to start with something to drink while you look at the menu?"

The fact Yvonne knew their names, and they knew hers, was a testament to just how much Preston and his Stingrays teammates hung out here.

Sunday's Side was the restaurant attached to their preferred watering hole, Pat's Pub, and it was Preston's favorite place for breakfast. He didn't have a clue what the cook, Riley, put in her blueberry pancakes to make them so light and delicious, but he would walk a hundred miles across the desert on his knees for an order.

"I'll have a coffee," Victor said. "Black."

Preston didn't usually drink coffee, but he was having a hard time giving a shit what he drank or ate at the moment. "Same."

Yvonne smiled as she flipped the cups already on their table, filling them with the pot she'd carried over with her. "Okay. Do you need a few minutes, or are you going with the usual?"

Yep. They were here a lot.

Victor, also a huge fan of the pancakes, spoke for both of them. "The usual. Tall stacks with the side of bacon."

Yvonne chuckled. "Y'all really should consider trying something else. I promise it's all good."

Ordinarily, Preston was the one carrying on the polite conversation with Yvonne, as Victor was a grumpy bastard on a good day. Preston must've look more pissed off than he realized, considering Victor was taking one for the team and handling all the chitchat, he and Yvonne sharing some pleasantries and talking about the season. Yvonne was part of the Collins clan who ran the restaurant and pub, and if there were bigger Stingrays fans in the city, Preston hadn't met them yet.

Once Yvonne left to put in their order, Victor leaned back, his arms resting on the top of the booth. "Alright. Spill."

"Nothing to spill," Preston lied.

Victor studied his face hard, then growled. "Sure, there isn't. Listen, when the guys heard we were going to breakfast this morning, they appointed me their fucking spokesperson, even though I said *fuck no*."

"Spokesperson?"

"The guys want to know what the hell is going on with you, man."

Preston didn't want to talk about any of this. Not his depression. Not Chelsea. Not that fucking asshole who was kissing her.

He thought he'd been pretty good at shielding his blues, but if his teammates had noticed…

Time to deflect.

"What do you mean?"

Victor frowned, annoyed at the way he was playing dumb. "You've been a fucking sad sack since Thanksgiving. Usually, you're more annoying than that Will Farrell *Elf* character at the holidays, and today you walked in here looking like somebody just fucking punched your mother. So what gives?"

"I'm just not feeling it this year. Not feeling a lot of things lately," Preston confessed. Especially not today. Not now that he'd seen Chelsea with that man.

Victor studied his face closely. "You think it's some sort of midlife crisis thing?"

Preston had considered that when he realized his struggles were mental, not physical. But he'd dismissed the idea fairly quickly. Because even if that was the case, the usual cures wouldn't help because he already owned a shit-hot car, and he loved his condo overlooking the Inner Harbor. So, it wasn't like he could buy himself happiness or move.

On top of that, he had a decent social life with plenty of good friends—both his teammates and his neighbors—so he wasn't hurting for company when he wanted it.

He'd even thought perhaps his sadness had been the result of losing Johnny and June back in September. He'd bought his beloved clownfish right after he signed with the Rays, and they'd been a part of his life for fourteen years. Just before Thanksgiving, he'd purchased two new clownfish and an even larger aquarium, and while he'd grown fond of the new fish, they weren't the magic fix he'd been hoping for.

Which meant the problem was exactly what he hadn't wanted to admit, not even to himself.

Chelsea.

"I'm only thirty-five. Too young for a midlife crisis."

Victor didn't reply, probably because he didn't appear to agree.

While he really didn't want to talk about his doldrums or the Chelsea sighting, Preston was kind of glad Victor was the elected spokesperson. Because of all Preston's teammates, Victor was the one most likely to relate to some of the shit that had been mucking his thoughts lately. He and Victor weren't just the oldest guys on the team; they were two of the longest-standing Rays, both playing for Baltimore for over a decade. So, they had a shared history as far as their careers went.

Maybe it wouldn't be the worst thing to talk about some of the other, easier things he'd been thinking about recently.

God knew he wasn't ready to deal with what he just saw down the street.

"How long do you think you're going to keep playing?" Preston asked.

Victor's brows rose so high, they nearly disappeared into his hairline. "You thinking of retiring from hockey?"

Preston quickly shook his head, even though he wasn't as sure of that answer as he might seem. "I've been at this for fifteen years, and believe me, I'm starting to feel every minute of that. In my back, my knees, my ankles."

Victor smirked. "Tell me about it. Hockey takes its toll. But come on, man, we're not past our prime yet. Shit. I feel like I'm just hitting my stride."

Preston agreed with that. With each passing year, Victor got stronger and stronger. The guy was a beast on the ice, and there was no better defenseman in the league than Victor Reed.

"You are," Preston agreed.

"And so are you," Victor added.

Preston wasn't so sure about that. While his playing hadn't declined, he felt as if he'd reached a plateau these past couple of years. If he asked his teammates and coaches about it, they would say they had no problem with that plateau because he was still a rock-solid left-winger. He knew that. If his playing had slipped, he would have been the first one to put in more fucking hours in the gym and on the ice…or, if it came to it, make the decision to walk away. He was a competitive asshole, but he was also a team player who believed in earning every penny of his ridiculously generous salary.

Preston leaned back and sighed. "I'm not sure it's the physical wear and tear of the job that's getting me down. I think it has more to do with work/life ratio."

Victor snorted. "You been talking to the team shrink?"

Preston chuckled miserably. He probably *should* talk to the shrink, but as soon as he thought it, he dismissed it. Fuck that jazz.

"What the fuck are you talking about, work/life ratio?" Victor pressed.

"It's hard to have a social life during the season," Preston explained.

"Bullshit. We go out plenty. You're not talking about fucking partying; you're talking about fucking. As in, you aren't getting any. And we all know why."

They *did* know why. All of his teammates knew about…her.

Preston rubbed his eyes. He'd already opened up to Victor, so why not go for broke? He needed advice.

"I just saw Chelsea. Fifteen minutes ago."

If Preston had been in a better frame of mind, he would have laughed at Victor's outright shock, his wide eyes, his mouth hanging open.

"Chelsea? *Your* fucking Chelsea?" he asked loudly.

Preston had long ago stopped noticing the way Victor dropped the F-bomb into sentences the way some people used commas, but the same didn't hold true for the two elderly women at the table next to them, who were shooting very disapproving glances.

Unfortunately for them, Preston didn't have it in him to curb Victor's foul language today. "She's not my Chelsea."

His response seemed to catch Victor off guard. "She's not?"

Preston shook his head. "Nope. Chelsea belongs to the guy I just saw her locking lips with down the street."

Victor grunted in response to that information. "Well, that explains your award-winning disposition this morning. Are you sure it was Chelsea? I mean, isn't she supposed to be in Paris?"

"I'm positive it was her, though I don't have a clue why she's not in Paris or how she ended up in Baltimore."

Victor rubbed his jaw, which, even now, first thing in the morning, was covered with a five-o'clock shadow. Victor swore his beard grew back before he even finished shaving. "Back up and start at the beginning."

"I decided to walk here rather than drive."

Victor scowled. "In that jacket? It's cold as a witch's tit out there."

They got another dirty look from the old ladies, but Victor either didn't see or didn't care.

"The wind didn't pick up until I was on my way here. I walked down a different street from my usual because it sheltered me from the cold better, and I saw a sign for a new bakery."

At Victor's blank expression, Preston explained, "Chelsea's childhood dream was to open her own bakery. She planned on calling it Sugar and Spice."

Victor cracked his neck, the action a regular habit that drove Preston crazy. "Never ceased to be amazed by how much shit you remember about a chick you hooked up with for one night a year ago."

Preston ran a hand through his hair. "I remember everything about Chelsea."

"So you saw the bakery," Victor said, getting them back on track.

"It's not open yet, but the sign is already there. I stopped short when I saw the words Sugar and Spice Bakery."

"And then what?"

"I was standing across the street. Before I could walk over

and check it out, another man stopped in front of the bakery, waving to someone inside."

"Chelsea," Victor said.

Preston pointed to the tip of his nose. "Yep. I don't know who the guy was, but I could tell they were close. Like, *really* close."

"Did you go over and talk to her?"

"No," Preston replied. "I was going to, but then the guy started kissing her and I…"

"You couldn't watch it, so you fucking stormed off."

He and Victor had been teammates for a damn long time, and it showed. The guy knew him well.

Victor smirked. "So how the fuck do you know the guy's a boyfriend? Maybe they've just gone on a few dates. Maybe it's nothing serious. How hot and heavy was this kiss?"

Preston didn't have a clue because the second the other man laid his lips on hers, he turned around and got the hell out of there. "As you said, I didn't stick around to watch."

Preston considered the body language between Chelsea and the other man. They had stood close to each other, but Chelsea hadn't hugged the guy when he showed up or acted overly excited to see him. Of course, he'd been at a disadvantage, only able to see the man's face during their interaction, which told him the guy was seriously into her.

Maybe Chelsea wasn't as into the guy as he was her. That initial smile of hers *had* looked forced.

Or…

Maybe that was just wishful thinking.

Preston threw his head back, glaring at the ceiling. "What if he's her boyfriend? What if it's serious?"

"Only one way to find out."

Preston's groan prompted Victor to roll his eyes.

"Jesus fucking Christ, Romeo."

This time, there was no missing the dirty looks the old women shot their direction. Victor acknowledged them with a single nod of the head, which Preston knew was as close as they were going to get to an apology.

Victor leaned closer to the table, his voice only slightly quieter when he said, "You've been crying in your fucking beer over that girl since last year."

Preston scoffed. "I haven't been crying in my beer," he lied. Because he had been doing that.

"Have you slept with anyone else since Chelsea?"

Victor already knew the answer, so Preston treated it as a rhetorical question. After all, the fact every single one of his teammates not only knew Chelsea's name but that he hadn't been able to get her out of his mind, date anyone, sleep with anyone else, or freaking move on from the greatest one-night stand in history, was a testament to how much he'd talked about her in the past year.

"Dude. You were obsessed enough that you went looking for her."

He had. Or at least, he'd done as much as he could, though Preston wouldn't say he'd launched a full-scale search. In truth, all he'd known to do was call Elio and Gianna to see if they remembered a Chelsea, who'd come to the Ugly Christmas Sweater party with an Allyson.

Neither of them did. Gianna had a list of people who'd bought tickets, but she didn't have a clue whose tickets Chelsea and Allyson had used—since they'd gotten them from a friend of friend—so his one and only lead had been a dead end.

He'd kicked himself for not insisting she let him drive her home, because at least then he would have had an address to work with. Instead, he'd had nothing except her first name, Chelsea, and the undying belief that she was his soul mate. The soul mate he'd let slip through his fingers.

If he'd known the morning she left that he would still feel like this twelve months later, he would have continued to demand her last name and phone number, and he wouldn't have taken no for an answer.

"Don't you think you owe it to yourself to talk to her and find out if she's as fucking crazy about you as you are her?"

Preston wanted to do that, but the same fear he experienced when he'd seen her on the street with that guy returned. "What if she doesn't?"

"Then you move the fuck on. Find a puck bunny and fuck her." Victor acted like that was the obvious solution, but for Preston, it wasn't. Not at all.

"Don't you *ever* wish for more, Vic?"

Victor, unlike him, seemed to be enjoying an extended bachelorhood, riding the single train all the way into his thirties.

He considered his question. "You mean like a relationship?"

Preston nodded.

Victor grimaced. "You know what your problem is, Romeo? You view relationships as some sort of golden goose when, in reality, they're hard fucking work and not all they're cracked up to be."

It was a well-known fact that Victor had had his heart thoroughly broken a long time ago, though it happened before his time with the Stingrays, so no one knew much about the elusive mystery woman. It was also well-known that he'd been a jaded, down-on-love fucker ever since.

"Obviously, you haven't been paying attention to Blake and Coulton lately. Those guys reek of happiness and hot sex."

Victor rolled his eyes. "Honeymoon phase. Both of them."

"Maybe so," Preston said, "but I want what they have." And he wanted it with Chelsea.

"No maybe about it," Victor countered.

Two of their teammates, Blake Wright and Coulton Moore, had fallen head over ass in love. Blake with his next-door neighbor and best friend, Erika, while Coulton had found his lady love, bartender Ainsley, in a run-down tavern in Cherry

Hill, of all places. While Victor had a point that the relationships were brand-new, Preston was certain both men had found exactly what they were looking for. And what he was pretty damn sure he would have found with Chelsea, if they'd had more than one damn night.

"There's nothing stopping you from finding a girl except *you*, Jacobson. If it's Chelsea, then great. If it's not, then it's time to get your head out of your fucking ass and start looking."

Leave it to Victor to tell the hard truths.

Because his friend was right. The only one holding him back from finding what Blake and Coulton had was himself.

The problem was, he'd spent this entire year comparing every woman he met to Chelsea. Every single one of them had come up lacking…big-time.

"You're right," he admitted. "Fate's giving me a chance to settle the Chelsea thing once and for all. I shouldn't have walked away without talking to her. If she's single, then I'm going to ask her out. If she's not, then…I'm moving on."

Given how much it hurt to say those words, it was safe to say, he was nowhere near ready to actually do that.

"Good man."

Yvonne delivered their pancakes and the two of them discussed their last game as they tucked into the delicious meal.

Once they finished eating, Victor resumed the relationship conversation. "If the Chelsea thing falls through, talk to Tank. I'm sure he can point you in the right direction as far as finding an eligible lady to date."

Preston snorted. "Date? Is that what we're calling it?"

He had no intention of asking Tank for help. As one of the team's resident playboys, Tank had cut a swath through the Rays' seemingly endless supply of puck bunnies. He wasn't all that discerning, and he sure as hell wasn't dating them.

Preston would look on his own…eventually.

"More coffee?" Yvonne asked when she noticed their empty plates.

He and Victor shook their heads, so she gathered up the dirty dishes. "I'll bring the check."

Now that Preston had decided to talk to Chelsea, he was anxious to see her again. That limited view of her from across the street hadn't been nearly enough. Even faced with the prospect of having his heart broken, he couldn't stay away from her.

"Thanks for breakfast." Victor placed his napkin on the table and leaned back, groaning and assuming a pose that—were this Thanksgiving—was typically paired with the unbuttoning of the jeans.

Preston slipped his credit card into the padded wallet when Yvonne set it on their table. "Wanted to treat you, since you're opening your house to me for the holidays."

"Not necessary but appreciated just the same. Guess it wouldn't be nice if I didn't warn you that Pip and my sister can be a fucking lot. So while it's cute that you thought the invitation was me being nice and worthy of a free breakfast, my initial thought was more along the lines of fresh meat."

Preston chuckled, perfectly aware that for all his bluster, Victor adored his sister and niece. As in, sun-rises-and-sets-on-their-shoulders kind of adoration. "I'll be fine. Anyone else take you up on the offer to join?"

Victor, one of the few Stingrays who was a Baltimore local, typically invited all the guys on the team who didn't have time to make trips home for the holidays.

Preston, Seattle born and bred, usually made the cross-country flight to spend the day with his family, but adding an extra trip mid-season always left him super jet-lagged. This year, his energy had waned enough, thanks to his depression, that he didn't even consider traveling home. Instead, he and his parents were mailing the gifts and doing Christmas morning via Face-

Time. After that, he was spending the rest of the day with Victor and his family.

"Yeah. I've got quite a few of the boys coming this year. Should be a good time. Lucas, the idiot, is still insisting on the Nerf gun war."

Lucas, aka Rookie, was their newest teammate, fresh from the AHL.

"Like I want to spend the next six fucking months picking up stray Nerf bullets around my house," Victor grumbled.

"You have a housekeeper who will most likely be the one finding the bullets. Besides, I think it sounds fun. A new tradition."

"A new tradition," Victor scoffed, shaking his head. "Because suddenly we're all fucking twelve again."

"Guess I should warn you, the second Lucas said Nerf war, I went online and bought myself a sweet Elite Blaster, twenty-five dart drum gun that fires five darts per second."

Victor sat straighter, scowling. "Tell me you're fucking joking."

Preston shook his head, forcing this lighthearted conversation, even though his heart wasn't in it. "I'm a competitive guy, Vic. In it to win it. Always."

"Jesus. You realize I'm going to have to fucking buy one of those for Pip now, right?"

"Actually, you aren't. I bought two. Second one is already wrapped. My Christmas gift for her."

Victor narrowed his eyes. "You trying to one-up me with my niece at the holidays?"

Preston might worry about the menace in his buddy's voice if he wasn't a hundred percent certain Victor had already broken the bank buying Pip every little thing her heart desired. "I think you've got the role of favorite uncle locked for life, even with my sweet-ass gift."

"Fucking machine gun." Victor sighed. "She'll love it. Wish I'd thought of it."

Victor slid out of the booth, rising. "Well, I gotta run. Told Pip I'd take her Christmas shopping so she can buy something for her mom. Good luck with Chelsea."

Preston gave him a salute, signing the credit card slip Yvonne had just returned with before standing as well. "I'll see you later."

He pulled on his jacket and bid Yvonne goodbye, then stepped back out into the cold air, pointing his feet in the direction of Sugar and Spice Bakery.

His first thought was here goes nothing, but he quickly revised it.

Here goes everything.

CHAPTER SIX

AN HOUR EARLIER...

Chelsea glanced up when she spotted someone standing outside the large front window of the bakery. She groaned aloud when she saw Rick waving at her from the sidewalk.

"Jesus Christ," Ethan muttered.

"Ethan, we've talked about this."

Her best friend shot her a look that said more than words could.

"We're just friends," she added, even though that wasn't going to help her case.

"Friends," Ethan said, like the word tasted nasty. "He doesn't want to be your friend, Cupcake. He wants you back."

Chelsea shook her head. "No. He doesn't. Rick and I grew up together, just like you and I did. We have a long—and yes, complicated—history, but he's apologized, and he's gone the extra mile since then. I told him all we can be is friends, and he agreed."

"He lied. Because the guy keeps coming back like a hungry mosquito," Ethan muttered.

Chelsea rose. "I'm going to go talk to him."

"Notice how he's not walking in here? He's too afraid to face me because he knows I see through his bullshit."

Chelsea rolled her eyes. "He's faced you countless times in the past five months. He's probably avoiding you because you've been extremely unpleasant, bordering on rude every single time."

"Only bordering?" Ethan asked in dismay. "Dammit. I'm going to have to double down on my efforts."

Chelsea tried hard not to laugh because it would only encourage her bestie. "Stay here."

Ethan didn't bother to reply, just turned his attention back to the brochure of industrial countertops they'd been perusing.

She walked outside, smiling at Rick, who was admiring their new sign. If anyone would have told her a year ago she'd not only forgive Rick for jilting her but open the door to a friendship, she would have called them crazy.

Unfortunately, Chelsea didn't realize she'd forgotten to put her jacket on until she'd stepped out into the chilly December air. "Hey, Rick. What's up?"

"I stopped by your parents' house earlier to return the snow-blower my dad borrowed from yours. Dad's is on the fritz again."

Chelsea laughed. "It's been on the fritz for twenty years."

Rick chuckled. "I know. Which is why I'm giving him one for Christmas. Getting tired of hauling your dad's back and forth just because my car is a practical size."

"I still can't believe your folks bought a MINI Cooper."

"Mom thinks it's cute. I think it's a pain in the ass."

"So what brings you here?"

"Your mom told me the sign was up. I wanted to see it. It looks great, Chels."

"It does, doesn't it?" The two of them took a moment to admire it.

By the time she moved back to Baltimore in July, the Rick and

Vanessa love affair was over, ending shortly after Valentine's Day. She hadn't been home more than a week before he came to see her. She'd told him to take a hike that time—and the next twenty times he'd shown up, issuing apologies she had zero interest in.

The road from there to where they were now had evolved slowly—like a snail's pace slowly—as Rick persisted. The man who'd only been somewhat present when they were dating had suddenly become extremely attentive and considerate. Something she didn't given two shits about nowadays.

However, their mothers were best friends, which meant their families did stuff together all the damn time. No longer ghosting her, Rick somehow managed to be where she was. It would have been easier to hold on to her anger if he hadn't been in her face all the damn time and so…apologetic and nice.

But that wasn't how things worked out. She and Rick had been thrust together at the summer picnic her mother threw together to welcome her home. Then he'd shown up at one of her parents' fall firepits with his mom and dad. Their families had also celebrated Thanksgiving together and had plans for Christmas.

Somewhere around mid-October, Chelsea realized that anger took a lot of energy, so she simply let go of hers, even though the same couldn't be said for Ethan and Allyson. Regardless of her best friends' opinions—of which they had many, many heated ones—she told Rick she forgave him.

And she did.

But that didn't mean she forgot. She'd made it very clear they would never be anything more than friends, and while she didn't say it aloud, that friendship deal was limited to something that was actually more glorified acquaintance due to the fact she didn't trust him. The trust was dead and buried and there was no resuscitating it. So she would be cordial, nice, and friendly, but that was all she had to offer him.

"I was wondering if you wanted to go out to dinner Friday night," Rick asked, leaning in uncomfortably close.

"Dinner?"

"I know you're busy these days, but I think you deserve a night off."

Chelsea hesitated for a lot of reasons. "I really don't have time to go out right now."

"Chelsea. It's been ages since we've had the chance to do anything together...just the two of us."

That was true—and by design. All her time spent with Rick was in the presence of other people, their parents or mutual friends...or "unmutual" friends, as in the case of Allyson and Ethan. What he was proposing sounded too much like a date.

"I don't think it's a good idea."

Rick seemed to take her rejection in stride. "I understand. It's just...there are some things I'd like to talk about."

Shit.

Chelsea didn't like the way Rick was looking at her. She knew all his faces, and this one told her Ethan was right. Rick didn't want to just be her friend.

"I feel like we've said it all." She hoped he'd read her tone and cut this conversation off before it veered too far into the danger zone.

"You're right. We have. So maybe I should just show you."

"Rick." Before Chelsea could reiterate all the reasons why the two of them were—to quote Taylor—never, ever, ever getting back together, Rick grasped her shoulders and pulled her forward, his lips landing on hers.

Shock held her still for maybe five seconds before her brain re-engaged and she shoved him away, furious. "What the fuck is wrong with you?!"

Rick had been all contrite smiles, but her refusal seemed to awaken his frustration. "Dammit, Chelsea! What else do you want from me? I've apologized. I've been a good friend to you.

I've brought gifts, helped you and your parents out around the house. I even offered to invest in your business."

He had, and she'd shut that down *hard*. "I don't need your money."

Rick brushed off her comment. "So you keep saying, but I don't know what else you expect me to do."

Expect? She didn't expect anything of him.

"I'm not making you jump through random hoops, Rick, and there are no expectations. I thought we were reestablishing a friendship."

He sighed, looking almost dejected, something she wasn't sure she'd ever seen from him. "I know I hurt you, and I get that you want to punish me, but—"

"Punish?" Chelsea crossed her arms around herself, freezing in the bitter wind. She really should have grabbed her coat. Figures he'd picked the coldest day of the winter to drop all this on her. "I... *No*, that's not what I'm doing." She didn't have the energy for this. She was existing on less than five hours of interrupted sleep a night. Her tank was empty, which was probably why she was letting Rick's comments slip in and sucker punch her. "I'm not trying to punish you."

He lifted one shoulder, clearly not believing her.

So yeah...she'd handled everything with him completely wrong. Awesome.

"Will you at least consider my invitation to dinner?"

She shook her head.

"Just as friends," he quickly added. "I won't bring any of this up again."

It was too late for that offer, because there was no coming back from what he'd said. Not for her. Friendship was her bottom line, and he'd made it very clear he was hoping for more.

"I can't do dinner with you."

Rick fell silent, which wasn't exactly a good thing. She could practically see the wheels spinning, which meant his courtroom lawyer brain was calculating the best way to get what he wanted. So she could expect to be subjected to relentless texting, well-thought-out arguments, or, worst of all, pressure from their mothers.

Because while she'd stupidly thought Rick was okay with them just being friends, his mother, Angie, had made it obvious she was not fine with that relationship status, both subtly and *not* so subtly pushing for a reconciliation. She was still determined to see her baby married to Mom's, even after all the shit that went down. Mom wasn't actively pushing for that, but she wasn't exactly discouraging Rick's drop-by visits.

"I hope you'll change your mind."

She wouldn't change her mind, but she was all about the path of least resistance right now because it really was fucking cold out here.

So, she said nothing.

From this point forward, she would avoid Rick like the plague…somehow.

Rick leaned toward her again, but this time she was prepared, taking a big step back while shooting him a warning look.

He took the hint, not pushing his luck. "I'll text you later."

She nodded, wondering what kind of fallout she could expect if she blocked his number again. She'd been an idiot to unblock it in October. She'd clearly been stupid about everything in regards to Rick.

He gave a quick wave of farewell and walked away.

Turning toward the front of the bakery, she looked at the sign, recalling how excited she'd been when she saw it this morning for the first time. Now, it was sullied, ruined by her idiot ex-fiancé.

She smiled gratefully when Ethan came outside with her coat.

It wasn't until she'd pulled it on that she noticed Ethan's dark scowl. "Did that fucker kiss you?"

Chelsea closed her eyes wearily. "I hoped you hadn't seen that. Yes. He did. I gave an inch with the forgiveness/friendship bullshit, and now he's trying to take the mile."

"I told you when he started sniffing around in July he wanted you back."

Ethan had, but at the time, Chelsea had thought the idea ridiculous, certain she'd never even speak to the asshole again.

"You're perfectly justified to say 'I told you so,'" she muttered.

It spoke to just how good a friend Ethan was that he didn't take any pleasure in being right. "I'm sorry, Cupcake. I know there's a lot of pressure from your families, but Rick burned the bridge between you with his actions. I don't think it's possible to be friends."

"You're right. It's not. I've been an idiot."

Ethan grinned and wrapped his arm around her shoulders, tugging her close. "Nope. You are a sweet person, who always sees the best in people. It's why I love you."

She appreciated the compliment. Then Ethan went on to add, "You're also currently sleep-deprived and stressed to the max, so you're working with half a brain."

"Less than half," she grumbled.

"This is why I've had to stick around all this time. You need my jaded cynicism, astute observations, keen insights, and fully functioning brain to keep you safe."

She laughed, soaking up a few more seconds of Ethan's warm hug before stepping away. "Where would I be without your brilliance?"

"Luckily, you'll never have to find out because I'm true blue. Yours for life."

She knew that all the way to the depths of her soul, and it helped her shake off the last few crappy minutes. "Thanks. And now, I'd really—REALLY—like to not talk about Rick anymore. He's ruining my Zen."

Ethan looked like he wanted to persist, but then he took in her exhausted expression and relented. Because unlike Rick, Ethan could read the fucking room. "Okay. I agree. That asshole doesn't deserve even a second thought."

"Good. Because we have bigger things to discuss."

"Like?" Ethan asked.

"Are we insane?"

"In general?" Ethan retorted. "Yeah. Probably."

"No, asshole. You know what I'm talking about. I mean…" Chelsea paused, then realized he was right. "Okay. Yes, we're insane in general, but I was referring to this." She gestured toward the ornate lettering on the front plate-glass window of the building she and her best friend were now renting with an option to buy.

"Oh…nothing about this is insane. It's perfect."

Ethan had been saying those same words—on repeat, because she was hormonal and needy—since they'd decided to go all-in on this dream.

"I'm being serious, Ethan. This is a humongous life change, coming on the heels of—fuck me—so many life changes." If she thought about how much things had changed, she'd start to hyperventilate because seriously! It was a fuck-ton.

"A year and a half ago, I was about to walk down the aisle with the clueless wonder who just left."

Ethan held up his hand. "We do not speak of the dark times."

They really didn't. Not anymore.

Not since last December.

Because those dark times had been erased by a big, friendly, sexy-as-sin giant.

Maybe erased *and* replaced was more accurate, because God knew she hadn't forgotten a single solitary second of her time with Preston.

He had given her the best night of her life, resuscitating her confidence and her libido, before she ventured out into what she'd thought was an exciting new future in Paris.

Well, she'd gotten exciting and new.

Just not in the way she'd expected.

Glancing through the plate-glass window, she spied her future, sleeping peacefully in the stroller Ethan had parked right by the door before bringing out her coat.

"All I'm saying," Chelsea continued, "is a broken engagement, a move to Paris, an unexpected pregnancy, followed by a return to Baltimore was already insane enough. To follow all that by starting a new business might officially make us—well, *me*—totally insane. I have a three-month-old." This time, she gestured to the stroller instead of the window.

Ethan brushed her concerns away now, just as he had every single time she questioned the wisdom of this venture. "Fate picked the timing, Cupcake. We would be fools to walk away from what was clearly meant to be."

She studied the name of their dream bakery, painted on the window of the shop in bright colors.

Sugar and Spice Bakery.

Seeing the words displayed there was powerful, overwhelming, amazing, and she had to admit that it did feel like perhaps destiny had led them here.

A year ago, they'd set this dream aside, declaring it a silly wish made by kids, while she planned her escape to Paris and Ethan accepted a large promotion with the marketing firm he'd worked for since graduating from college...even though the job bored him to tears.

At the time, they had somehow managed to convince themselves that they were making adult decisions, doing the smart thing, focusing on their careers instead of pipe dreams.

That was a year ago.

Now?

Now everything was completely different. Those adult choices had been chucked aside, as they took a major risk attempting to live the lives they'd always imagined for themselves but hadn't had the courage—or cash—to go for.

At least, not until the fate Ethan spoke of reared its head.

Then he shot her a too serious, too terrified look. "Besides, if we don't do this, Aunt Agnes will haunt us until the day we die."

Chelsea laughed even though there was no arguing with that. Because Aunt Agnes would. Nor was there much room for debating fate.

Because on the same day Chelsea discovered she was pregnant, Ethan's beloved great-aunt Agnes passed away.

Aunt Agnes had never married or had children, which was a shame because she would have made the world's greatest mother. She'd lived in a gorgeous house on the river in Patapsco Park, just outside Baltimore. Her home was far too large for just one person, but that was due to necessity because it was overflowing with costumes and props from Agnes's time as an actress in New York, maritime memorabilia from the two years she'd sailed around the world, as well as countless treasures from her travels to every continent on the planet, including Antarctica.

Whenever she was home, she planned elaborate, fun weekend sleepovers for "her favorite nephew" Ethan—he was her only one—as well as the two "nieces of her heart"—her and Allyson. Aunt Agnes had "adopted" them as her own when they were young kids, and she'd never wavered in her devotion and love, never forgetting birthdays or special occasions, sending postcards and souvenirs from her travels, wearing a huge, oversized Kentucky Derby hat to their high school graduation ceremony as she cheered the loudest from the front row.

Weekends with Agnes were some of the best times of Chelsea's life.

Agnes didn't own a television, something that had horrified them the first time they went to stay at her house, when they were just seven years old. Allyson nearly had a panic attack when she realized she couldn't watch Nickelodeon. However, that horror didn't last more than the first hour, as Agnes pulled out her extensive hat collection and the four of them spent hours trying them on, inventing names and accents for each "character."

After that, she, Ethan, and Allyson lived for sleepovers with Agnes, having countless adventures with the playful, attentive woman, which included sledding down the stairs on an inflatable raft, taking long cruises down the river on her pontoon boat, and holding their own dance-offs that kept them up way too many hours past their bedtime. They may have been the kids, but Agnes's imagination left theirs in the dust as they acted out extravagant stories—always in costume, of course.

When they got too old to play, Agnes created amazing, challenging scavenger hunts that took them entire weekends to solve. And it was Agnes who encouraged Chelsea and Ethan's dream of opening their own bakery. She'd nurtured that desire by including "bakery time" in their sleepover activities, Ethan serving as a sometimes unforgiving, strict boss, barking orders at Chelsea as she slaved away creating the delicious pastries and pies Agnes and Allyson—her most dedicated "customers"—consumed.

Coming back home to Baltimore in July had been a bittersweet return because, while Chelsea had missed her hometown during the months spent in Paris, the city didn't feel the same without Agnes.

The fate Ethan referred to was the substantial amount of money Aunt Agnes left, not only to Ethan but to her and Allyson as well.

In her will, she had *strongly* suggested that some of the money she and Ethan received be used for Sugar and Spice

Bakery, informing them life was wasted on adults, and she'd raised them better than to make life choices based on society-driven common sense and fear of failure.

Then she reminded them that the most important decisions weren't made with the head but with the heart. Which, when they discussed it, both she and Ethan admitted they'd let their heads be the driving forces behind their "adult decisions." Chelsea had come clean about using the move to Paris to avoid Rick, and Ethan said he'd thought at the time that money and security were more important than happiness.

When Ethan called to tell her Agnes had passed, he'd been unaware that the entire time they were on the phone, Chelsea was staring at the two lines on a pregnancy test.

She'd spent the rest of that night alone, wavering between shock over the baby growing inside her, and grief over losing one of her favorite people on the planet.

A month later, Ethan called again, telling her about the inheritance and how Agnes wanted them to use some of the money to start their bakery, and that was when she'd dropped her own little bomb.

"She would love this," Ethan mused, admiring the sign before glancing inside the shop window. "And him." Ethan was completely enamored of her son, and he'd vowed the moment he heard she was pregnant that he was going to be her baby's Aunt Agnes. As far as promises went, Chelsea couldn't think of a better one.

"I wish she could have met him," Chelsea added sadly, shivering when a frosty blast of wind hit them. "We should probably go inside. It's cold out here."

Ethan snorted, aware her desire to go back inside wasn't based on temperature as much as she couldn't bear not being right beside her baby every minute of the day—and night.

He opened the door and they walked inside, slowly pushing the stroller back to the lone table in the place. It was a card table they'd borrowed from Chelsea's parents, along with the two camp chairs they now dropped down into. For the moment, this was their "office," the place where they would make all the plans for opening this shop on Valentine's Day.

"Best baby ever," Ethan said, looking into the stroller.

"He really is. Except, well…if I could get him to sleep through the night, he'd be a hell of a lot more perfect."

Ethan ran his finger under one of her eyes gently, no doubt tracing the dark circle there. "He's a growing boy, always hungry. He'll get there in another two or three months, especially when you start him on solid foods. You just have to hang in there."

Ethan spoke as if he was an authority on the subject, despite not having a child of his own. Of course, that made sense, considering he'd read every single book and article ever published about babies, taking his role of godfather and honorary uncle very seriously.

"Probably gets that from his father, who was a big guy. Lots of growing to do," she mused. Then she laughed. "Oh, and from me because I'm always hungry."

Ethan rolled his eyes. "We can attribute his hunger to you. But those eyes…"

Gray eyes. Distinctive. Beautiful. Every time she saw them, her heart panged painfully as she remembered…him.

The best thing Chelsea had ever done was spend the night with Preston, and she still felt that way even now. The past year might have had a lot of ups and downs, panic and stress and sleepless nights, but they were worth it.

Because of that night. And because of her baby.

However, the dumbest thing she'd ever done was not get Preston's last name or his phone number. After returning to Baltimore in July, she'd called the Rittenhouse Hotel, hoping she could convince the front desk clerk to give her Preston's last name. Despite her pleading and—yes, she wasn't too proud to admit it—tears, the clerk would not be moved.

From there, Chelsea called the haunted inn, even though she'd known from the start that would be a dead end. Preston had admitted to getting his tickets the same way she had, through a friend. The woman working the front desk of the inn, Tory, was more helpful than the Rittenhouse clerk, going so far as to search the entire list of tickets sold for the event, but sadly, no one with the first name Preston had purchased one. Which was just what she'd expected.

"I hate that Preston doesn't know about him."

Ethan had to be as sick of that comment as the "are we insane?" one. Because she had repeated it daily since discovering she was pregnant.

"I know, Cupcake. But you have to let that go, stop beating yourself up over it."

She appreciated his reassurances, but they did nothing to combat the guilt she felt over being so stupid. Personally, she blamed *Serendipity*. She'd woken up the morning after that incredible night with Preston and done her best Kate Beckinsale impersonation, telling him it was for the best if they walked away clean from their magical one night.

Now, the idea that Preston was out there, walking around Philadelphia, oblivious to the fact there was a part of him living here in Baltimore, made her physically ill if she thought about it too hard. He deserved to know he was a father.

"Put it away, Chels." Ethan placed his hand on top of hers. "You tried to find him."

A couple of long, pleading, somewhat embarrassing phone calls where she admitted she didn't know the last name of her baby's father didn't feel like much of an effort, but what else could she have done?

Ethan was right. She needed to put that regret away. She glanced at the "Bakery Plans" notebook in front of her, flipping it open. They needed to make hay while the sun shined. Or in this case, while the baby slept.

While she'd enjoyed her time in Paris, there was no denying she'd been terribly homesick…and despite her efforts, her French sucked. So after three months in the City of Lights, when she discovered her pregnancy, it hadn't been a hard decision to make plans to return home to have the baby. After all, in Paris, she would have been alone, and here, she had family and friends to help her.

Of course, returning home hadn't been without its challenges. For one thing, she was a twenty-six-year-old single mother living at home with her parents. She loved her mom and dad, she truly did, but after being on her own the past six years, moving back into her childhood bedroom was a bit of culture shock. As was trying to parent with her mother, who, while helpful, had definite opinions on basically everything Chelsea should be doing.

She was grateful for her parents' help and how they'd welcomed her home with open arms, but something was going to have to give, because Chelsea wasn't sure how much longer she could bite her tongue whenever her mom offered advice about how Chelsea should be living her life…on every subject. From childrearing to Rick. From the bakery to Chelsea's still-present baby weight.

Lately, Mom was harping about the fact Chelsea wouldn't be in the boat she was if she wasn't so impulsive and thought things through before acting.

Too much more time spent under that roof and Chelsea wouldn't have any tongue left.

She rubbed her eyes, blinking a few times when the words in the notebook grew fuzzy. She was existing on limited sleep, all of it coming in two-hour stints, as she still woke several times a night to feed the baby.

These days, her mom—a part-time teacher's aide—was

watching her son two days a week, Allyson caring for him whenever her work schedule allowed, and she and Ethan covering the rest of the time together here. That worked fine for now, as they were in the planning stages of the new business, and she could do a lot of that with a baby on her lap. It wouldn't be possible when she was baking in the kitchen, and Ethan was overseeing the counter, working with employees, and managing the business side.

She put thoughts of daycare out of her mind. She wasn't mentally prepared for it. The idea of leaving her baby boy with strangers stressed her out. The problem was, she wasn't sure she would be any better prepared come February, and the time to start looking at her options was now…or like months ago.

"You doing okay?" Ethan asked. "Manage to get any sleep last night?"

She shrugged. "The usual."

"So, no." He gave her a sympathetic smile. Ethan and Allyson had been delighted by her move back home and, once again, they'd been her rocks, walking beside her as she weaved her way through pregnancy, delivery, and now motherhood.

Ethan placed his hand on her arm. "You know your mom would take a shift, or a whole night, just so you could actually make your way into REM sleep."

"I know she would, but I'm trying not to ask her to…" Chelsea stopped talking, hating the way she sounded petty, given all her mother had been doing for her.

"I know Ellen is driving you mad. You don't have to stop talking, just like you don't have to feel guilty for your feelings. I'm surprised you haven't lost your shit with her."

Chelsea's shoulders slumped. "I don't want to be ungrateful, because Mom and Dad really have gone to bat for me, taking it in stride when their single daughter got pregnant by a one-night stand—a man whose last name she doesn't know—and decided to move back home. It makes me feel like they're deserving of some patience."

Ethan laughed. "There's some patience, Cupcake, and then there's the patience required for Ellen Murphy."

Chelsea groaned. "She's still pissed I didn't give breast-feeding more of a shot. She's annoyed as hell about us starting this bakery. And apparently, it's my fault he's not sleeping through the night yet," she said, gesturing to her son. "She always knows better than me, and it's making me mental."

"She *thinks*," Ethan interjected. "She *thinks* she knows better. Something that drove you up the wall when we were teenagers. I can only imagine how much worse it is now. You know, the offer to move back in with me—"

Chelsea raised her hand, cutting him off before he could issue the now-familiar offer. "You and Justin are still in the test-drive on this cohabitation thing. Me moving in with a newborn would cramp your style."

No one had been more surprised than Chelsea when her commitment-resistant bestie had not only fallen in love but invited his new squeeze to live with him.

"Justin loves the little munchkin as much as me," Ethan started.

"Thank you. But no. My plan remains the same. I'll live with my parents until summer, once we've gotten the bakery off the ground, and then I'll find a place of my own. Ellen and I are hanging in there just fine."

They were hanging in there by the skin of their teeth, but admitting that wouldn't help her win this debate with Ethan.

"So, let's talk kitchen equipment." Chelsea pointed to the list she'd compiled, ready for a new subject.

The bakery was a *major* bone of contention between she and her mother, who disagreed with Chelsea's decision to use the inheritance to start a business. Oddly enough, Mom wasn't pushing Chelsea to use the money to move out. Probably because that would limit her attempts at controlling everything Chelsea did as a mother.

Instead, Mom thought the money should have been put into a college savings fund. And while Chelsea had done that with some of it—Agnes had been an extremely wealthy woman—she ultimately decided she wanted to honor Agnes's request that the money be spent toward the bakery. After all, Chelsea could spend the next however many years of her life working barely better than minimum-wage bakery jobs, *or* she could turn the money into an investment, offering a better future for her and her baby.

For the next hour, she and Ethan debated which pieces of equipment they absolutely needed prior to opening the shop and which were things that could wait until they were more established.

"Dough sheeter? What the hell is a dough sheeter?" Ethan asked.

Chelsea was about to explain why that piece was on her must-have list when the front door to the shop opened. The bell Ethan hung above the door approximately five seconds after they got the keys to the place—claiming it was old-school charming—rang out.

"Sorry," Ethan said, glancing toward the front. "We're not op—"

Chelsea looked up from her list when her best friend stopped talking, her attention sliding to the door.

She gasped, momentarily distracted by Ethan gasping as well.

Surely her eyes were playing tricks on her.

She rose slowly, afraid to blink in case she was imagining *his* presence, aware Ethan was doing the same, his moves mirroring hers as if they'd choreographed it.

"Preston," she and Ethan said in unison.

What the hell?

Ethan didn't know Preston. He hadn't been at the holiday party.

Then, Ethan did her one better, because he didn't stop speaking, adding a last name to the first.

"Jacobson."

Chelsea's gaze flew to her best friend. "You know him?"

"Of course," Ethan replied, not taking his eyes off Preston until…

She saw the second the light went on as her best friend's back straightened, Ethan's gaze traveling from Preston, to her, to the sleeping baby in the stroller behind them.

"*Preston?*" Ethan asked her.

She nodded just once, before turning as Preston walked into the bakery, the door closing behind him. He hadn't said a word. Rather, he looked curious—and confused—by her interaction with Ethan.

Meanwhile, she couldn't stop herself from drinking him in, because how the hell did he manage to get even hotter in the last year?

"Chelsea," Preston said, as he approached the table, standing close enough that she could reach out and touch him. His gray eyes were locked on her face, and she got the sense he was having the same trouble. Too afraid to blink, to believe. "I never thought I'd—"

A tiny cry distracted him, and Preston's attention went to the stroller he just now noticed. His brow furrowed as she turned, bending over to pick up the baby, before facing him once more.

"Hey, hey, little man," Ethan said, stroking the side of the baby's face. "Don't cry."

Preston was studying them closely, but damn if his poker face wasn't rock solid. She didn't have a clue what he was thinking.

She cleared her throat. "Preston," she said, though his name came out rough and tight, as she fought to speak. All she wanted to do after discovering she was pregnant was find him so she could tell him about the baby.

So why, when he was standing right in front of her, couldn't she?

"Um…"

Months of guilt were washed away in an instant, replaced by…fuck…

Everything.

Nervousness, happiness, relief…and even fear over his reaction.

What if he denied or rejected his paternity?

What if he didn't?

Chelsea didn't know what to make of the fact that the second question scared her more than the first. For the first three months of his life, her baby had been just that—hers. Now, however, that was all about to change, and it terrified her.

Since she and Preston both looked like deer in the headlights, Ethan took over, reaching into the small cooler she'd brought with her, pulling out a bottle of milk, and handing it to her as the baby continued to fuss.

Her gaze traveled between the men. "Ethan, how do you know Preston?"

"Preston Jacobson plays for the Baltimore Stingrays, Cupcake." Ethan ran a fingertip down her cheek, grinning. "You really should've said yes when I invited you to all those games. Especially the ones since the start of the season…in October. I could've even loaned you his jersey," he added in a whisper she hoped Preston couldn't hear.

Ethan was literally the world's biggest Stingrays fan on the planet, attending as many home games as he could afford, and the owner of more jerseys than the players themselves probably had. He'd been trying to drag her and Allyson to games for years, but they'd always turned him down, comparing going to a hockey game to pap smears, trips to the dentist, and helping a friend move. They'd made a game of coming up with a long list of shit they'd much rather do.

To be honest, Chelsea wasn't as opposed to attending a game as she was giving up the gag over *not* going.

If she'd gone in October…

Preston didn't acknowledge the introduction.

Instead, his eyes were locked on the baby in her arms.

"It looks like congratulations are in order, Chelsea," he said stiffly.

Oh no. Did he think that she and Ethan were a couple? And that the baby…

This was bad.

Really, really bad.

CHAPTER SEVEN

"PLEASE LET ME STAY," Ethan murmured.

Preston vaguely recalled that Chelsea had a gay best friend named Ethan, so while this man wasn't the father, that meant the guy from earlier…

Fuck. Was that guy her boyfriend? Her husband? Preston couldn't see her ring finger, thanks to the baby blanket covering her hands.

"No," Chelsea replied, under her breath. Obviously, she was trying to keep her conversation with Ethan private, despite the fact Preston was standing right there and could hear every word.

"I'll go over there and stand in the corner. You won't even know I'm here. I won't say a word, promise." Ethan made no effort to lower his voice. In fact, he was looking at Preston as he spoke to Chelsea. "Preston Jacobson," he added, shaking his head in disbelief. "And my sweet little Cupcake. Unbelievable."

Preston didn't have a clue what Ethan was talking about, but he was clearly exasperating Chelsea, who blew out a hard sigh.

"Don't you have something to do in the kitchen or somewhere else?" she asked pointedly.

Ethan shook his head. "Nope. You're not going to talk loud enough for me to hear you all the way in the kitchen."

Chelsea closed her eyes briefly, as if praying for patience. "Go away. Please."

Ethan's smile widened, and he finally decided to include Preston in the conversation. "Tell you what I'll do. Preston, why don't you and Cupcake take some time to reconnect? My apartment is only six blocks away. I'm going to run home really quick. If you're still here when I get back—and I think you will be—I have approximately ninety-seven things I'd love for you to sign."

Ethan's request was so unexpected, Preston couldn't help but chuckle, despite the fact his heart was splintering into a million pieces. He'd spent a year thinking about Chelsea, wishing he could see her, talk to her, and the whole time, she'd been moving on with her life, falling in love, and starting a family.

"Ethan," Chelsea said. "Seriously. Go. Away."

"I'm going, I'm going. Super nice to meet you," Ethan said, shaking Preston's hand effusively. "Seriously, huge fan. *Huge.*"

Preston nodded, even though his attention was locked on Chelsea, who was feeding the baby. The baby blanket was too high for Preston to see the little one's face, so it was impossible to gauge the child's age. Considering they were together a year ago, and she wasn't dating anyone else at the time, the baby would have to be a newborn.

Ethan left the bakery and, given how fast he was walking, Preston suspected the man hadn't been joking about returning with things for him to sign.

"Do you have time to sit and talk?" Chelsea asked.

Preston nodded, aware this conversation was likely to be painful. The idea of Chelsea happy and in love with someone else shouldn't hurt as much as it did.

It was only one night.

He'd repeated those same five words to himself countless

times over the past twelve months, but they never stuck, never gave him the power to push her out of his mind.

Preston took the seat Ethan had just vacated, watching as Chelsea sat as well, adjusting the baby slightly before popping the bottle back in his mouth. Ethan had referred to the baby as "little man" when he comforted him, and that tracked, given the blue blanket and the dinosaur-clad arm he could see that was reaching up toward the bottle. Not that the child was old enough to hold it himself.

"You're a mother," he said, kicking himself the second the words crossed his lips.

Hello, Captain Obvious.

"I am. I…um…" She looked down at the baby, her cheeks flushed.

"Paris didn't work out?" he asked, when her pause lingered. Chelsea was clearly as uncomfortable with this reunion as he was.

She shook her head. "No. I knew I would need help when the baby came along, so moving home was the wisest option."

"Baltimore is home? Not Philly?"

"Allyson and I drove to Philadelphia for that party. The original plan had been to crash at her cousin's house afterward."

Original plan. The one that had changed when she'd suggested the two of them leave the party together.

"Quite a coincidence. I'd been planning to spend an hour or so at the party, have a beer with my buddies, then drive back home to Baltimore that night."

She shook her head in disbelief. "Huge coincidence. How did you find this place? Me?"

"Dumb luck. I had breakfast with a teammate this morning, and I was walking to the restaurant when I saw the sign on the window." Preston gestured toward the front of the building. "You said your dream bakery would be called Sugar and Spice."

She smiled. "I can't believe you remembered that."

"I remember everything from that night." The second he said the words, Preston wished he could call them back. But only until…

"So do I," she whispered.

That confession from her would have lit up his insides like a Christmas tree if she weren't holding someone else's baby.

"Preston," she started, her face too serious, suddenly.

He drew in a deep breath, preparing himself. She was about to address the baby-sized elephant in the room.

"I tried to find you," she said, her words catching him off guard.

He liked the idea that he'd made enough of an impression that she looked for him. Of course, given the baby in her arms, that impression hadn't been lasting. Not like his twelve months —and counting—obsession.

"I tried to find you too," he confessed.

She grimaced. "You didn't buy a ticket for the party. I called the inn, but no one named Preston had purchased one."

"I didn't have a ticket at all," he admitted. "My buddy, Elio, runs the inn with his wife, Gianna. They invited me to come, since I had an afternoon game in Philly that day. He was the one I called and talked to, to ask about you."

Chelsea leaned back, her shoulders slumping. "The front desk clerk I spoke to—her name was Tory—didn't know you."

"She wouldn't," Preston confirmed.

"And the clerk at the Rittenhouse Hotel was an asshole. Completely refused to give me your name."

It sounded like she really had been searching. "Why were you looking for me, Chelsea?"

Chelsea fell silent as her gaze slid down to the baby in her arms. She pulled the empty bottle from his mouth and set it on the table. As she did so, the blanket shifted. The baby wasn't a newborn. Preston didn't know a lot about babies, but his buddies—Elio included—had kids, so he could tell this baby was likely a couple, three months old.

Preston leaned forward, gently tugging the blanket down so that he could see…

Large gray eyes darted in his direction.

The same color eyes Preston saw in the mirror every morning.

"Chelsea," he whispered.

"I swear I tried to find you!" There was a desperation in her tone that gave Preston the answer to the question he hadn't asked.

"Mine?"

She nodded, glassy tears shining in her eyes. "I wanted to tell you, but…"

Preston couldn't stop staring at the baby in her arms. "He's mine."

"Yes."

"A son," he murmured, stunned.

Holy.

Fuck.

He had a son.

"What's his name?"

Chelsea's lips tipped up in a small, tremulous smile. "Lennon."

"Jesus Christ," he whispered. "That's the best name I've ever heard."

She laughed, but it was a shaky one, more nerves than joy.

Preston rested his elbows on his knees, shock taking over. His entire body went numb as a million truths crashed on his head at the same time.

He had a son named Lennon. With Chelsea, the woman of his dreams.

He was a father. He was a father. He was a father.

It was that realization that started playing on repeat as if his brain was trying to force the rest of him to catch up and get with the program.

While shock rendered him speechless, nerves were impacting Chelsea differently as she suddenly started talking fast. "He was born on September first. A Virgo."

"Like you," he murmured.

"God. You really do remember everything. He came a week early. He was nine pounds, four ounces, and twenty-two inches long. I was glad he didn't wait any longer to be born because… well, look at that head."

Preston couldn't take his eyes off the child, who was the most adorable baby he'd ever seen in his life. And yes, he was definitely prejudiced.

Chelsea hastily rambled on, shooting fact after fact at him. "He's currently off all the charts for height and weight. A big boy, like you. He was born with dark hair, but most of that's fallen out and what's growing in now is closer to your shade. And his eyes…"

"They're gray. Like mine." Preston's gaze locked with Lennon's, whose hands were swinging around wildly. He reached out, thrilled when his tiny son grasped his finger and held tight.

"He's the best baby ever," she continued. "Hardly ever cries, always smiling, and so, so sweet. He's not sleeping through the night yet, but that's just because he's always hungry."

Preston soaked in every word. Part of him was grateful for the recap, but it didn't feel like that was her intention. Instead, it was like Chelsea was trying to sell him on his son.

She bit her lower lip. "I know this is unexpected, and I know we used condoms… But I swear, he really is your—"

Did she think he didn't believe her?

"Chelsea. Stop. I know he's mine. I know you wouldn't lie about something like this. We might not have spent a great deal of time together, but I know that much for damn sure."

"It's just…I didn't know you were a professional hockey player. That's cool, but…I mean, maybe women… Shit. I'm saying everything so badly." Her face was bloodred, and her eyes were downcast. Her stress was currently giving his shock a run for its money.

Preston thought back to that night. "The first condom slipped," he said. "I didn't think about it at the time, but I should have."

She nodded. "So should I."

"And we weren't exactly careful in the shower," he added.

She looked visibly relieved. "I was three months pregnant before I even realized. I kept blaming the missed periods and nausea on the stress of moving to Paris, because I was super homesick. When I found out…well, that was when I tried to find you."

"Can I…" Preston couldn't stand it anymore. He wanted— *needed*—to hold his son.

"Hold him? Oh my gosh. Of course." She lifted Lennon, carefully passing him over, though Preston noticed her hands were trembling.

The second she put Lennon in his arms, something he didn't even realize was askew clicked into place, and he was overwhelmed by a happiness he'd never experienced in his life. Not even when the Rays had won the Stanley Cup nearly a decade earlier.

His heart raced and his vision blurred as he held his son for the first time. Honestly, it was taking everything he had not to fall apart. Not because he was upset but because it felt as if he'd just been handed the most precious gift of his life. His heart was so full, he worried it might burst.

Lennon looked up at him as Preston ran the tip of one finger over his soft, pudgy cheeks. Chelsea wasn't lying about him being off the charts. The chubby baby was an armful, surprisingly heavier than he expected. He recalled his mom telling him that he'd been her roly-poly little baby, joking that it took her ages to dig through the rolls to find his neck just so she could wash it during bath time.

Preston huffed out a breathy laugh when Lennon smiled at him.

"He's perfect," he whispered. "Chelsea, he's perfect."

She swallowed heavily, her voice still wobbly. "I know."

"Hello, Lennon," he said to the sweet boy. "I'm your daddy. You and I are going to have so much fun together. I'm going to teach you how to ice skate and how to play hockey and how to ride a bike and drive…"

Chelsea sniffled, reaching into the baby bag to pull out a tissue. Wiping her eyes and nose, she gave him the most sorrowful look he'd ever seen. "I'm so sorry, Preston."

Preston's brows creased. "Why?"

"Because you missed his birth, and the first three months of his life, and…" She paused, sucking in a trembling breath. "I never meant to keep him from you. I just didn't know what else to do. I bought a ticket to the holiday party in Philadelphia for Allyson this year. It's being held again in a couple of weeks. She was planning to drive there on the off chance you showed up. I was hoping she could get your name and number so I could call you. Of course, Ally, being Ally, she's spent the last month inventing all these elaborate kidnapping schemes if you refused to give her the number. She's probably going to be a little disappointed to know I've found you, now that I think about it."

Her words fell out so quickly, Preston struggled to keep up.

"It was the only thing I could think of to do. I just…God, I'm so sorry," she repeated.

"Chelsea, sweetheart. Breathe." Preston reached out with one hand to grasp hers, giving it a squeeze. "You gave me a *son*. He's healthy and happy and perfect, and that's all because of you. *I'm* the one who's sorry. Sorry that you had to go through the pregnancy, the delivery, and all the sleepless nights without my help."

"You don't need to apologize," she said.

"Neither do you."

They fell silent as Preston continued to hold her hand while they stared at their son together.

"Look what we made," he whispered, grinning at her. His shock slowly started to recede, replaced by wonder and delight.

She returned his smile, though it looked forced.

"I guess we have a lot to talk about," Chelsea said after several more minutes of simply admiring their son.

They had so much to talk about that Preston couldn't begin to imagine where to start. Well, that wasn't true. He knew exactly where to start. "I want to be a part of his life."

A tear slid down Chelsea's cheek. "I'm glad," she said, her words not matching her emotions. "Honestly. I want you to be a part of his life, too. God," she said, wiping her eyes with the tissue. "I don't know why I'm crying."

Preston squeezed her hand again. "We don't know each other that well. We had one night together a year ago. It makes sense that might scare you."

Her lower lip trembled. "It shouldn't. I mean, I don't regret that night at all, Preston. Not even now. That night with you gave me Lennon."

"Us," he interjected. "It gave *us* Lennon."

She blinked rapidly, but it didn't stop the tears from falling. "For so long, he's been mine. From the moment I knew he was growing inside me, he's been mine. Just mine."

"I know that. But from now on, I'm asking that he be ours. I'll be a good father to him, Chelsea."

"Okay, yes. Of *course* yes. You want to spend time with him," she said, more to herself than him.

He nodded, because that was exactly what they needed to talk about, and it was bound to be a tough conversation, especially if there was another man in the picture. Preston didn't bring that up, waiting for her to mention it.

While they'd shared a powerful connection last year, it appeared there was someone else in her life now.

"I realize I'm asking you to share him with someone who's little more than a stranger," he started.

"You don't feel like a stranger to me. You never did. It's just…with him…" She lowered her head, her shoulders shaking slightly as she tried to pull herself together.

"I'm not going to take him away from you, Chelsea." He sought for a way to reassure her.

"I know that. I know I'm overreacting."

"I don't think you are," he said. "As I said—we don't know each other that well."

"He's the most important person in my life," she explained. "I would die for him."

Preston looked down into Lennon's now-sleeping face. "So would I."

Chelsea stared at him, long and hard, and the tears slowly stopped. "You would, wouldn't you?"

"I love him. I've known him all of ten minutes and I'm so in love with this baby, I can barely breathe."

Chelsea started crying again, but this time they looked like happy tears. "That's the most wonderful thing I've ever heard. I feel the same way."

"We'll figure this out, Chelsea. I promise. We'll find a way to raise him together. Co-parenting."

"I'd like that. Despite me falling apart—I'm blaming hormones—I have to admit it's been tough. My parents help a lot, but I try not to impose on them too much."

Preston wasn't sure what to make of that. Where was the other man? Why wasn't he helping her?

"I want to do everything right for him," she continued, "but there are just so many hours in the day, and I spend the majority of them feeding him, bathing him, changing diapers, then trying to do the mundane stuff like laundry and sterilizing bottles while he's napping. Mom helps a lot, but my dad works long hours, so I hate to ask him for help—even though he'd give it if I needed."

"Well, now you have me to help with that," he said, ridiculously excited about the idea of caring for his son, even though he was pissed off if some other guy was leaving her to do everything on her own. "Although, I don't know how to do half of what you just said."

She smiled, though it was far too brief for him. Then her anxiety crept back in. "Do you want to get a lawyer or..." She sighed. "I have no idea how to do any of this."

"Let's try to sort it out on our own first. If you'd be more comfortable drawing up something legal, we can do that, but for now, why don't we start with the basics and move from there. We should probably address our expectations for each other and our hopes in regard to time spent with him."

"Okay. Yeah. That makes sense."

"What are you doing tonight?" he asked.

"Same thing I always do. Bath, bottle, bedtime," she replied.

"You have your own place?"

Chelsea grimaced. "Unfortunately, no. When I returned to Baltimore, it made sense for me to move back in with my parents, financially and because I needed help with Lennon."

So she wasn't living with the guy. Preston wasn't sure why that fact made him feel better. No, not better. Hopeful. If she and Mr. Man from the Street weren't in a serious relationship, Preston was throwing his hat in the ring. Because he was determined to expand on what they'd started last year.

Chelsea kept talking. "Living with them works...for now. They welcomed me home with open arms, and they're over the moon with their grandson."

Grandson.

God, Preston couldn't wait to call his own folks. Of course, knowing his mother, she'd be on the next flight from Seattle to Baltimore. Soooo…maybe he should put that call off until he and Chelsea made some concrete decisions. The upcoming conversation was already going to be difficult with the two of them trying to agree on who got him when. He wanted to have some answers regarding all of that before he told his parents, because Mom would sure enough ask those questions.

"Could we meet for a late dinner tonight? To discuss where we go from here?"

She nodded. "Lennon typically goes down for the night at seven and, if I'm lucky, he sleeps until about midnight. My parents will be home to watch him, so how about seven-thirty?"

Preston wished he could be there for bath, bottle, and bedtime, but the two of them needed time to sort things out first. "How about Pat's Pub? Have you ever been there?"

Chelsea shook her head. "No, but I've heard good things about it. I can meet you there."

They fell silent again as Preston gently rocked his son. Lennon had fallen sound asleep, cooing the sweetest sounds as he breathed. It was almost like he was singing.

"I don't know if I can walk away from him," Preston admitted.

"I get that. I hate being away from him. I swear I spent the first month after he was born staring at him twenty-four seven. I have approximately seven million pictures and videos of him."

"Will you send them to me?" Preston asked, as he pulled his phone from his back pocket. "All of them."

"I will, but it might take a few weeks," she joked.

Preston unlocked his phone with his face, then handed it to her. "Put your contact information in?"

She did, then she sent a text from his phone to hers before handing his back. Grabbing hers, she added him as well.

Preston glanced at the contact info. "Chelsea Murphy."

He had it. Her name and her phone number. At last.

Then he glanced at Lennon. "Lennon Murphy?"

She nodded. "I didn't give him a middle name. I thought if I ever found you…" She shrugged. "I figured we could add your name."

Jesus. She really had hoped to find him. Saving room to give his name to Lennon was the sweetest, most thoughtful thing he'd ever heard. "Thank you," he said, sincerely grateful.

"So…you're a hockey player, huh?" she asked. "I didn't realize you'd actually made that childhood dream come true."

"I did. And now…" Preston looked around the building. "Yours is coming true too."

"Ethan and I inherited some money late last spring from Ethan's great-aunt. She encouraged us to open the bakery in her will. Agnes was a huge part of my life, and I still can't believe she's gone. Without her, we'd never had been able to do this."

"It's a great space on a cool street. Lots of foot traffic."

"That's what Ethan said," Chelsea agreed. "He handled finding the property, since I had my hands full with this sweetheart. Ethan has been incredible through all of this. He's nuts about Lennon. I asked him and Allyson to be the godparents. They were both with me in the delivery room. I hope that's okay. I know you don't know them."

"It's fine, Chelsea. Honest. I'm glad they were there for you. And I can tell Ethan's crazy about the baby." Again, no mention of the other man. Maybe Victor had been right. Maybe the guy kissing her was new to the scene or things weren't that serious between them.

"The bakery has caused some discord between me and my mother, because she thinks I'm taking too big a chance and I should be saving the inheritance for Lennon, but…" Chelsea waved her hand. "Sorry. I'm a nervous talker. Scratch all of that. You don't want to hear my silly drama."

Actually, he did. He wanted to know every single thing there was to know about her, her life, and Lennon.

The attraction he'd felt toward her the night of the holiday party was child's play compared to now. He'd spent a year trying to tell himself he was building Chelsea up bigger in his mind, imagining she was prettier, funnier, sweeter than she'd actually been.

Sitting with her now, he could see that—if anything—he'd downplayed his memories. Because she was still just as open and honest and genuine as she'd been at the party. He never had to second-guess with her, never had to wonder or worry that she was playing him because of his career or his ridiculously large bank account. And motherhood really freaking suited her. She'd gained weight during her pregnancy, enhancing her gorgeous curves, adding a healthy glow to her skin.

She was still an incredibly beautiful woman, even with the dark circles under her eyes. For some reason, he was as attracted to those as anything else, because it was proof she was spending her sleep-deprived nights taking care of their son.

"There's nothing wrong with pursuing a dream, Chelsea. I spent my entire childhood determined I was going to be a professional hockey player. Talk about an unachievable dream. You want to know what made the difference for me?"

She nodded.

"No one laughed at or dismissed me. No one told me I couldn't do it. Instead, my family supported me, even though it was a financial strain and a huge time commitment. You've been dreaming of this since you were young, right?"

"I have."

"Then you should go for it."

"But you don't think the timing is," she gestured toward Lennon, "a little insane?"

He chuckled. "I think it's safe to say the timing will never get any better. Unless you're okay with waiting until Lennon moves out. Because you're a mom for life."

Her eyes widened. "Oh my God. You're right. When I first got back to the States, my old boss said I could return to my job at his bakery, but when I looked at the hours and the pay—barely better than minimum wage, with no benefits—I realized just how hard it would be with a newborn baby. As my own boss, I'll have a bit more freedom to set my own schedule."

"That makes sense."

"Not that I won't still have early hours. My days start at four a.m."

Preston feigned a horrified face, pleased when Chelsea laughed. It was the first time she'd laughed freely, the sound unfettered by nerves.

"Figuring out childcare is one of those things I've been struggling with. I should already be looking. We're opening the bakery on Valentine's Day, and while I've got things sorted until then between me, my mom, Allyson, and Ethan for now, once this place opens…I hate the idea of leaving him with strangers."

Preston leaned back in his chair, shifting slightly to a more comfortable position. Lennon stirred, and, for a moment, he feared he'd woken him up, but then the baby sank deeper into his arms and continued sleeping. "So we'll add childcare to the list of things we need to talk about. Because I'd like to be included on that list of people who take care of him. My schedule during the season is a bit hectic, between games, workouts, practices, and road trips, but there are still plenty of hours during the day when he could be with me."

"You want to take care of him?"

"He's my son, Chelsea. I want to spend as much time as I can with him. Oh, and I'll need a list of things I should buy for him for my place. I mean, I know I need a crib and high chair and car seat, and maybe a changing table, but what else? I want to make sure I have everything he needs."

"You're buying furniture for your place?"

"Well, yeah. I might need a diaper tutorial, and directions on how to give him a bath, and a feeding schedule, and…" Preston stopped, aware that while he was getting carried away, excited by the idea of having his son with him, Chelsea had suddenly gone chalk white.

He lifted one hand. "I'm going too fast."

She didn't respond for a moment or two. "You are, but I understand why. You've already missed so much time. It makes sense that you want to be with him. I'm…" She ran her hand through her hair. "I'm going to try to…"

"I shouldn't have started this conversation here. We both need some time to sort through all of this. I got carried away."

"And I love that," she confessed. "Even though it scares the shit out of me."

Preston put one of his hands over Lennon's ear. "Language. I can see we're going to need to add a swear jar to the discussion list," he joked.

She laughed. "Oops."

"Don't be scared, Chelsea. We'll find a way to make this work for both of us."

"I've played out every scenario imaginable about how you would react if I ever found you and told you about Lennon. This has been way better than all of them."

"You've made me happier than I've ever been in my life. I'm still reeling a bit, but this is truly the best thing that's ever happened to me, and I was with the Rays the year we won the Stanley Cup."

She shifted toward him, placing her hand on top of the blanket, peering down at Lennon.

"Thank you for our son," Preston whispered, leaning forward. Chelsea met him halfway, their foreheads touching, their child between them.

They remained there for a few minutes, simply watching Lennon sleep.

When they parted, Preston glanced at his phone and groaned when he saw the time.

"You need to leave?"

"I have workouts in an hour and a half, and I need to run home to change." Preston, who never called in sick, never took a day off, was tempted to call out. After all, other guys had taken paternity leave when their babies were born. Lennon might be three months old, but today was his birthday as far as Preston was concerned.

"That's okay. Ethan and I have a little more work to do here, though I suspect he'll be worthless when he gets back. He wasn't exaggerating when he said he was a huge fan."

Preston shrugged. "I don't mind fans at all. Love them, in fact."

"It's going to take me some time to wrap my head around the fact you play for the Stingrays."

Preston laughed. "Good. I'd hate to think I'm the only one floored by this reunion of ours."

Chelsea giggled. "Guess we both left that hotel with some big-ass secrets."

"I guess we did."

As if they'd summoned him, Ethan returned, the door to the bakery swinging open, the bell tinkling.

Ethan stumbled in with two giant duffel bags stuffed to the gills.

"Ethan!" Chelsea chastised. "You can't ask Preston to sign all that."

He tossed the bags on the floor by the table, and Preston got the sense the man didn't care if he signed any of it. He'd merely been seeking an excuse to return. Given the pensive look Ethan shot in Chelsea's direction, it was clear he truly was a good friend, more concerned about her right now than getting his shit autographed.

"Everything good?" He glanced between Chelsea and Preston, his eyebrows rising when he realized Preston was holding his son.

"I'm a father," he said proudly. "I'm going to have to stop on the way back to my place to buy some cigars."

"He's happy," Chelsea added. "He wants to be a part of Lennon's life."

"Of course, you do. That baby is the GOAT." Ethan grinned, slapping Preston on the shoulder. "Congratulations, man. I'm still dying over the fact that the whole time Chelsea was looking for her Preston, I was cheering you on from the cheap seats."

Preston laughed. "I'll have to set you up with better seats for the next game. Can't have Lennon's godfather sitting in the cheap seats."

Ethan's eyes widened. "Seriously? I mean, only if it's no problem. Although, something tells me I'm going to need an extra ticket, because chances are good I'm *finally* going to get this one to come with me." He jerked his thumb in Chelsea's direction.

"I hope she does." Preston glanced down at the bags. "Listen, Ethan, I'm afraid I need to leave."

"No problem," he said, good-naturedly. "Now that I know you're going to be around, we have all the time in the world for you to sign my stuff. We'll take it in batches," he joked, "so your hand doesn't wear out."

Preston smiled widely. For too much of the past year, he'd been down in the dumps, overcome with loneliness and longing for Chelsea. All of those heavy feelings were history, replaced with pure joy.

Sure, they still had a lot of stuff to figure out, but just knowing Chelsea and Lennon were going to be a big part of his life from this day forward, was enough to hold the anxiousness he should be feeling, at bay.

"I suspect our paths will be crossing a lot," he reassured Ethan, praying that was true. "So tonight at seven-thirty?" he said to Chelsea, reconfirming their dinner plans.

She nodded and lifted her arms, intent on taking Lennon back.

Preston hesitated. He hadn't lied earlier. Walking out of this building, away from her and Lennon, was going to be one of the hardest things he'd ever done.

Chelsea must have sensed his struggle. "I'll send you a bunch of pictures and videos this afternoon, I promise."

"Okay." Preston bent his head, lifting the still-sleeping baby so that he could place a soft kiss on his forehead. "Daddy will see you again, very soon."

Even as he spoke, he knew it wouldn't be soon enough. Five minutes from now wouldn't be soon enough.

Chelsea gently took Lennon away from him, tucking him into her arms, and the sight of her holding their child took his breath away.

Preston cupped her cheek. "I'm so glad I found you. Both of you."

Chelsea blinked rapidly, her lashes wet again with unshed tears. "I'm glad you did, too."

Unable to hold back, Preston decided if there was even the tiniest chance, he was going all in with this woman. Letting her walk out of that hotel room was the biggest mistake of his life, so he wasn't going to play it safe or cool this time around. There was too much on the line. "This is probably going to sound silly, but...I missed you."

"Goddamn, that's romantic," Ethan murmured.

Chelsea huffed out a breathy laugh as she rolled her eyes at her best friend. Then she looked back at him. "I missed you, too."

Preston kissed her on the cheek when he really wanted to place one on her lips. Then he gave Lennon another kiss on the forehead.

"I'll see you later."

She nodded.

Somehow, he found the strength to walk away from them. Turning at the doorway, he twisted around and gave them a wave, then headed outside.

The Preston who left the bakery was completely different from the one who'd walked in.

He was a father.

He had a son.

He found Chelsea.

God willing, the life he longed for was starting right now.

And he couldn't wait.

CHAPTER EIGHT

CHELSEA WALKED into Pat's Pub, trying to beat back the anxiety that had been growing ever since Preston said goodbye earlier. For months, all she'd wanted to do was find him and tell him about Lennon. Now that she had...she was freaking the fuck out.

She'd been fine-ish at first, because she'd still been at the bakery with Ethan, who had sung Preston's praises up one side and down the other. And a lot of what he shared about Preston hadn't just been about his skill on the ice. Though God knew she heard more than enough of those stories as well, as Ethan recounted amazing Preston goals from years past. Ordinarily, she tuned her best friend out when he was on one of his long-winded hockey discourses, giving her unrequested replays and analyses, but this afternoon, she'd been practically spellbound.

What had interested her more, however, were the details about Preston's charitable work. Ethan followed all the players' social media—as well as the team's—so he lost no time pulling up Preston's, showing her post after post of him working with underprivileged kids, reading in kindergarten classes, visiting fans in the hospital, and auctioning off sports memorabilia to raise money for very worthy causes.

She'd left the bakery feeling much better about tonight's meeting.

Then she'd gotten home...to her mother.

When Chelsea explained to her parents that she'd found Lennon's father, and that he wanted to be a part of his son's life, she honestly thought they'd be thrilled. And for the most part, Dad was. He obviously wanted to meet Preston, but he knew how important it had been to Chelsea to find him, and how much guilt she'd suffered over not being able to tell him that he had a son.

Mom, however, went the opposite direction, unwittingly putting the fear of God in her. Her comments hadn't helped her nerves when her mother started listing off Chelsea's own unspoken fears one by one.

Mom had latched on to Preston's career as a hockey player, worrying that he was a playboy with a slew of baby mamas scattered around the country. Then she'd managed to work in the fact that he'd be on the road for the majority of the year, so he'd be a much-absent, unreliable source of help. From there, she expressed concern over Preston's wealth, and how it would allow him to hire a successful lawyer who might find a way to "take Lennon away from us," if that was what he decided he wanted. That thought was terrifying as shit.

"Chelsea."

She glanced up and saw Preston was already there, seated in a booth. He waved her over, his smile so friendly and kind that she almost instantly felt calm again. She wasn't sure what magic he possessed, but she had recognized the man's ability to put her at ease a year ago, and it was still there.

She crossed the quaint pub, claiming the bench seat across from him. "I can't believe I've lived in Baltimore my whole life, and I've never been here."

"This pub has become a sanctuary for the Stingrays. We come here to celebrate our wins, and occasionally we drag our sorry asses here to drown our sorrows after a loss," Preston explained.

"I'm going to do you a favor and not share that information with Ethan, or he'll be camped out here after every game from now until the end of time," she joked.

Preston laughed. "Go ahead and tell him. Being godfather to our son should come with some perks. I'd be happy to introduce him to my teammates. How was the rest of your day? Get a lot of work done?"

She shook her head. "It was exactly as I predicted. After you left, Ethan spent the next two hours breaking down your entire career with the Stingrays for me, and to make matters worse, it was done show-and-tell style, because he wasn't kidding about having ninety-seven things for you to sign. I saw way too many jerseys, trading cards, posters, pucks, and pennants this afternoon—not to mention the highlight reels of your best plays on YouTube."

"Oh my God. I'm not sure whether to apologize or call Ethan to thank him for talking me up."

"Both are probably in order," she mused.

"I'm sorry."

She laughed. "I'm kidding. You're an amazing hockey player."

"How could you tell? As I recall, you come from a football family."

Once again, Chelsea was touched by just how much of their one night together Preston recalled. She'd obsessed over those hours more than she cared to admit, so it was nice to know she wasn't alone.

"I'll have to correct that mistake. Or perhaps it's safer to say, my dad will correct it for me, because when I told him who you were, he looked more than prepared to change allegiances as far as sports is concerned. Trust me when I say, that's a big damn deal."

Preston leaned back in the booth, looking equal parts pleased and uneasy. "So you told your parents about me?"

"I did."

"And?" he prodded.

"And, obviously, they want to meet you." Chelsea wasn't sure how much to add to that. While Dad was pretty accepting, Mom was going to be tough to win over. Mainly because Rick hadn't just been attempting to worm his way back into *her* life. He'd shown up at her parents' place shortly after Chelsea's return to Baltimore with a check that he'd handed to her dad to cover all the money they'd lost on the wedding, offering them the same "heartfelt" apology she'd gotten.

Mom had held on to her anger for a while, but when Rick kept coming back with flowers and small gifts for her and Lennon, Mom had forgiven him.

Not that that was surprising. After all, it wasn't just Rick pleading his case to her but his mother, Angie, as well. Mom and Angie had basically raised her and Rick together, jokingly planning their wedding from the time they'd been babies, so Mom had softened up way faster than Chelsea.

Dad—bless him—was reserving *his* judgment, agreeing with her that actions spoke louder than words. Rick's actions on their wedding day had been deafening. His apology little more than a whisper in comparison.

"I would like to meet them," he replied.

Given the fact she and Preston were a one-night stand with consequences, it felt awkward to discuss meeting parents with him, but since nothing about this situation could be called normal, she decided to just roll with it. "Did you talk to your parents yet?"

Preston shook his head. "No. I wanted to call them immediately, but I was afraid my mother would hop on the first plane from Seattle to meet Lennon. I figured we needed to chat first."

Chelsea understood Preston's uneasiness, because the idea of meeting his parents made her ridiculously nervous. These kinds of introductions felt like a three-months-into-the-relationship thing. Not a "Hey, Mom and Dad. This is the guy I hooked up with after the party and who's now my baby daddy" thing.

"Hi, Padraig," Preston said, as the bartender came over to their table.

"Hello, Preston. Sorry it took me so long to get over here. We got slammed at the bar with a bunch of ladies out barhopping for a bachelorette party."

Chelsea glanced over where the bartender was pointing, grinning at the large group of giggling women indulging in blowjob shots. Given how loud they were talking, it was a safe bet this wasn't their first stop in the hop.

Preston did the introductions. "Padraig, this is Chelsea. Chelsea, Padraig."

She and the bartender shook hands.

"It's nice to meet you," she said.

"You too, Chelsea." There was something about the way Padraig said her name that made her wonder if the two of them had met before. Or it did, until he sent a questioning look in Preston's direction. It was a strange exchange, especially when Preston grinned and nodded. Then it felt like Padraig knew who she was because of Preston…but that couldn't be right.

"What can I get you two to drink?"

"I'll have a PBR," Preston said, before looking at her.

"Just an unsweetened iced tea for me." She lifted one shoulder at Preston before adding, "Need to be sharp for the midnight feeding. And the three a.m. one."

Padraig's brows rose briefly, then he nodded. "I'll grab those drinks. Give you two some time to decide what you want to order." He handed them the menus.

Chelsea wasn't sure she could eat. Those butterflies in her stomach had turned into frogs, jumping around out of control. "What's good?" She pretended to look at the menu, when really she was fighting to calm down.

She must have given something away, because rather than answer, Preston reached across the table and grasped her hand. "It's okay, Chels. It's just me. I'm the same guy you met a year ago. I know the situation is…" He paused, searching for a word.

"Fucked up?" she offered.

He laughed. "I was going to say unique."

"Ah, ever the optimist." Chelsea turned her hand in his, squeezing it back. "But thanks for that. I'm letting my nerves get the better of me."

"I meant what I said earlier. I'm sure we can find a way to work this out so that both of us are happy. In fact, we won't stop until we figure it out."

She took a deep breath and released it, drinking in his confidence. "Okay. Sounds like a plan."

"And for the record, the fish and chips here are amazing."

She put down her menu. "That sounds delicious." Then, because she was too nervous to start talking about the hard stuff, she landed on a harmless subject. "It really is a cool place."

Preston spent a few minutes giving her a brief history of the pub and the family that ran it. Apparently, Pat's Pub and the adjoining restaurant, Sunday's Side, had been established by Pat and Sunday Collins, and it was now being run by their children and grandchildren.

"I'll have to bring Ethan and Allyson here sometime. They'd love it."

"Speaking of Ethan." Preston pulled out his cell phone. "I want to make a note to remind myself to request tickets to the next home game for him. The team has a box for family and friends. I can get him a spot in there."

Chelsea brushed a stray lock of hair out of her eyes. She was way overdue for a haircut, but she couldn't seem to find the time to do anything for herself nowadays, every minute spent with Lennon. At some point, she was going to have to learn how to take her eyes off her baby and start functioning in the real world again. "I stand corrected on Ethan. Forget this pub. If you get him those tickets, he'll set up camp in that box and never leave."

Preston shook his head in amusement.

Padraig returned with their drinks, and Preston ordered the fish and chips for both of them.

"Good choice," the bartender said. "I'll put that order in right now. Wave me down if you need anything else."

Preston thanked Padraig, who returned to the bar, typing their order into the computer.

"So, tell me more about your job. I've never met anyone who played a sport at the professional level." Chelsea was legitimately curious about his career, but at the moment, she was using that safe topic as another way to avoid discussing the harder items on tonight's agenda.

"I started playing professionally when I was twenty. I was drafted by a West Coast team, played there for a year, then I got traded to the Rays. Been here ever since."

"So you're not a local, then?"

Preston shook his head. "Nope. Born and raised in Seattle."

"Must be exciting, playing for the NHL, traveling all over the country."

He shrugged, then took a sip of his beer. "The travel isn't all that great. Lots of time in transit and no time for sightseeing. Most of what I know about the cities we play in involves the arenas and the airports."

"I never considered that."

One of the women with the bachelorette party broke away from the group, clearly en route to the bathroom. She stopped by their table, flashing Preston a smile and breathy "hello" that was such a glaringly obvious come-on, it took all of Chelsea's willpower not to roll her eyes, especially when the woman leaned over, ensuring Preston got a good look at her tits.

"I'm a huge fan."

Preston, to his credit, nodded briefly and offered a quick "thanks," before turning his attention back to Chelsea.

Annoyed at being dismissed, the woman huffed and walked away.

Chelsea rested her chin on her hand. "Let me guess…you have women throwing themselves at you like that all the time, right?"

Preston glanced behind him in the direction the woman walked, as if he hadn't even really noticed her. Then, the shameless devil's eyes sparkled with pure mischief. "I will admit that's one of the perks of the job."

"Mm-hmm," she hummed. "Are you sure? Because she was giving you a bird's-eye view of her tatas and you barely noticed."

"Dime a dozen," he muttered. "She doesn't hold a candle to you."

"Still smooth with the lines, I see," she said, trying to fan the flames on her libido because, woo boy, Preston always knew the right things to say to fire up the old girl parts. And that was saying something, considering she'd basically just shoved a watermelon through her hoohah three months earlier.

While they waited for the food, he regaled her with stories of the road and the extremes some of the "puck bunnies," as he called them, went to in order to get his attention. Some of the stories were horrifying enough that she was ashamed to call herself a woman.

Soon, the conversation switched from puck bunnies to the hijinks he and his teammates got up to; then he shared some of his favorite moments during big games.

He was passionate about what he did, and it shone through. While she might have expected him to be cocky, there was a humility to him as he praised his teammates rather than bragged about his own achievements.

"Okay. I think you've convinced me to watch a hockey game," she said.

"Excellent," Preston replied as he pulled out his phone. "I'll be sure to request a ticket for you as well. And Allyson?"

She hesitantly nodded. "If that's not a problem. She'd hate to miss the fun." Then Chelsea recalled herself. "What am I saying? I can't go to a hockey game. I have Lennon."

"You're here tonight," Preston pointed out.

"Yeah, but that's…out of necessity. To be honest, this is the first night I've gone out since he was born. I know the day is coming when I need to, but…"

"You're a good mom."

Chelsea flushed under his praise. Then her nerves kicked in again, and before they could travel too far down that path, she changed the subject again. "Do you miss Seattle?"

One side of his mouth tipped up in an almost grin that let her know he *knew* what she was doing, but mercifully, he went along with it. "I go home a few times a year to visit my parents, but after so many years here, I've come to think of Baltimore as home. And you? Baltimore born and raised, you said?"

Chelsea nodded. "I was born at Hopkins."

"Didn't go off to college?" he asked.

"Nope. Went to culinary school here, while working at a donut shop. So, apart from those months spent in Paris, I've lived here my whole life. Allyson, Ethan, and I have been best friends since second grade, and my parents still live in the house I grew up in. How's that for boring?"

"You couldn't be boring if you tried."

Chelsea didn't know what to make of Preston's compliments. They rolled off his tongue so easily—and so sincerely. She hated herself for choosing that moment to recall Mom's comment about professional athletes being indiscriminate playboys. Was he just saying what he thought she wanted to hear? "Thanks, but you might want to withhold judgment on my boringness until you know me better."

Padraig returned with their food. "There's ketchup, salt, and malt vinegar there." He pointed to the condiment holder on their table. "Need another round?"

"Yes, please," Preston said.

Padraig nodded, leaving them alone once again. They ate in silence for a couple of minutes, Chelsea following Preston's lead, sprinkling her fish and fries with malt vinegar and salt. One bite of the fish, and she decided Preston had undersold just how good it was.

"So," he began, and Chelsea knew they'd reached the end of the small-talk portion of the evening.

"So," she repeated.

"Thanks for the videos and pictures." Preston glanced at his phone. She followed his gaze and realized he'd already made one of the photographs she shared with him this afternoon the background. She was touched by the choice, because it didn't just include a photo of Lennon—of which he had at least a hundred to choose from—but one of the two she'd sent that included her. "I spent a full two hours before coming here tonight looking through all of them. Goddamn, we made one cute kid."

She laughed. "We really did. Those chubby cheeks of his…"

"Adorable. I hope he has your dimples."

Chelsea bit her lower lip. "I don't have any idea how we go about this."

Preston took a quick sip of the new beer Padraig quietly dropped off, and, for the first time, she got the sense that he was as nervous as she was. "I guess the best thing to do would be to say what we want, then decide if those desires are workable for both of us."

Chelsea agreed that was reasonable, but when it came to her

—nope—*their* baby, she wasn't exactly reasonable. "What do you want?" she forced herself to ask.

Preston sat up straighter. "I don't want to be an every-other-weekend dad. I meant what I said at the bakery. I want to be a part of his life, a real part. I was hoping we could share custody of—"

He stopped talking when Chelsea failed to hold back what was essentially a half gasp, half sob.

"Chelsea." Preston took her hand again. "Joy, wait. Please don't panic."

His use of her nickname from a year earlier slowed down her immediate alarm, but only for a second or two. "I'm sorry. It's the word custody." God, what if Mom was right? What if his end game was to take Lennon away from her? "I hate it."

"You're right. That was a shitty word to use. Makes it sound like we're divorced or something. What if we just say co-parenting?"

"You want a lot of time with him," she said. "Equal time?"

God, she couldn't even leave Lennon long enough to get a haircut.

"Not immediately, Chelsea. Lennon doesn't know me. I get that. What I'm asking for right now is a chance to get to know my son…with you around, of course."

"Okay." That was a fair request, one she couldn't exactly turn down.

"I have a game out of town tomorrow in Boston. We're leaving at the crack of dawn, but I'll be back the next day by noon. I was hoping we could have a family date."

"A family date." Chelsea toyed with one of her fries, trying to wrap her head around the idea of Preston calling them a family. Is that what they were? Or what he hoped they would become? Did co-parenting fall under that heading?

Ugh. This was all so confusing, and she wasn't helping

matters by overreacting to his requests by making her own fears known.

"The idea of spending a single night away from Lennon kills me, Preston. I can't even begin to process how I'd do that. I don't think I can."

Preston leaned back, considering her words. "I get that. And I understand it. Completely. Chelsea, leaving that bakery today, without knowing when I'd see my son again…it hurt more than I can say. I know that must seem strange to you but—"

"It doesn't," she hastened to interject. "I'm glad you felt that way. Well, I'm not glad you were hurt, but glad to know how much you care about him."

"My schedule is chaotic at best while I'm in season, and you're trying to launch a new business, so time isn't exactly on our side right now."

"No," she agreed. "It's not."

Preston clicked on his phone, opening the calendar app, turning it sideways so they could both see it. "Why don't we start slow? Organize the first visit."

Chelsea pulled her phone out of her purse and opened her calendar as well. "Okay, well, we've already planned a date—a family date—for the day after tomorrow."

"Are you working with Ethan that day?"

"Only in the morning."

"Great." Preston typed the words Family Date on his calendar. "So what if you and Lennon come to my place around one? I can send you the address."

"Your place?"

"I want us to spend as much time as we can together, and I want you to see my condo, tell me how to baby-fy it. I suspect it will be easier to take care of him if we're at home. I could come to your parents' house if you—"

"No," she interjected, unwilling to subject Preston to her mother's fifth degree so soon in their reunion. Given Mom's unflattering list of concerns, it would be better to give her time to accept Preston's presence in Lennon's life. "No. It would be better at your place."

"Great. We can order in lunch and dinner and just hang out. You can teach me all the things," he said with a grin. "Like diaper changing and when naptime happens and how he likes to be held, stuff like that. I've already ordered a playpen and some toys that'll arrive before your visit, so maybe—"

"You what?" Chelsea thought she might've heard him wrong. He'd only discovered he was a father eight hours ago.

Preston gave her that same sexy, charming grin that had turned her head the night of the holiday party. "I pulled up an internet site on essentials for babies five minutes after walking out of the bakery. Spent the rest of my walk home reading reviews, then placing an order. I only ordered the playpen to start because I want your opinion on the crib, car seat, high chair, baby tub, and other stuff. But I figured the playpen was a good place to start because it's versatile. It's adjustable so it works as a bassinet, too, and it even has a changing station attachment."

Chelsea shook her head, trying to process the fact he'd already gone to so much effort. "I think it's sweet that you've already bought stuff."

"Is there anything else I need to buy for him before our date? Diapers? Wipes? Maybe a playmat for the floor?"

"No," she said. "I can bring all of that with me."

"Okay. We can do some online shopping for the rest of the stuff while we're at my condo."

Chelsea figured she should respond to that, but right now, her mind was whirling over everything he'd said. For someone who claimed they could start slow, Preston seemed to be doing the exact opposite. He was moving at warp speed, and she was struggling to keep up.

The problem was, they couldn't really take this as slow as she might be comfortable with because Lennon wasn't going to stop growing. It wasn't fair of her to let Preston miss out on any more of their son's tiny, daily milestones, simply because she was unable to share him.

They fell silent for a few minutes, each of them finishing their dinner and drinks. It wasn't an awkward silence. In fact, it felt deliberate on Preston's part. Like he could tell she was over-wrought, and he was giving her time to calm her thoughts.

She and Rick had known each other all their lives, and he'd never been able to read her like this man, who'd known her…God, what? When she did the math, she figured she and Preston had spent less than twenty-four hours together. Yet, it felt like more. Felt like they were years beyond that.

Probably because they'd made those hours count, holding back nothing from each other. She'd opened up to him that first night together about things she'd never told anyone, and he had done the same. If Chelsea was prone to flights of fantasy, she'd think perhaps the two of them were soul mates, that they'd known each other in a previous life.

Then she did an internal eye roll.

Yeah, right. That's totally what's happening here.

Padraig came back to clear the table. "Do you want some dessert?"

Preston looked at her, and Chelsea shook her head.

"Just the check," he said.

Padraig went back to the bar, returning quickly. Preston slid him a credit card, despite Chelsea reaching for her own wallet.

"Let me go halfsies," she insisted.

Preston refused. "Nope. I invited you. I'm paying."

"Then I'll pay for the takeout for our family date."

The look Preston gave her said he had no intention of agreeing to that.

Padraig returned, he and Preston making small talk about tomorrow night's game in Boston as he signed the receipt.

"Good luck," Padraig told him, before turning to her. "It was really nice to meet you, Chelsea."

"You too," she said, once again getting the feeling that Padraig knew her somehow. She glanced at the time on her phone. "I should probably head home. This is the longest I've been away from Lennon, and…"

Preston grinned. "You miss him."

"It's silly, I know, because he's most likely been asleep the entire time I've been away, but…" She stopped herself from saying more because it occurred to her she was pouring salt in Preston's wounds, complaining about being away from Lennon for a few hours when he'd missed so much time with his son. Months.

"Text me your address?" she asked.

Preston picked up his phone and did so immediately. Chelsea's eyes widened a bit. She knew the area where he lived. It was an upscale neighborhood on the waterfront.

"We'll be there at one," she promised.

"I can't wait. Come on. I'll walk you out." Preston reached down, helping her out of the booth, a shiver of—God—desire snaking down her spine when he placed his hand on the small of her back. She hadn't had sex since their one night together, and she hadn't felt a drop of arousal since then. Granted, she'd been sick for three months—morning sickness was no joke—and then big as a whale during the final trimester. After Lennon's birth, an exhaustion that went bone deep took over, more powerful than anything else.

Preston, with his simple, innocent touch, had reawakened the dragon, and she was suddenly salivating for more.

He walked her all the way to her car, the two of them standing next to it on the curb. She turned to face him, glancing up at her big, friendly giant just as he bent his head down to her.

She drew in a surprised, thrilled breath when he placed a soft kiss on her lips. It was slow and sweet and nowhere near enough. Chelsea was tempted to grab his shoulders, drag him back down, and show him how to do it properly, because that attraction she felt for Preston last year had only grown in the twelve months since. Grown until it was nearly as large as the Stay Puft Marshmallow Man in *Ghostbusters*.

Fortunately, her brain kicked in just in the nick of time, and she pulled back, instantly sorry when she saw…disappointment?…flash in Preston's eyes.

She shoved that regret aside because they were about to begin co-parenting their son. That had to take precedence over everything else, including her raging hormones. Things between them right now were nice and peaceful and friendly, and she had to make sure they stayed that way.

Chelsea hated that her mom's negativity was worming its way in, planting poisonous seeds in her thoughts.

But how nice would Preston be if they gave in to the sparks that were clearly still there, and things went south? Would he fight her for Lennon? The word *custody* was powerful enough to cause her to take a big step back.

"Thanks for dinner," she said, hating how thin her voice sounded.

Preston frowned, studying her face, sensing the change in her. The man was too damn observant for her good.

"You're welcome. Good night, Chelsea."

"Good night, Preston." She climbed into her car on unsteady legs, her stomach cramping as uncertainty and fear reared their ugly heads.

Until she and Preston were on steadier ground, she needed to keep her distance from him physically and emotionally. Which meant no more hand-holding and no more kissing and no more dreams of picking up where they'd left off last year.

Because it was her son's future on the line.

CHAPTER NINE

PRESTON HAD JUST FINISHED WIPING down the kitchen counters, tossing the sponge into the sink, when he heard a knock on his door. He gave his condo—which had never been cleaner—one final glance before crossing the large open-design living room/kitchen/dining area to answer it.

He was more excited than a kid at Christmas.

Swinging the door wide, he quickly darted forward, grabbing one of the oversized bags Chelsea carried.

"Why didn't you text me from the car?" he asked, taking a bouncy baby chair and second bag from her. "I would have helped you carry all of this up."

Chelsea was lugging enough stuff he wondered if she was planning to move in, not that he'd complain about that. Once he'd relieved her of everything except Lennon, who was sound asleep in his carrier, he led her into his condo.

Her eyes widened when she saw the large floor-to-ceiling windows that overlooked the Inner Harbor. "Wow. That's some view."

Preston placed the bags on the floor, then reached out for Lennon's carrier, peering down at his son. He'd been less than worthless the past two days, every spare moment spent staring at the photos and rewatching the videos Chelsea had shared with him. She had sent more yesterday, while he was on the road, keeping him in the loop on Lennon's past thirty-six hours. It had been awesome.

His teammates, once they'd overcome their shock, were happy for him. First, because he'd found Chelsea again, and secondly, because of Lennon. However, he couldn't help but feel like some of the happiness they directed his way was premature. Because while he'd found Chelsea, he by no means had her back.

The other night at Pat's Pub, he'd considered asking her about the man on the street countless times, but something had stopped him.

No. Not just something.

Fear.

He was afraid of finding out the man meant something to her, that she was in love with him. Their dinner at the pub had been little more than two old friends reconnecting, and while it was nice, it hadn't been enough for him.

So he'd stupidly decided to test the waters by kissing her after walking her to her car.

For a split second, she'd responded to the kiss. But then, as if someone had dumped cold water over their heads, she backed away. It wasn't confirmation that there was another man in her life, but it sure as shit felt like it to him.

Regardless of the uncertainty surrounding Chelsea, one thing was still definite…and amazing…and wonderful.

He was a father.

So this morning, as he and his teammates disembarked from the bus, Preston passed out cigars, the guys slapping him on the back and congratulating him as he showed off even more pictures.

"How long has he been asleep?" he asked, itching to hold his son again.

"Not long. He conked out in the car, which FYI is your first Lennon lesson. If he's fussy and nothing seems to soothe him, go for a drive. It never fails to put him to sleep within minutes."

"Good to know. It occurs to me I should find a notebook and pen."

Chelsea laughed. "I think you'll be able to retain what I tell you. Most of it is common sense. The rest I figured out through trial and error."

Preston placed the baby carrier on the couch, sitting next to it so that he could study Lennon's face as he slept. "I can't get over how perfect he is. Like, he's seriously the cutest kid ever, right?"

"One thousand percent," Chelsea said, agreeing readily, glancing over at the playpen.

"I set it up to be a bassinet. Was that right?"

"That's perfect." Walking to it, she ran her hand over the soft blanket he'd laid atop the padded cushion of the bassinet. "I'm going to move him over here. It's not good for them to sleep in the carrier for too long."

Preston watched as she oh-so slowly unfastened and lifted him out of the carrier. Lennon stirred a bit, but she rocked him gently as she walked to the playpen. Placing him in it, she pulled the second blanket he'd bought over their baby. Lennon remained asleep through it all.

Preston was relieved that Chelsea seemed more at ease today than she'd been at Pat's Pub. He'd spent a fretful couple of nights, afraid he'd pushed her too hard. First, in his requests regarding Lennon, and then, when he'd stole that kiss by her car.

Reconnecting with Chelsea again had reinforced his belief that she was the one, that she'd been made for him, his perfect mate, but that didn't mean she felt the same way.

Preston had made that soul mate comment so many times over the past year to his friends, family, and teammates that he'd started to question himself, thinking he'd overplayed his feelings toward her.

He would never question them again.

Love at first sight was real.

Period.

End of sentence.

"While he's napping, would you like a tour of the place?"

Chelsea nodded. "I would."

He gestured at their surroundings. "Obviously this is the great room, and the main reason I bought this place. I love the open concept and, as you pointed out, the view."

"It really is killer." Chelsea walked over to the windows, looking toward the water.

Preston pointed to the small marina just below them. "See the boat second from the shore on the right?"

"Yes."

"That's mine." He hadn't lived in Baltimore more than a month before he'd fallen in love with being out on the water. Within six months of being traded to the Stingrays, he'd bought the boat, spending a great deal of his summer cruising down the Patapsco River to the Chesapeake Bay, where he fished from his deck, soaking in the sunshine and sea air.

"That's not a boat, Preston. It's a yacht."

He laughed. "Not quite, but when Lennon gets older, I plan to take him out fishing with me."

Chelsea looked at him, smiling. "That sounds wonderful. Ethan's aunt Agnes had a boat as well, but hers was nowhere near as big. She would take me, Ethan, and Allyson out on it, though our fishing expeditions were usually fraught with drama."

"Drama and fishing don't mix."

She gave him a gorgeous grin. "You've never gone with Ethan, who refused to stab poor defenseless worms, or Allyson, who screamed bloody murder whenever we actually managed to land a fish."

Preston laughed. "You didn't add to the drama?"

"Hell no. I'll have you know I'm an excellent fisherwoman. I baited Ethan's hooks and took the fish off Allyson's before setting them free. All the while, Agnes lay back in her lounge chair, drinking Aperol Spritzes and laughing her ass off at us."

"Agnes sounds like a lot of fun. Is this the woman who had all the hats and no television?"

Chelsea's eyes widened. "I forgot I'd told you that story."

He and Chelsea had spent hours in that hotel room last year, alternating between the hottest sex of his life and sharing childhood stories. He remembered being fascinated by Chelsea's adventures with Ethan's aunt.

"She'll never get to meet him," Chelsea said sadly, glancing over at Lennon. "Aunt Agnes would have loved Lennon."

"I'm sure she would have."

"Ethan has sworn to take on her role in Lennon's life, exposing him to the same adventures and games and scavenger hunts."

"Then I'm glad I managed to score tickets for him. I know I mentioned the team box, and I can definitely get him a spot there whenever he wants, but I thought for this first time, he might prefer being center ice, lower bowl, near the glass. Best spot to really feel like he's part of the action." Preston walked over to the kitchen counter, retrieving the envelope with three tickets for tomorrow night's home game. "I know you're not sure if you can make it, but there's one in there for you just in case. And for Allyson, of course."

Chelsea accepted the envelope. "Oh wow. It was so sweet of you to think of her, and I know Allyson will go. Ethan's done nothing but sing your praises since he met you at the bakery."

Preston noticed she didn't say anything about her attendance, but he didn't push, even though he really wanted her there. Hockey was a huge part of his life, of who he was, and he wanted to share that with her, wanted her to see him out on the ice.

"My dad and I watched the Boston game last night."

He smiled. "Oh yeah. What did you think?"

"I was blown away, because that sport is seriously nuts."

"Nuts how?" he asked, chuckling at her wide-eyed expression.

"How in the hell do you skate like the wind, all while pushing a puck down the ice and getting shoved into the boards by other giants, then manage to get that teensy puck by the biggest giant in the rink and into the tiny net? It's nuts!"

"I guess it is. But it's fun."

"How sharp are the skates?" she asked.

"Razor sharp."

She shuddered, then narrowed her eyes, looking at him more closely. "How many of those teeth aren't your originals?"

Preston laughed loudly. "A few, but I'm not revealing which ones until at least our eighth date. Don't want to scare you away."

Chelsea's brows furrowed slightly, leaving him to wonder about her reaction.

Was it the word *date* that was tripping her up? Granted, today wasn't a traditional date, but in his mind, it was exactly what it was. He'd invited her because he wanted to get to know Lennon, but he also wanted to spend time with her.

He considered tackling the subject of the other man again, then changed his mind. They had approximately twelve million other fish to fry before he could propose that they pick up where they'd left off last year. Dammit.

Preston led her across the room to the large shelf he'd had built especially for his aquarium. His mother was deathly allergic to both dogs and cats—all pet dander did her in—so the only pet he'd been allowed to have as a child was a fish. Which was fine with him, because in his mind, there was nothing more peaceful than watching fish swimming around.

"Oh, is this Johnny and June?" Chelsea asked.

Preston shook his head. "Sadly, I lost both of them in September. I got them when I first moved here, so they were with me for fourteen years. I took their loss pretty hard."

Chelsea was shocked. "Fourteen years?"

"Some clownfish can live more than twenty years in aquariums. I got these guys around Thanksgiving."

"Let me guess," she said, her eyes sparkling. "Harry and Meghan? Beyonce and Jay-Z? Taylor and Travis?"

Preston was amused by her guesses and slightly nervous about answering the question. "Nope."

"Well, don't keep me in suspense."

Preston pointed to one of the fish. "That's BFG, and over there, hiding in the aquarium plants, is Joy."

Chelsea's humor gave way to something different, but just as nice. She looked...touched. "You named them after us?"

"The night we spent together was one of the best of my life, Chelsea. And I felt that way before I learned about *him*." He gestured toward their son. "Now it's not *one* of the best but *the* best. Because it gave us Lennon."

Chelsea didn't reply, but he wasn't concerned about her silence because she didn't appear to disagree. It was more like he'd rendered her speechless...in a good way. There was a glassy sheen of tears in her eyes that she tried to blink away.

He placed his hand on her back, turning her toward the hallway. "Come on. We better finish this tour before Lennon wakes up." He guided her down the hall, pointing out the laundry room, his office, and then the guest room. "I was thinking of turning this into the nursery. It's right across from my room."

Chelsea entered the guest room, running her finger along the dresser.

"There's plenty of room in here for a crib, and I could set the changing table up on the dresser. I was planning to paint those shelves white to brighten the room, and they're large enough for books and toys. For now, I was thinking of leaving the bed." He didn't add that he was hoping to convince her to spend some nights here with Lennon. In his ideal world, she'd be in bed with *him*, but they were a long way away from that, especially if…

"Chelsea, are you seeing someone?" he blurted, before he could chicken out again.

She seemed surprised by his question, so much so she didn't see his immediate relief when she instantly shook her head. "No. No one. You?"

Preston had to fight to draw in air because her answer knocked all the breath from his lungs. He wasn't sure who he'd seen kissing her on the sidewalk, but it was clear, given her direct response that the man meant nothing to her.

He didn't even try to hide his smile, which was clearly too big for the situation, because Chelsea gave him a look. He probably appeared unhinged, but he didn't care. She wasn't dating anyone. She was single.

Despite the mountain of issues standing between them and Preston's hopes for their future, he suddenly felt excited and ready to tackle every concern until he reached his true goal, the one he hadn't said to Chelsea yet.

He hadn't lied about wanting to spend every minute he could with his son, but what he hadn't said was that he wanted Chelsea to be there too. Preston didn't merely want to co-parent. He wanted them to be a family—a *real* family.

"I'm not dating anyone," he replied.

"Still a hopeless romantic?" She licked her lips somewhat nervously.

"Something like that."

They stared at each other for several long moments. Preston was tempted to cut the distance, to go to her, but her posture was too stiff, too…uneasy. He wasn't sure what was going through her mind, but clearly something was holding her back.

After a minute or two, she cleared her throat. "It's a lovely room, Preston." Chelsea was slipping back into that anxious state, so he opted for distraction.

"And this," he said, leading her across the hall, "is my bedroom."

She followed him, her eyes taking in everything. "It's so nice in here. Tasteful. Elegant, even."

"What were you imagining?" he asked with a grin. "Black silk sheets? Mirrored ceiling? Notches on the bedpost?"

She smirked. "Only the first two. I didn't think you'd be tacky enough to keep count with tick marks."

Preston wrapped his arm around her shoulders, ruffling her hair playfully. "Smart-ass."

She tried to bat his hand away, the game ending when they heard Lennon's cry from the living room.

Walking back down the hall, Chelsea started to pick him up, then stopped herself. "You want to hold him?"

Preston nodded eagerly, stepping next to her so that he could bend down to lift their son from the bassinet. Lennon had stopped fussing the moment he saw them, his tiny hands waving wildly. Picking him up carefully, Preston nestled the tiny baby in the crook of his arm, overwhelmed once again by the sheer power of his emotions.

This kid was fucking everything.

Chelsea smiled at the two of them for a moment, then walked back to the bags they'd left on the floor.

"What the heck is in all the bags?" Preston crossed over to stand next to her, swaying as Lennon looked at him.

"Going anywhere with a baby is no small production," Chelsea said, opening the first bag. "I got two playmats at my baby shower, so I thought I'd bring one to leave here. Saves you buying one yourself."

Preston watched as she snapped a couple pieces together, then placed it on the carpeted floor. "Would you prefer I put it in the guest room?"

"No. It's great right there." Preston figured Chelsea would look at him like he was nuts if he told her how much he loved seeing all the baby stuff—and her and Lennon—in his space.

Chelsea took several bottles of milk out of a smaller cooler. "Mind if I put these in the fridge?"

"Not at all."

Returning, she opened what Preston assumed was the typical diaper bag. Inside, in addition to diapers and wipes, he saw burping cloths, a couple more sleepers, and a pacifier. "He probably needs to be changed. Want to do the honors?"

While he had two nieces, he hadn't seen them more than a handful of times while they were still in the diaper phase, so he'd never changed a diaper in his life. "I'm going to need you to talk me through it."

"You got it."

He placed Lennon on the changing pad attached to the playpen. It took him a ridiculous amount of time to get the small baby's legs out of the sleeper. "He's got one hell of a kick," Preston observed.

"He's a strong one, all right. Just like his daddy," Chelsea added.

Once Lennon's legs were free, Preston pulled the tabs on the diaper, peering inside and breathing a sigh of relief when he realized this diaper only contained pee.

"You got lucky," Chelsea mused. "Because once you smell baby shit, it imprints on your olfactory senses hard."

"Something to look forward to," he replied sarcastically.

"Okay. Just grab his ankles and lift him…"

Preston followed her directions, doing as she said. Tugging the wet diaper out, Chelsea quickly slid the clean one under him as Preston held on to the squirming infant. "It's like wrestling an alligator."

"It really is," she agreed. "And you have to move fast

because I've been soaked by more than a few of your son's Old Faithful impersonations."

Preston laughed. "Oh, so he's *my* son when he pees on you."

"Absolutely."

Preston rolled his eyes, while inside he was doing somersaults, delighted that Chelsea seemed a little more at ease with him assuming the father role.

It took another couple of minutes for him to wrangle Lennon's legs back into the sleeper and get it zipped.

"What's next?" he asked.

"He's probably getting hungry. It's been a few hours since his last bottle. Ready for the feeding tutorial? It's way easier than the diaper one."

"Hit me with it."

Chelsea grabbed a bottle from the refrigerator, then showed him how to prop his arm up on a pillow to make it easier to hold Lennon. The second Preston offered him the bottle, Lennon latched on, gulping the milk down like he was starving.

Chelsea giggled. "You would think I never feed him."

"Another thing he gets from me. I have a big appetite."

Chelsea sat down next to Preston on the couch, tucking one leg under her as she faced him and Lennon. "You're doing really well."

"Thanks."

"So…have you told your parents about him yet?"

He nodded. "I called them yesterday morning. And it was just as I suspected. They want to meet him. They're insisting on coming for Christmas now. I told them I needed to talk to you first."

"They should definitely meet him," she said quickly.

What Preston *didn't* say was that his parents were just as excited to meet Chelsea. He and his folks—despite the distance—were close, so they knew all about the woman he'd met at an Ugly Christmas Sweater party who'd stolen his heart, then vanished into thin air. Mom cried when Preston told her he'd found her, equally convinced she was the one for her too-long-single son.

"Mom is over the moon. My brother has two girls, so Lennon is their first grandson. Given it's been just over twenty-four hours, it's probably a safe bet that she's made six Target runs and bought at least fifty outfits for him."

"That's sweet."

"I guess at some point, we should talk about the holidays. Are you going to be in Baltimore?"

"Oh yeah. I'll be here. He's too little to travel with, given all the stuff I'd need to pack for him. I mean, you see how much I needed to bring today, and you helped me out by providing the playpen/bassinet/changing pad thing."

"It *is* quite the haul. So, maybe you and Lennon could come here on Christmas Day for a little while to meet my parents. Or we could come to you," he offered.

"We'll come here, and we can stay as long as you'd like. I'm taking breaks from my mom whenever I can get them." Chelsea closed her eyes and sighed. "God, I'm sorry. I don't mean to keep sounding so ungrateful when it comes to my mother."

"What's going on with her?" This was the second time Chelsea had mentioned being unhappy with her mother.

"I love my mom," she started.

Preston chuckled, because he knew that sentence wasn't going to end there. "But…"

Chelsea threw her hands up. "But she's driving me up the wall. She's always been strong-willed and opinionated. The two of us butted heads for most of my teen years. When I moved out, first with Rick and then with Ethan, things got better. Mom and I get along great when our interactions are limited. You know, a phone call here or there and maybe a few visits a month."

Preston could see where this was going. "But now, you're living under the same roof."

"With a baby. *My* baby," Chelsea stressed. "Or, well, I mean ours. Mom has strong opinions about how to take care of a baby, and some…okay, *most* of them are pretty old school. Like she thinks I shouldn't immediately go to Lennon when he cries in the middle of the night, insisting that's the only way to get him to sleep through the evening. But I'm not letting him cry."

"I agree with you." Preston hated the idea of Lennon lying alone in a bed, upset.

"And lately, after his three-a.m. feeding, I put him in bed with me and leave him there instead of putting him back in his bassinet. We both sleep better and longer—but oh my God, Mom loses her shit over that. Even though I've read lots of positive things about family beds."

Preston made a mental note to start reading articles about babies. "I like the sound of a family bed, too."

"She's also pushing me to start him on solid foods, but the doctor and baby books all say it's too soon. It's just…" Chelsea leaned back on the couch, closing her eyes exhaustedly. "It's been a lot."

"It sounds like it." Since Lennon had finished his bottle, Preston pulled it out of his son's still-sucking mouth.

Chelsea reached over, helping Preston guide the baby to his shoulder after placing a burp cloth there. She shifted closer, gently patting Lennon on the back as a demonstration. Preston followed her lead, both of them laughing softly when the baby let out a gigantic burp.

She took Lennon from him, rising to walk over to the playpen. She put him inside, smiling. Preston joined her, placing his arm around her shoulders and pulling her close.

"You're doing a great job, Chelsea. I'm sorry if your mother doesn't make you feel that way, but all you have to do is look at that healthy, smiling baby to know it."

She turned toward him. "Thanks, Preston."

They were standing close, but neither of them sought to

move away. Instead, Preston used the hand still resting on her shoulder to move her nearer. He did it slowly, giving her a chance to pull away.

Chelsea didn't resist, allowing him to close the distance.

"Chelsea," he whispered, his lips a mere inch from hers. "I'm going to kiss you."

Her lips tilted upward, her tongue darting out to lick her lower lip. "That's a bad idea."

Preston didn't agree, but it proved there was something going on in Chelsea's head that was holding her back. Unfortunately, he wasn't strong enough to put on the brakes...yet. "Tell you what. We can discuss why you think that after."

She nodded just once. "Okay. After."

That was all the permission he needed. Preston wrapped one hand around the back of her neck, the other gripping her hip. He'd dreamed of kissing her again for too long to take this slow. In his mind, they'd kissed a million times since last December. The light kiss outside the pub hadn't been anywhere near enough for him.

Chelsea's hands flew to his shoulders before sliding through his hair. She fisted it, pulling as if afraid he'd let go.

If he had his way, he was never letting go. They could live out the next sixty years right here, in this spot, just like this.

Their tongues found each other at the exact same moment, and Preston drank down her hungry whimpers. Passion took over as he deepened the kiss, moving his hand from her hip to her ass, pressing their lower bodies together so that she could feel the effect she was having on him.

Chelsea released him with a loud intake of air, drawing in a deep breath before slamming her lips back to his.

Jesus. She was so sexy.

She hadn't held anything back that night they'd spent together, giving him everything she had. It had been heady and amazing.

This kiss proved time hadn't dimmed their attraction to each other.

When she nipped his lower lip, it proved to him just how big this thing between them had grown.

They broke apart briefly, both panting for air, glancing down to discover Lennon had fallen back to sleep.

Preston, still hungry for her, kissed her again, slowly pushing her backward as he did so, not stopping until they reached the couch. He placed a hand around the front of her throat, using that hold to push her down onto the cushions. Chelsea followed his unspoken commands, sitting down, then lying back as he climbed over her, caging her beneath him.

Her legs parted to make room for him, wrapping around his waist as she tilted her hips upward to brush his crotch, his cock, constricted within the tight denim.

He remained over her, holding himself with bent elbows on the cushions, the kissing going on and on and fucking on.

Chelsea gripped his back and shoulders, then her hands danced lower to his waist, slipping underneath the hem of his shirt. His cock grew harder when she stroked the bare skin of his chest, her nails lightly scoring circles into the skin around his nipples.

Preston cupped her breasts over her shirt, moaning at their larger size.

Chelsea broke the kiss, blushing uncomfortably. "The baby weight isn't going away."

He tipped her head up with a finger beneath her chin, forcing her to meet his gaze. "You are the sexiest woman on the planet."

She looked like she wanted to protest that, call him a liar, but something in his eyes must have convinced her that he was telling the truth.

Unfortunately, that wasn't enough to convince her to keep going. She bit her lower lip, squirming slightly as the legs that had been wrapped around his waist fell away. "We shouldn't have let this go so far."

He frowned, recalling her belief that the two of them kissing was a mistake. "Why not? I wasn't lying when I said I looked for you, that I missed you. Chelsea, I haven't stopped thinking about you since that night."

Chelsea rested her hand flat against his chest, applying pressure until he lifted himself off her, the two of them sitting next to each other on the couch. They were still relatively close, but compared to their previous position, it felt like they were miles apart. "Preston, my hesitance doesn't have anything to do with us."

He frowned, confused.

"It's because of him." She pointed toward the playpen where their son slept. "We spent one night together, and, yes, it was incredible. But it was still just one night. It would be the height of irresponsibility to start something between us."

"Because of Lennon."

"Because it wouldn't just be our hearts at stake if things didn't work out. I mean…we're getting along now and working together to co-parent. If our relationship turned contentious… Lennon would suffer for it."

He hated every single word she said, even though he understood. He didn't agree with her, because in his mind, this relationship had what it took to go the distance. Preston knew a year ago she was the one, and that belief had only grown stronger with each passing day. But he didn't know how to convince her of that because—dammit—her concerns were valid.

"So I think it would be best if we kept this thing between us…" She paused, looking for a word.

It didn't matter to him which word she used. He knew they were all going to suck.

"Platonic," she finally landed on.

Yep. It sucked.

Preston considered pushing the issue, but in the end, he realized the best thing he could do, for now, was respect her wishes.

While the two of them still shared that powerful connection he'd felt the moment he met her, what they didn't possess was a long history or any real time spent together.

So, Preston was going to have to give her that. Going to have to put his desires on the back burner while he gave Chelsea a chance to get to know him.

"Okay," he said, relieved that he'd landed on the right answer when she gave him a genuine smile, pleased he wasn't fighting her.

"We owe it to Lennon to take things slow, to navigate our way through being parents together," he added. "But, Chelsea, that doesn't mean I'm giving up on us. I'm just postponing the inevitable until you figure out what I already know."

She frowned. "What's that?"

"This thing between us?" he replied, taking her hand in his, lifting it to his lips so that he could kiss her palm. "It's serendipity."

CHAPTER TEN

"I CAN'T BELIEVE THIS!" Ethan was literally bouncing on their way into the hockey arena. "I mean, getting you both here at the same time is pretty much a dream come true, but the fact we're sitting in the team's box. I'm more excited than Thor at a two-for-one sale on hammers."

She and Allyson laughed, and while she didn't admit it, Chelsea felt exactly the same way. And not just because she was a pretty big fan of hockey these days but because she would finally get to see Preston play in person.

Of course, it didn't hurt that the entire arena was buzzing, fans of the sport happy to be there to cheer on the home team. She'd promised to buy her dad some sort of Stingrays souvenir from the gift shop, so she made a mental note to check it out before they left.

Preston had texted several times today to make sure she was still coming and to give her instructions on how to get to the box. Then he'd gone the extra mile and set them up with valet parking, yet another reason Ethan was practically coming apart at the seams.

As a true Stingrays fan, Ethan typically managed to attend at least one home game a month. He and Allyson had used the center-ice tickets a couple weeks earlier, but Chelsea had opted to stay home, foolishly thinking that might help her maintain a friendly yet platonic distance from Preston.

That idea had failed spectacularly. And she wasn't mad about it.

It had been seventeen days since Preston walked back into her life.

Seventeen amazing, glorious, spectacular days since he'd walked into the bakery and effectively flipped her entire world on its head. Or maybe her world had been on its head prior to him, and his arrival had tipped her right-side up again.

Preston hadn't lied about wanting to be a part of Lennon's life. The two of them had created a shared, color-coded spreadsheet on Google, where they each filled in their work schedules. Preston's schedule was highlighted in green, hers in yellow. From there, they filled in the blanks with "family dates," all marked in blue. With the exception of two multiday road trips, Preston had found time, even if it was just a few minutes, to see Lennon on thirteen of those seventeen days. And he never failed to FaceTime from the road to check in and get some screen time with his little man.

On days where they had lots of time to spend together, they typically hung out at Preston's condo. Whenever it was just the three of them, he took over practically all of their son's care, feeding him, changing his diapers, singing silly songs to him, and holding him in front of the aquarium, so Lennon—who was now obsessed with fish—could watch them swim.

Even better, Preston took care of *her*, something no one had done since…well…since she was a child. He fed her, watched her crappy reality shows with her, and even encouraged her on two occasions, after sleepless nights with Lennon, to take naps in the guest room. She felt more well rested than she had since their baby was born.

She'd been too close to the end of her rope prior to his arrival in their life, her exhaustion and stress off the charts. Between her mother's criticisms, Rick's unexpected—and unwanted—kiss, and the lack of sleep, she'd been on the verge of a complete meltdown.

Preston showing up should have been the tipping point.

But it wasn't.

That wasn't saying she hadn't initially been stressed out and worried about what his presence in Lennon's life would mean, but those emotions had never really become full-blown. Because of that magical something the man possessed that set her at ease…even when he was the one freaking her out. Preston calmed her down, quieted all the noise in her head. She'd noticed that ability the first night they met, thinking perhaps she'd imagined it, or it had been a result of the wine, and then later, the super-hot sex.

For the past seventeen days, there had been very little wine and no sex, and the man still had his finger on her volume button, turning down the racket until every bad thought simply evaporated in the silence that remained.

As they walked into the arena, Ethan gave Chelsea a rundown on how different this experience and the one two weeks ago were from his usual trips to the games. He'd also supplied the jersey she was currently wearing. She, of course, was adorned in Preston's number and name, the jersey practically hanging to her knees. Allyson, meanwhile, had bought her own a couple of weeks ago, choosing one based solely on the jersey number—sixty-nine.

Allyson was forever destined to have the sense of humor of a thirteen-year-old boy.

Chelsea couldn't help but be touched by all the effort Preston had gone to tonight to make it a special occasion for her and her friends.

"Here we are," Allyson announced when they found the box.

"I cannot believe we've got box seats." Allyson, who was usually the life of every party, was a bit subdued tonight. Not because she didn't share their enthusiasm but because she was completely overwhelmed. "I'm pretty sure every member of my family is watching this game tonight. My cousin Alan said he'd try to get a picture if he sees us on TV."

Chelsea had been okay until they got to the box, but as they entered, she felt her nerves kicking in. She hadn't fully thought through the implications of sharing the space with family and friends of Preston's teammates. What was she supposed to say if someone asked her who she was there to see? Did she refer to Preston as a friend or...

God knew she wasn't introducing herself as his baby mama.

As they stepped in, Ethan's eyes nearly bugged out at the array of snacks and beverages—all free—set up along the back wall. "Do you know how much a beer costs at the concession stand?" he murmured.

Chelsea rolled her eyes, wondering if he was going to spend the entire night breaking down every difference between attending the game as a random person versus as a VIP, which is what they definitely felt like.

The box wasn't overly crowded. Preston had mentioned there were a handful of spouses/girlfriends/parents who came to every home game, while the rest attended when their schedules allowed. There were six other people already in the box, all standing together, chatting as they drank beer or wine. Their arrival didn't go unnoticed, and two women peeled away from the group to greet them.

"Hey," an attractive woman said. "I'm Erika Nelson, and this is Ainsley Hall. Would one of you happen to be Chelsea?"

Chelsea lifted her hand. "That's me."

Erika smiled widely. "Preston texted me this afternoon to say you and your friends were coming. You must be Ethan and Allyson."

Everyone shook hands, greeting each other amiably.

"Are you here to root for someone in particular?" Ethan asked Erika.

"Blake Wright is my boyfriend, and Ainsley's dating the goalie, Coulton Moore."

Ethan, true to character, gushed about how talented both players were, even turning around and pointing with both thumbs to show Ainsley that he—like her—was wearing Moore's jersey. "We match!"

Given she'd only watched a half dozen games, Chelsea was grateful Ethan was there to carry the hockey portion of tonight's conversations. Because she had basically nothing to contribute. She listened politely as they chatted about the upcoming game, who was benched due to injuries, who they expected to see on the starting lineup, and how much they all hated Florida—tonight's competitor.

Allyson asked if there were assigned seats in the box, and Erika told them they were welcome to sit wherever they liked. She even suggested, since it was their first time, that they take the first row of the box so they had a great view.

Ethan loved that offer enough that he quickly walked down to claim a spot, waving Allyson down to point out something of interest on the ice.

Chelsea started to follow, but Erika stopped her. "I'm so glad to finally get to meet you, Chelsea."

She smiled, even though she got hung up on the word *finally*. She and Preston had only reconnected a little over two weeks ago, so *finally* felt like a strange word. To make matters worse, Chelsea had never heard Erika's or Ainsley's names. Hell, she only vaguely recalled Preston mentioning Blake and Coulton in passing. Considering most of their conversations centered around Lennon—because Preston was as obsessed with watching their baby as she was—that wasn't exactly surprising.

"Blake told me about your son, and he showed me a few of the pictures Preston shared. Lennon, right?" Erika asked.

Chelsea really was a million miles behind. "That's right."

"Coulton has showed me nothing, dammit." Ainsley asked to see a picture, oohing and aahing over Lennon's undeniable cuteness. The more the two women talked about and gushed over Lennon, the more relaxed Chelsea began to feel.

Allyson left Ethan hanging by the railing of the box to grab drinks. "You want a glass of wine, Chels?"

She requested red, like Erika was drinking. Ainsley, meanwhile, was drinking a beer.

"So how long have you been dating Blake?" Chelsea was ready to change the conversation to something other than herself.

"Officially? Only a few weeks, but we've known each other for years. Blake and I live across the hall from each other. Or, I guess I should say *did*."

"Did?"

Ainsley answered for Erika. "Blake and Erika moved in together a couple weeks ago."

"I lost the coin flip," Erika joked, "so now all my stuff is at Blake's, and I'm just waiting for my lease to run out before we add my name to his. It works out because it makes things easier for Corky."

"Who's Corky?"

"Blake and I found a puppy outside our building in the fall, and we decided to co-parent her. We credit her for encouraging us to change our status from friends and neighbors to boyfriend/girlfriend." Erika pulled her phone out as she spoke, her actions prompting Ainsley to roll her eyes good-naturedly.

"She probably has more pictures of her dog on her phone than you do of Lennon. And Blake has more than *her*," Ainsley joked.

Erika shoulder-bumped the other woman, but it was clear

they were friendly enough that the teasing rolled right off. Chelsea liked both women very much, and she appreciated the efforts they were taking to make sure she felt welcome.

"Oh my God. That is the sweetest dog ever," Chelsea gushed sincerely, grinning at how adorable the tiny little thing was, nestled in Blake's arms.

"Right? I swear they should put her picture on cans of dog food," Erika said. "And Lennon should be the next Gerber baby."

They all laughed. Allyson handed Chelsea a glass of wine, then lifted the two cans of beer she got for her and Ethan. "Going to go deliver this. Something tells me I'm going to need ALL the beer tonight, because Ethan only has a million and twelve things he *needs* to tell me about the Stingrays and the arena. Stupid me, I thought he'd covered it all the last time we came, but apparently he hasn't even scratched the surface."

"Lift your can when it's empty and we'll keep the alcohol flowing," Ainsley offered.

"You're my girl," Allyson said, giving Ainsley a sideways fist bump so she didn't spill the beer before returning to Ethan.

"So no baby or dog pics on your phone?" Chelsea asked Ainsley.

"God, no. I'm in the same boat as Erika. Coulton and I are in the *very* beginning stages of our relationship. We haven't even been an official item a month yet, and we only started living together at Thanksgiving."

Chelsea tried—and failed—to school her expression because damn…who moved in together right as they started dating?

Ainsley smirked. "You can say what you're thinking, because I know that's hella fast. The shacking-up together thing was a combination of my necessity and Coulton's relentlessness."

"He decided she was the one and never looked back," Erika said. "It's super-romantic. Blake was the same way. Once he decided I was the one, there was no stopping him. One minute,

I'm living across the hall, the next, he's smuggling all my clothes out and hanging them in his closet. Preston's ways are rubbing off on the rest of the guys. All except for—"

Ainsley and Erika looked at each other, saying, "Tank," in unison before cracking up. "Oh…and Victor," Erika added.

Chelsea recalled Preston mentioning Tank and Victor, as well as her mom's comments about professional athletes. "Preston mentioned there were a lot of women…"

"Puck bunnies," Erika said, crinkling her nose. "The Rays have a fair amount of female groupies who hover around the fringes, hoping to catch their eye. Luckily, our guys don't pay them any attention anymore."

Chelsea got the sense she was included in that "our guys" comment. Then something else Erika said came back to her. "What did you mean, when you said Preston's rubbing off on Blake and Coulton?"

"The guys seem to be following Preston's lead. Coulton met Ainsley and never questioned from that day on that she was the one for him. You know that all the guys call Preston 'Romeo', right?" Erika asked.

Chelsea nodded. He'd confided that their first night together. "He calls himself a hopeless romantic."

"Not so hopeless anymore," Erika said. "Now that he's finally found you again."

Again with the word *finally*. Chelsea didn't know how to respond to that. "I'm not sure I follow."

Erika exchanged an uncomfortable glance with Ainsley. "Um…I've already had two glasses of wine tonight. Maybe I've spoken out of turn."

She appeared sober as a stone.

"What did you mean when you said it was 'finally' nice to meet me?" Chelsea's curiosity was getting the better of her.

Erika sighed. "Now I *know* I've said too much."

Ainsley smirked. "Well, it's too late now. When Coulton and I started going out, he filled me in on all his teammates, telling me little things about them and their lives. He told me Preston had met the woman of his dreams at a holiday party last Christmas, and that he'd been hung up on her ever since. That was you, right?"

Chelsea nodded, somewhat dumbfounded. "Hung up on me?"

Erika pursed her lips, then apparently decided there was no point in shutting up now. "He hasn't gone out with anyone in a year. Not since he met you."

Chelsea's mouth fell open, shock kicking in. Preston had sort of alluded to that...she supposed. Telling her he'd missed her, that he thought about her all the time. But to eschew *all women* when she knew he had an abundance to entertain himself with? That couldn't be true.

Could it?

"Damn. As if I needed another reason to be a Preston Jacobson fan."

Chelsea turned around, surprised to discover Ethan and Allyson standing behind them. They'd clearly heard the last part of the conversation, hence Ethan's comment.

Allyson grinned sheepishly at Ainsley, waving her empty beer can. "First one went down way too fast. Thought you might judge me."

Ainsley laughed. "I used to work in a dive bar. No judgment from me, I promise."

"Preston didn't want anyone after you," Ethan said, his gaze locked with Chelsea's. While Mom was still Team Rick, Ethan was all in on Preston. "And you were the same."

Chelsea snorted. "I was trying to navigate my way in a new country, then I was pregnant, and then I was caring for a newborn. It's not like I had loads of time to rock the dating scene."

"And if you had?" Ethan's brow rose, letting her know she

still would have been obsessed with Preston, even if she hadn't had his baby.

She pursed her lips because she hated lying.

Before anyone could say anything more, the announcer asked everyone to rise for the National Anthem. She, Allyson, and Ethan made their way to the front row, Ainsley and Erika claiming the seats right behind them in the second row.

Chelsea expected to be distracted by everything she just learned, but the second the announcer introduced Preston as part of the starting lineup, she was spellbound. Watching him in person was way better than on TV, and it was official—she was a hockey fan for life.

Ethan sat between her and Allyson, explaining the parts of the game they didn't understand, and Chelsea was amused by Ainsley's extremely colorful language whenever one of the Florida players did something she considered dirty.

The five of them took turns grabbing rounds for the others, while putting a serious dent in the snacks. They cheered loudly when Blake scored a goal in the first period, groaned when Florida tied it up in the second, and lost their minds when Preston scored late in the third period, putting the Rays back in the lead. By the time the final buzzer sounded, Chelsea was riding a high unlike anything she'd ever experienced.

As they rose from their seats, she hugged Erika and Ainsley, feeling like she'd just made two new friends. They exchanged numbers so that the three of them could find a day to attend another game together. Erika's attendance was dependent on her work schedule. She was an ER doctor, and Ainley was apprenticing to become a tattoo artist.

As they left the box, Chelsea's phone pinged with an incoming text from Preston.

> You guys want to join us at Pat's to celebrate the win?

Chelsea glanced at the time, torn. It was only nine-thirty, and while she really, really wanted to see Preston, she also missed Lennon.

"Please say yes," Ethan said over her shoulder, reading her text. "Lennon's asleep."

She sighed. "I know he is, but..." If tonight was like every night the past week, Lennon would wake up between midnight and one a.m. for a bottle, then go right back down, sleeping until five or six. It had been bliss.

"If you go, we can go," Ethan said, gesturing to him and Allyson. "Without looking like stalker fans."

Chelsea smirked. "There's no hope you won't look like a stalker. You're already drooling at the prospect of hanging out with the Rays."

"Cupcake," he pleaded. "Do it for me, please? This is seriously a once-in-a-lifetime opportunity."

Chelsea laughed. "Are you ever going to outgrow peer pressure?"

"Never!" Ethan replied dramatically.

"Fine. But, for the record, I don't think this is a once-in-a-lifetime thing." Maybe that was a lofty statement, but Chelsea knew it was true. Preston was committed to Lennon, and by extension, her. Because he was an amazing guy, his kindness also extended to her friends.

Chelsea texted Preston back.

Sure. Meet you there?

Preston replied with a thumbs-up.

See you there in an hour.

She added her own thumbs-up to the thread, then texted her dad—there was no way she was texting Mom—to let him know she was having a drink with Ethan and Allyson and would be home later.

Dad said exactly what Ethan did: Lennon had been asleep for hours and they were perfectly capable of doing the midnight feeding. Then, bless him, he told her to stay out as long as she liked and to have some fun.

With the exception of that late dinner with Preston, Chelsea hadn't gone out on her own at all since Lennon's birth because all of her "dates" with Preston had included their son.

Slipping her phone back into her pocket, she gestured toward the parking lot. "Dad extended my curfew," she joked. "So it looks like we're moving the party."

Allyson and Ethan high-fived as Chelsea giggled, and then they waited as the valet retrieved their car. Chelsea was the designated driver, only having the one glass of wine before the game started. She'd never been a big drinker, and she was even less of one now, since the idea of caring for a crying baby with a hangover sounded about as much fun as weeding a garden full of poison ivy.

Padraig waved to Chelsea when she and her friends walked into Pat's Pub. She led them over to the bar.

"Hey, Chelsea. I was wondering if I was going to see you again," he said.

She introduced him to her friends, then Padraig gestured to a long table near the rear of the pub. "I set up a place for the Rays and fans back there."

"They always come here after wins?" Ethan asked.

Padraig shook his head. "Not always. Sometimes they come after they lose too," he replied with a grin. "And they always give me a heads-up. Tank texted as soon as they got back to the locker room. You're welcome to grab a seat. The groupies arrived early and grabbed a spot next to the team's table."

"Puck bunnies?" Allyson asked, mainly because she'd just learned the term and, for some reason, it amused her.

Padraig chuckled. "Yeah."

Chelsea couldn't help but notice that *all* the people currently waiting at the table next to the reserved one were female. Unfortunately, Erika and Ainsley weren't included in the group. Neither had indicated they were coming, so Chelsea assumed they were doing some private celebrating with their boyfriends.

She couldn't help but wish the same were true of her and Preston. Not that their private celebrating would include any of the fun stuff, since she'd insisted they needed to maintain a platonic relationship.

Being a responsible adult really sucked.

"What are you drinking?" Padraig asked.

Ethan ordered a pitcher of PBR, and they headed back to the table. They claimed the end of the table. The puck bunnies checked them out as they sat down, but their attention didn't last long, since it was obvious they didn't view them as a threat.

Chelsea felt like a slouch in her oversized Rays jersey. The other women all looked like they were headed out for a night of clubbing, in their short skirts, low-cut dresses, and ridiculously high heels. They'd also taken special pains with their hair and makeup, all of them looking like they'd sprung from the glossy pages of a fashion magazine.

That was when she realized it wasn't just Lennon holding her back from Preston.

Rick had done a number on her self-esteem when he'd skipped their wedding, riding off into the sunset with someone else, however briefly. Someone tall and willowy and beautiful. How could she expect to hold Preston's attention when he was surrounded by women who looked like this all the time?

Chelsea toyed uncomfortably with her ponytail and considered pulling the band out.

"Those women wish they were *half* as gorgeous as you," Allyson murmured, leaning close enough that no one could hear except her and Ethan. "Twenty bucks says Preston only has eyes for you when he gets here."

Chelsea gave her friend a grateful grin. "You have to say that. You're my bestie."

"Even if I wasn't, it would still be true. Look how hard they have to try. You realize you have something they don't, right?"

"Do I want to know what that is?" Chelsea asked.

"Natural beauty."

"Thanks, Ally." She smiled, then wrapped her arm around Allyson's shoulders. "I needed to hear that."

"Speaking of other things you need to hear," Ethan starting, leaning closer. "I know you've been holding yourself back from Preston, and I understand why. But, Cupcake, you sacrificing your own happiness isn't going to help Lennon. He might just be a baby, but I read an article that said they can sense the emotions of their caregivers. It impacts his emotional development."

"When do you have time to read all this stuff?" she asked.

Ethan chuckled. "I'm not changing diapers and doing midnight feedings, so it frees up a few hours."

"So what are you saying?"

"I'm saying," he stressed, "that I want my godson to be surrounded by happiness and love. If you're stressed or scared or lonely, there's a good chance he'll pick up on it."

"Wow. Way to go for the jugular," she muttered.

"You deserve to be loved, Chels," Allyson added. "Don't be so quick to dismiss Preston because you're afraid he'll hurt you like Rick did."

Chelsea was grateful for their advice. "I'll think about every-thing you said. Promise."

Padraig delivered their pitcher as more fans drifted in. Chelsea recognized a few of them from the box, the new arrivals joining their table. They were much nicer than the puck bunnies. Given the Stingrays' win, everyone was in a festive mood, recounting some of the more exciting parts of the game.

When Preston and several of his teammates arrived, the pub cheered. Preston was stopped every few steps by fans, slapping him on the back and congratulating him on the game-winning goal. Throughout it all, he kept looking back at her, smiling.

He'd almost reached their table when he was intercepted by one of the gorgeous puck bunnies who'd dismissed Chelsea and her friends earlier.

"You were amazing tonight, Preston," the woman said, plastering herself to his side.

"Thanks, Mindy."

God, Preston knew the woman's name. Had the two of them—

Chelsea shut down that line of thought.

"Let me buy you a drink and we'll celebrate," Mindy offered.

Chelsea had heard the expression *bedroom eyes*, but she'd never actually seen them. Mindy practically radiated sex, and as much as Chelsea wanted to hate the woman, she couldn't deny she was beautiful.

"No thanks," Preston said, disentangling himself from Mindy with practiced ease. "I'm celebrating with my girl tonight." He was looking straight at Chelsea, her heart doing cartwheels at the way he called her *my girl*.

She could've pointed out that wasn't entirely accurate, but she didn't want to. At. All. Because it sounded too fucking good.

Allyson shoulder-bumped her. "Told you so."

Finally, Preston made it all the way to her. He didn't say anything. Instead, he tugged Chelsea up and into his arms, giving her a big hug before pulling away slightly, cupping her cheeks, and kissing her on her forehead.

"God, you look pretty tonight."

She practically melted when he spun her around, her back pressed tight to his chest, his muscular arms enclosing her in a way that made her feel safe and horny all at the same time.

"Lucas, this is Chelsea," he said to one of his teammates.

Then he pointed to Allyson and Ethan, who stood as he introduced them.

"Nice to meet you," Lucas said to her, before turning to Allyson and giving her a sexy grin that was pure flirtation. "Nice jersey."

Allyson leaned closer, as if imparting a secret. "Thanks. I picked it because of the number." Then she backed up that announcement by wiggling her eyebrows in an outrageously hubba-hubba way, her silliness catching Lucas off guard.

Preston laughed loudly, and Ethan groaned.

Chelsea and Allyson looked at both men, confused.

Ethan gestured to Lucas. "That's *his* jersey."

"Oh!" Allyson replied with a shameless laugh. "Lucky you. Did you pick it because it had some deep, personal meaning for you?"

Lucas shook his head, his interest piqued rather than deterred, then he moved closer to Allyson. "Can I buy you a beer?"

She nodded and mouthed "oh my God" to their group, when Lucas turned to walk to the bar, then she followed. Chelsea couldn't help but agree, because Lucas was sex-on-a-stick hot.

Ethan snorted. "Didn't take her long," he observed.

"It never does," Chelsea added.

"Allyson is hilarious," Preston said, still chuckling. "Lucas might have his work cut out for him."

Chelsea rested her hands on Preston's arms, which were still looped around her waist. The petty part of her couldn't resist sneaking a peek at the puck bunnies. Mindy was obviously looking at her in a different light, possibly realizing she was too hasty in her dismissal, while the other women were staring at Allyson and Lucas with clear envy.

"Having fun?" Preston murmured in her ear.

She loved being held by him this way but she wanted to see him, so she twisted, delighted when he kept his hands on her waist. "You were incredible, Preston. And I'm now a believer. Hockey is the greatest sport."

He gave her a kiss on the cheek. "I loved knowing you were there, in the stands watching me."

She blushed, thrilled to her toes by his admission. That, paired with Erika's insider information about Preston's feelings for her, and Ethan and Allyson's advice that she seek her own happiness as well as Lennon's, meant Chelsea's attraction—okay, horniness—was currently off the charts.

Lifting on her tiptoes, she gave him an impulsive kiss. She meant for it to be quick, but Preston wasn't just fast on the ice. His grip on her tightened as he extended the kiss, drawing it out. His tongue swiped her lower lip, and she obliged by opening her mouth. Lifting her hands to his shoulders, she pressed her body firmly against his, recalling the way he'd caged her beneath him on the couch.

While Chelsea rarely drank enough alcohol to get drunk, the same couldn't be said for Preston's drugging kisses. When he wasn't kissing her, her brain functioned just fine. But the second his lips landed on hers, she was wasted, all reasonable thoughts drowned in lust and desire.

Preston broke the kiss, his forehead pressed to hers. "I'm trying to play by your rules, Joy, but it's not fucking easy."

He had been…for the most part. While he hadn't kissed her since that day on the couch, he'd still been seducing her with touches she couldn't exactly chastise him for. Because friendly hugs, a gentle hand on the small of her back as they walked, and holding her hand could all fall into the platonic range. If they were done by anyone other than Preston.

"Maybe…" she started, as that impulsive side her mother kept bitching about emerged. "Maybe just for tonight, we could bend the rules. A little bit," she stressed.

Preston's smile was pure wickedness, and she was here for it.

"I'm very good at bending the rules," he whispered in her ear.

Then he spent the rest of the night proving just *how* good he was, as he insisted she sit on his lap, even though there were plenty of chairs at the table. Preston snuck countless kisses, some on her lips but just as many on her cheek, behind her ear, on the side of her neck. One of his hands drifted beneath the jersey, stroking her back in a slow way that was maddeningly sensual. And while those touches were enough to stoke her embers into a flame, his whispered words—half compliments/half list of all the ways he wanted to take her—added enough fuel that her body was a raging bonfire by the time the celebration ended.

Preston wrapped a firm arm around her waist as he walked her, Ethan, and Allyson to the car at the end of the night.

While her friends—both tipsy as hell—giggled and climbed into the car, Chelsea leaned against the driver's-side door, facing Preston. Driving away from him tonight was going to be harder than walking away from him in that hotel last year had been.

There was no denying she wanted him.

Physically.

Sexually.

However, the part of her that hadn't completely caught up to the others was the emotional bit. Because she was still trigger-shy, suffering from PTSD, and racked with indecision. Not to mention, she was letting her mother live in her head rent-free.

"I know we were only bending the rules tonight," Preston said, as if he could see the direction her thoughts had drifted.

"I..." she started, feeling as if she owed him some sort of explanation for why she was still holding back when she'd made it very—VERY—clear her attraction to him was off the charts.

"All your reasons for holding back are still there, Joy, and there's nothing wrong with that. We're taking this at your speed, I promise."

And just like that, the pressure she'd been feeling simply melted. Like magic.

Preston tilted his head. "What?"

She'd whispered the magic part aloud. But she didn't know how to explain how he seemed to have some mystical power that quieted all the chaos inside her, so instead, she just said, "Nothing. Never mind."

"You still okay to come Christmas Day?" he asked. "I could always stop by your place with my parents for a little while, if that's easier."

Jesus. No part of that would be easier.

"Lennon and I will come to you," she said.

Preston had met her mom and dad earlier in the week, stopping by for an hour. Dad had been awesome, asking Preston a million and twelve questions about hockey, all of which he answered kindly. Mom was also polite, if reserved. She offered drinks and snacks, then hovered a bit too nearby as Preston held Lennon. It was a short visit, and one that would have been very awkward if not for Dad and Preston keeping the conversation rolling, while Chelsea sat on pins and needles.

She suspected future get-togethers would be easier, but not if she scheduled it on Christmas.

Even if it *had* upset her mother, Chelsea's decision to split the holiday between her family and Preston's had been a simple one to make. Mainly because it didn't upset Mom enough to convince her to uninvite Rick and his parents, despite Chelsea telling her point-blank she didn't want to see her ex.

Mom said it was too late to cancel on them.

To be honest, Chelsea was excited about spending part of the holiday with Preston, even though she was slightly nervous about meeting his parents.

"Great. I was hoping..." Preston lifted one of her hands, kissing the palm. "My parents are spending the night in a hotel. They always do, even though I always offer them the guest room. I was hoping…" he started again. "I've never been a part of Lennon's bedtime routine, helping with the bath, putting him to bed, doing the midnight feeding."

"You want us to sleep over?" she asked.

He nodded. "Yes. In the guest room," he hastily added. "You could consider it my Christmas present."

She laughed. "A sleepless night and changing shitty diapers is a questionable gift choice, but…yeah. We can stay with you that night."

He picked her up, spinning her around as she laughed.

"Put me down, you lunatic!"

Preston placed her feet back on the ground, then leaned toward her. "I'm bending the rules one last time." With that, he gave her the mother of all kisses, taking her lips with a hunger and passion that had her questioning whether she'd be "sober" enough to drive home.

They only stopped when her tipsy friends started cheering them on from inside the car.

When the two of them parted, she was breathless and flushed…and falling for him.

Hard.

So hard that the only thing her scarred, terrified heart could think was, if he left her the way Rick did…

This is going to hurt.

CHAPTER ELEVEN

"OH MY GOODNESS. Let me steal one more squeeze and then I swear I'm leaving."

Preston chuckled, and Dad rolled his eyes because this was the fourth "last" squeeze Mom had stolen, struggling—like Preston had the first time he'd met Lennon—to let the baby go.

Chelsea stood nearby, smiling widely, clearly touched by Mom's instant love for their son.

"We're all doing breakfast in the morning, Mom," Preston reminded her. "So you can snuggle him all you want over eggs and bacon."

Mom finally relented, handing Lennon back to Preston before turning to Chelsea, her arms outstretched. "Let me steal one more hug from you too, sweetheart."

Mom was a big hugger, always had been, and so far, over the course of the afternoon, Chelsea had been subjected to no less than a half dozen of her embraces. Not that she seemed to mind.

Just like she didn't this time.

Chelsea stepped forward, the two women hugging. "It was so nice to meet you, Grace," she said. Mom had insisted Chelsea call her by her first name rather than Mrs. Jacobson.

"You too, Chelsea." They parted, but Mom clasped hands with her. "Lennon is absolutely precious. You've given me the greatest gift this year."

After they parted, Dad stepped in, grabbing his own hug. "I'm glad you and Preston found each other again."

"Me too," Chelsea confessed.

"A beautiful family," Dad mused, his voice low, even though everyone heard him. Preston's gaze darted to Chelsea to gauge her reaction, and he was touched by the way she smiled, then wiped away a happy tear.

"We'll see you both in the morning," Preston said, opening the front door to his condo as his parents left, carrying bags filled with gifts from both him and Chelsea.

Mom and Dad hadn't been the only ones touched by the matching mugs she'd given them, adorned with a cutest picture of Lennon, his arms over his eyes as if exhausted. She'd added the words, "Not before my coffee," which had cracked them all up.

Closing the door behind Mom and Dad, Preston leaned against it, glancing down at Lennon, who was wide awake and squirming in his arms.

It had been a whirlwind afternoon, and probably the best damn Christmas of his life. Victor had understood when Preston canceled his plans to join his family, saying it was more important he spend Lennon's first Christmas with him. Then he assured Preston that Pip would *also* forgive him the second she ripped into the Nerf machine gun he'd passed on to Victor to give to her.

Preston chuckled as Chelsea walked over to the tree, shaking her head at all the gifts Lennon had received. He'd like to say it was his mother who'd gone overboard, but in truth, two-thirds of the presents had been from him.

He couldn't shake the feeling that he had a hell of a lot of making up to do for the three months he'd missed while Chelsea paid for everything. It was why he'd insisted she give him a complete list of everything Lennon needed, or would need, in the coming months.

Sitting next to the Christmas tree was a high chair adorned with a big bow. Chelsea confessed she'd moved that item down on her baby list, since Lennon wouldn't need it until he was able to sit up and hold his own head steady.

"You doing okay?" he asked. "I realize my mom and dad can be—"

"They're incredible," she interjected. "So, so nice."

He smiled. "So are yours." He meant that sincerely, so he was confused by Chelsea's incredulous expression. "Seriously," he added. "For a football guy, your dad is remarkably well-versed in the ins and outs of hockey."

Chelsea laughed. "He's become obsessed with the sport, subscribing to whatever app it is that lets him watch every hockey game played each night. I gave him a Stingrays jersey for Christmas this morning, and he pulled it on immediately, swearing it was his favorite gift. Or at least it *was*…until he got to yours."

Preston had dropped off a couple of gifts for Chelsea's parents, anxious for them to approve of him, not only for Lennon but for their daughter as well. "Not sure my gift counts, because you know I get those box-seat tickets for free, right?"

"Regardless, like Ethan, Dad flipped his lid and he's living for that game."

"Your mom was a little trickier," Preston admitted. "Figured she wouldn't be wooed by hockey merch. Hence the gift card."

"She and Dad are excited to try Pat's Pub, especially after I told them how good the fish and chips are. It was nice of you to think of them."

Preston walked to the refrigerator when Lennon started to fuss, grabbing a bottle before returning to the couch, sitting down to feed him. Chelsea drifted over to them, sinking next to him.

"Look at you, showing off your mad dad skills," she teased.

Preston chuckled, silently wishing he had more time to flex those father muscles. The more time he spent with Lennon, the more he suffered when they were apart.

He hadn't lied when he'd told Chelsea having them here all night would be the perfect gift. He loved the idea of having them under his own roof. For the first time since meeting his son, the world felt right, and he longed for them to be exactly what his dad had called them.

A family.

"Feeling better?" he asked. "When you first got here..."

Chelsea sighed. "My mother and I engaged in World War Three this morning."

Preston frowned. "Why?" When she didn't immediately respond, he figured out the answer on his own. "Because you were coming here?"

Chelsea lifted one shoulder, trying to play off the argument, but he'd seen the stress on her face when she'd arrived earlier this afternoon. At first, he'd chalked it up to nerves over meeting his parents, but he dismissed that idea pretty quickly when Chelsea and Mom clicked within minutes.

"She's taking longer to adjust to..." Chelsea waved a finger between him and Lennon. "This. To her, you're still a stranger, and she's quite protective of Lennon."

Preston had noticed Mrs. Murphy hovering whenever he held Lennon during his visits, but he hadn't really thought much of it. "That makes sense, you know. I mean, I've only met her a couple of times. Tell you what. After the holidays, I'll stop by your place more often, give her a chance to get to know me."

He'd expected his offer to set Chelsea's mind at ease, but damn if he hadn't missed the mark by a mile when she bit her lower lip nervously.

Then he recalled the guy who'd kissed her outside the bakery…and he wondered once again if there was someone else hovering on the fringes. Maybe someone her *mother* preferred.

"It's Christmas, and I really don't want to talk about my mom right now. We've been approaching the breaking point for months. Today, we hit it. Tomorrow, I'll talk it out with her, and then…" Chelsea leaned back against the couch cushions. Actually, she slouched, looking too exhausted for his peace of mind. "And then, I think I'm going to have to start looking for a place to live now. In addition to childcare."

It was on the tip of Preston's tongue to tell her she had a place to stay, but he knew Chelsea was nowhere near ready for that offer. He tried to tell himself it hadn't even been a full month yet, and he needed to be patient, but that was a damn hard thing to do.

Since he didn't want to encourage her to find somewhere else to live that wasn't his place, he decided to broach the other subject causing her stress. Because it had been on *his* mind as well.

"You having second thoughts about the childcare centers?" The two of them had spent the better part of one afternoon, while Lennon was napping, researching local childcare centers, then arranging appointments for times when they could visit together. The first visit was scheduled for just after the new year.

Chelsea shook her head, then shrugged. "Even if I am, it's not like there are a lot of viable options."

"We could revisit the nanny idea." Preston had suggested going that route after talking to Victor. His sister employed a nanny for Pip, and Victor said it worked well.

Chelsea had dismissed the idea, claiming it would be too expensive, and she wasn't swayed when Preston said he'd pay. Yet another instance when time wasn't on his side. Apparently, a few weeks as a father wasn't enough for Chelsea to agree to let him pay for a nanny she couldn't afford.

"We wouldn't need a full-time nanny, just someone flexible enough to work around our schedules," he added. While Chelsea's hours would be more fixed once the bakery opened, his would be all over the place during the season. "Victor gave me his sister's number. We could call and ask her how it works with her nanny."

When he made the nanny suggestion a week ago, Chelsea dismissed it out of hand. Tonight, it looked like she was considering it. "I guess it wouldn't hurt to talk to her."

Preston smiled because—whether she realized it or not—Chelsea was slowly starting to allow him more input regarding Lennon.

By trusting him to pick out a high chair.

By listening when he suggested a nanny.

By spending the night here so that he could learn the nighttime routine.

He'd noticed in the past few days that she'd also stopped giving him instructions, letting him take the lead in Lennon's care, confident that he knew what he was doing.

"Great. I'll ask Victor to let her know we'll call her soon."

She nodded, twisting to face him, the side of her head resting against the back of the couch.

Chelsea studied his face for a moment, and he got the sense she had something else on her mind, other than childcare. "Can I ask you something?"

"You can ask me anything."

"When you retire from hockey, do you think you'll move back to Seattle?"

No doubt, all the talk he and his parents had done over Christmas dinner about his hometown bothered her.

Preston shook his head. "No. I really do consider Baltimore my home now. It's where my friends are, where you and Lennon are. And most importantly, it's where my boat is," he joked.

Chelsea burst out in laughter, the loudness causing Lennon to flinch. "Oh no," she said, placing her hand on their son's chest. "I'm so sorry, baby. Did Mommy scare you?"

Lennon settled quickly, continuing to suck down the milk in his bottle like it was his last meal. Preston's mom swore he'd done the same thing when he was a baby, always guzzling every drop of milk, then seeking out more.

Of course, it was at that point Mom revealed she'd packed his baby album in her luggage, and she'd pulled it out, comparing the pictures he'd texted her of Lennon with ones of him when he'd been little. There'd been no denying Lennon took after him, something Chelsea good-naturedly joked about being unfair, considering she carried him inside her for nine months, before pushing his bowling-ball-sized head out of her body.

Preston would never forget the look of shock and amusement on Chelsea's face when Mom responded to that joke, saying "preach" and lifting her hand to Chelsea's for a fist bump.

"I guess I'm silly for worrying about something that's years in the future," Chelsea said, referring to his retirement from the sport.

"I'm not sure it will be years away," he confessed. With the exception of Victor, Preston hadn't told anyone he'd been thinking about retirement recently.

"Really?" Chelsea's tone told him just how much he'd surprised her.

"This past fall was not a great time for me. Usually I'm chomping at the bit for the start of each season, ready to hit the ice again."

"You didn't feel that was this year?"

He shook his head. "No. I've played in the majors for fifteen years, fourteen of them right here in Baltimore. Things I used to enjoy—like working out, the road trips to away games, hanging out with the guys after wins or losses—have started to feel more like, well, obligations, and not ones I necessarily look forward to. And it's only gotten worse since…" Preston looked down at the baby in his arms. "Him."

"Him?"

"And you," Preston added, going for complete honesty. "I hate anything that means I can't be with the two of you, even if it's just for a few hours."

Chelsea smiled, and for the first time, he got the sense there wasn't any of that ever-present doubt in her eyes. It felt like she truly believed what he was saying. "You're still brand-new to this parenting gig. The month after Lennon was born, I literally took three-minute showers because I hated that he was out of my sight. It gets easier with time. Or so Ethan tells me," she added with a giggle.

Preston didn't laugh, because there was too much truth to the joke. "That guy really is an authority on babies for someone who doesn't have any. He gave me a twenty-minute lecture on teething, telling me what to expect. When I asked how he knew so much, he said he'd hit me up with some links to good baby sites. He sent me thirty-two links, Chels. *Thirty-two*."

Chelsea closed her eyes, shaking her head, her smile growing even bigger. "He's read every word ever written about babies since finding out I was pregnant. And to be honest, I love him for it."

"He's a good friend, and the world's greatest godfather. You picked a good one." Preston reached over, squeezing her shoulder.

Lennon wiggled, letting out a long sound, like he was trying to join their conversation.

Chelsea looked at her phone. "Oh. It's getting late. Bath time for this little one. You ready for it?"

He nodded. "Hell yeah."

Chelsea talked him through the bath routine, showing him

how to check the water temperature, how to wash Lennon's hair, and then she pointed out all the bits that were easy to miss, like under his arms, behind his ears, and beneath those rolls in his neck. Lennon splashed, giving them a wide, gummy grin throughout. According to Chelsea, Lennon loved bath time.

From there, they put him in a clean diaper, onesie, and sleep sack.

Preston had also bought a rocking recliner for the nursery.

"This chair is amazing," she said, running her hand over the soft fabric. "You rock him while I clean up the bath stuff. I'll get another bottle ready for him. He won't drink much more, but it's the only way to get him to go to sleep."

Preston nodded, not needing to be asked twice. On her way out of the room, Chelsea turned off the overhead light, leaving him and his son alone in the soft, soothing light of the nightlight sitting on the dresser.

Preston rocked Lennon, who was sleepy after exerting all that splashing energy in the bath.

Before he realized it, Preston was humming, the tune to the lullaby his mom used to sing to him popping into his head. He wasn't much of a singer, but Lennon didn't seem to mind when he softly crooned, "Beautiful, beautiful, beautiful...beautiful boy."

They rocked in peace for a full fifteen minutes before Preston even thought to wonder where Chelsea was. He'd been so intent on the sweet, restful face of his son, he didn't realize she was leaning against the doorframe, watching them.

When he caught her gaze, he stopped singing, and she approached quietly, handing him the bottle. Then, without saying a word, she left the room, somehow knowing how precious this time alone with Lennon was to him.

Lennon drank this bottle more slowly, the sucking more for comfort than hunger, and before long, his eyes drifted shut.

Preston didn't rise immediately. Instead, he continued to rock, overwhelmed by a love greater than anything he'd ever known.

After a half hour or so, Chelsea peeked into the room. "Okay?" she whispered.

He looked up at her and nodded. Then he forced himself to rise, even though he would have been perfectly content to sit in that chair all night, rocking his son.

He carefully laid Lennon down in the bassinet next to the bed, hovering close for a moment or two to make sure he remained asleep. He made sure the baby monitor he'd bought was pointed in the right direction, checking the feed on the app on his phone, before following Chelsea back to the living room.

"You're a natural," she said softly.

He wrapped his arm around her shoulders after they sat down on the couch, tucking her tight against him. "Thanks for staying tonight. That was the perfect Christmas gift."

She lifted her face, her eyes shimmering with tears that told him she'd been as moved by the last hour as he had. They sat there, simply looking at each other, until he finally couldn't resist leaning closer and giving her a gentle kiss. It was a quick one, lasting no more than a few seconds, so it could be reasoned it was a friendly buss.

However, he knew that argument wouldn't hold up because of the powerful emotions behind it.

Preston drew the back of his fingers along her cheek, then forced himself to pull away. It was either that or shatter the hell out of her platonic rule.

He hid his satisfied smile when he got the sense it was taking her a moment to compose herself. The impatient part of him liked that, liked that she wasn't as immune to the sexual tension that radiated between them as she pretended.

Preston released a soft sigh.

"What's wrong?" she asked.

Tonight had reinforced his feelings regarding the future of his career. "I hate that I found you again mid-season," Preston admitted. "Knowing the bath and bedtime routine now is only going to make it harder for me when I have to hit the road again."

"Hockey is your job," she stated. "And you're great at it."

He appreciated the compliment, loving that she'd become a serious die-hard fan practically overnight. He'd established a habit the past couple of weeks where he called her the morning after a game, simply because he loved hearing her gushing recap. Or in the event of a loss, her "you'll get 'em next time" encouragement that was always combined with a list of the refs' shitty calls that cost them the game.

"It's been my passion for most of my life, but even saying that, I've always known that hockey isn't forever. It's not exactly a career you hang on to until it's time to start drawing social security."

She pondered that. "So you're really thinking of quitting?"

"It's considered retiring, and…" He shrugged. "I don't know. I'm one of the older guys on the team, so I've seen a lot of turnover, watched a lot of good friends walk away from the sport when their time was up. At thirty-five, I'm hitting the upper range, and my body is letting me know that. Most of my teammates are in their early to mid-twenties."

"What do you plan to do after hockey?" she asked.

"That's the million-dollar question, isn't it?"

She tilted her head. "You've really never given it any thought?"

"Of course I have," he reassured her. "I just haven't come up with anything I think I'd love as much as hockey. And," he smirked, "I wouldn't ever have to work again if I didn't want to. While I've treated myself to a nice car, an awesome waterfront condo, and a sweet boat—"

"As well as redecorating this place as a baby mecca," she interjected.

Preston chuckled, because he *had* gone overboard on the baby furniture. "Regardless of all that, I've socked away a hell of a lot of money and made some very profitable investments."

Chelsea narrowed her eyes. "Must be nice. The only money I have in the bank came from Aunt Agnes, and I'd give back every single penny of it just to have her still alive and well."

Preston gave her a comforting squeeze, aware of how much she missed Ethan's beloved aunt. "I know you would. I'm sorry I never got to meet her."

Chelsea rested her head on his shoulder again, and they sat together, content in the silence.

Preston considered all the things he wasn't saying aloud to her, things he knew it was too soon to be thinking, even though they'd taken root and weren't letting go. Like Chelsea, he wasn't comfortable leaving Lennon in the care of strangers either. That, paired with the thought that if he hung up his skates at the end of this season, there would be no off-season conditioning, practices, focused training. He would be free. Free to be…

He paused, because he'd never let himself think the words. Now, however, after rocking his son to sleep, they were flashing in his head like a goddamn neon sign.

Stay-at-home dad.

He'd considered countless second careers to follow hockey, and none of them had appealed to him even a fifth as much as the idea of raising his son.

But, as always, he couldn't say that aloud because time—fucking time—still wasn't on his side. He had to keep reminding himself that it hadn't even been three weeks since he'd found Lennon and Chelsea. Mainly because those three weeks had been crammed full of what felt like a lifetime of joy.

So, unfortunately, any desires he might feel in regard to his future needed to be put on the back burner until that trust Chelsea had gifted him a year ago was reestablished and strengthened enough to include Lennon *and* her heart.

"Want to watch a movie?" he asked after a few minutes.

She nodded.

Reaching for the remote, he turned on the television, scrolling until he found exactly what he was looking for. "*Serendipity*?"

She rolled her eyes, on to his game. "You don't play fair."

"Told you the first night we met. I play to win."

Chelsea laughed. "Guess I can't say you didn't warn me. Start the damn movie."

He pushed play, loving the way she snuggled even closer, his shoulder her pillow. As they watched, they discussed their favorite scenes, even spoke some of the lines aloud in unison with the actors. Chelsea seemed surprised by the fact he knew the movie so well, despite him saying so. No doubt she'd thought he was just saying things to woo her. He'd noticed since learning he played hockey professionally, she seemed to take him at his word less than she had the night at the party.

He was determined to get them back to that same level of trust.

When the movie ended, Preston turned the TV off, twisting to face her. "You were my most fortunate accident."

"Serendipity," she whispered.

He nodded, wanting her now more than ever. "Joy?"

"Yeah?"

"Want to bend that rule some more?"

She gave him a breathy laugh. "Just *bend*?" she asked, with enough emphasis on the word that he knew she wasn't ready to break the rule.

"Just bend," he vowed.

She didn't reply. Instead, she did one better, initiating the kiss, her hands finding their way to his shoulders, then his hair.

He loved the way she gripped it tight, tugging until his scalp stung, ensuring his lips didn't leave hers. Preston was a big fan of kissing. Always had been. He loved the intimacy of it, loved how much could be expressed by the simple act of touching lips.

But Chelsea took kissing to the next level. Because, while she was holding back from him emotionally, none of that hesitance was present when she kissed him. She was an all-in girl.

With one hand, he cupped her cheek as the other locked around her waist. He held her tightly, hoping against hope she would let these kisses linger. Hopefully, all the way to the midnight feeding. He wouldn't mind making out with her for a few hours.

When she shifted, he worried she'd hit her limit on bending…until she moved over him, straddling his lap.

Thank you, Santa Claus.

Apparently, he'd been a very good boy this year.

Chelsea released her grip on his hair, her hands sliding over his shoulders to his waist, gripping the soft cotton T-shirt he'd thrown on after Lennon's bath. Breaking the kiss, she gave him an adorably shy look, biting her lower lip for just a moment.

"Do you think it would be bending too much if you took your shirt off?" she asked, a blush blooming on her cheeks. "While your Christmas wish was the bedtime routine, mine is to see your b…chest again."

Her slip of the tongue made it obvious she wanted to see the whole package, but he didn't expect to get more than the kisses tonight, so it wasn't like he was going to put up a fuss.

Reaching behind his head, he gripped his shirt at the nape of his neck and pulled it off in one quick swoop.

Chelsea leaned back, her ass perched on his knees.

It took everything he had not to grasp that peach-shaped ass and pull her tight against his crotch. The only thing stopping him was the way Chelsea's eyes lit up as her gaze slid over his now bare chest.

"Sometimes…this past year…I told myself I imagined how hot you were," she whispered, as if revealing a secret.

The grin he gave her was half amusement, half understanding because… "I did the same thing," he confided. "I thought if I convinced myself you weren't as awesome as I remembered, I'd be able to move on."

Her gaze flew up, connecting with his. "It didn't work." She wasn't saying it didn't work for him but for her. Either way, she was correct.

He shook his head. "It sure as fuck didn't."

He toyed with the hem of her T-shirt. Like him, she'd changed into more comfortable clothes after Lennon's bath. Preston suspected she'd packed the silly holiday pajamas because they were practical and cute and, in her mind, not the least bit sexy. The long-sleeved tee was green with red sleeves with a colorful drawing of a reindeer, whose antlers were adorned with tree lights. The words "Lights Out" were emblazoned above it.

The holiday lights reminded him of the ugly sweater he wore the night he met her, recalling the way she'd made fun of him for affixing them with shipping tape.

As far as pj's went, hers revealed nothing, and yet they were sexier than any lingerie he'd ever seen.

"Is this a tit-for-tat situation?" he asked, wiggling his eyebrows when he said the word tit.

Chelsea huffed out a breathy laugh. "I suppose that's only fair."

Preston's cock thickened the second she'd nestled against him for the movie, riding at half-mast throughout the whole damn film. Now, it completed the journey to rock-hard, despite the fact he knew there would be no happy ending.

There wouldn't be until she realized what he already knew.

Their future together had been revealed that night in Philadelphia, and destiny had sealed the deal the day he'd walked into Sugar and Spice Bakery.

He knew it all the way to the depths of his soul.

But Chelsea wouldn't let herself see that yet. Not because she was being willfully stubborn or dismissive but because she genuinely believed she was protecting their son's heart. There was no way in hell he could be upset with her for that. Hence, the practicing of patience.

Chelsea started to take off her shirt, but Preston pulled her hands away.

"My present," he said. "I get to unwrap it."

Her face flushed a bright red, those dimples of hers appearing. Nothing Chelsea did was overtly sexual, and yet she was the most seductive temptress he'd ever met.

Lifting her shirt slowly, he savored every inch of skin he bared. He'd only just reached the bottom of her breasts when Chelsea's hands flew up to cover herself.

"I forgot—" she started. She covered her waist, and he assumed she was worried about her weight. She'd mentioned that concern last year, and again the first time she visited his condo.

"Forgot what?" he prodded, when she clammed up, suddenly uneasy.

"Since Lennon was born, I have stretch marks."

It was obvious she thought those marks were ugly, but knowing they were there did something to Preston he couldn't quite understand.

He gently grasped her wrists. "Let me see."

She closed her eyes and dropped her hands as he pulled her shirt off completely.

Just as she'd said, there were marks beside her stomach. Preston's heart raced as his mind drew a picture he hadn't considered before. "I wish I'd seen you when you were pregnant with him. God, I bet that was beautiful."

Chelsea's eyelids lifted, and she treated him to one of those expressions that said she thought he was off his rocker. "Imagine a beached whale and you'll know what I looked like. My stomach was out to here." She indicated a spot at least three feet away from her. "And my ankles were this big around." Again, she gave him fisherman-sized proportions. "And I waddled like a duck the entire last month. I promise you, no part of me was sexy."

If she was trying to turn him off, she was failing miserably, because at that very moment, Preston sent a wish out into the universe that he'd get to see what she was describing while carrying their second child…and hopefully third.

Gripping her hips, he guided her up, her ass lifting from his thighs so he could lean forward to kiss those marks. "I thought you were perfect before," he whispered, his tongue tracing the lines of her stretchmarks. "But now, you're a fucking work of art. Why would you try to hide something so amazing? These marks were drawn by you and Lennon, and I've never seen anything more gorgeous."

She gave him a wobbly smile, her eyes glazed with shiny tears. "How do you always know what to say to make me feel better?"

"Because I know you, Chelsea. I feel like I've always known you."

"I feel the same way."

The time for words passed, and Preston finished unwrapping his gift. She wore a soft sports bra, but he wasn't kidding about tit for tat, so he drew that off as well. By tacit agreement, their pants remained on.

Chelsea didn't resist or demure, letting him look his fill as she did her own exploring, her fingers drawing patterns over his chest.

The next hour was an experiment in torture and bliss as they kissed, licked, nipped, and touched. He worshipped her breasts, now larger, her nipples even more sensitive.

Chelsea slid closer, pressing down on his covered cock, the two of them dry-humping like teenagers in the backseat of a car.

Then Preston twisted them, pushing her to her back as she wrapped her legs around his waist, welcoming him between.

The change in position—though nowhere near enough—had both of them groaning. He hadn't intended to steal more than the kisses, but then the shirts had come off and his tenuous grip on control vanished.

Mostly.

Somehow, he managed to keep their pants on, aware if his hand slipped below the equator, he'd be powerless to stop.

Gyrating against her, Preston tried to find some semblance of relief, to no avail. His cock knew exactly how good it felt to be gloved by her pussy, and it wouldn't settle for less.

"God," Chelsea said, breathlessly. "Preston."

He was just about to suggest they not only break but shatter the damn rule, when Lennon cried.

Chelsea jerked, wiggling out from beneath him, trying to calm herself. It took a minute, but somehow they both managed to tamp down their arousal. Then, she gave him a crooked grin that told him she hadn't intended to let thing go so far as she pulled her shirt back on, and he responded to it with his own "oops" expression.

They both laughed breathlessly, rising when Lennon cried out again. Preston went to the kitchen for a bottle, while Chelsea walked down the hall to comfort their son.

When he arrived at the guest room, Chelsea was lying on the bed with Lennon tucked next to her. She gestured to the other side.

"You wanted to see the whole routine," she reminded him. "This is it. I feed him in bed and then we spend the rest of the night sleeping together like this."

He climbed onto the bed, grinning at how greedily Lennon took the bottle. He and Chelsea lay facing each other, neither of them speaking.

Preston drank in the moment, happier than he'd ever been in his life.

Within twenty minutes, Lennon and Chelsea were both sound asleep.

Closing his eyes, Preston made his New Year's resolution a week early. Because he was going to do whatever it took to keep these two with him forever.

His beautiful family.

CHAPTER TWELVE

"I'M A MASOCHIST," Chelsea muttered under her breath as she pulled a pan of cupcakes from the oven and set them on a rack to cool before getting started on the frosting. The batch was half test run, half she was too excited to wait to try all the new shit in the bakery's kitchen.

Chelsea had rung in the New Year with her parents and Lennon six days earlier, all of them watching Preston and the Stingrays play Calgary. She'd watched enough hockey by now that she knew nearly all the words to the Canadian National Anthem, which, as far as anthems went, was freaking awesome.

She sighed. While the cupcakes looked and smelled delicious, they didn't distract her from her current state of…yeah… masochism.

Because her thoughts were a chaotic mess.

She tried to tell herself that was understandable. After all, this morning, right now, was the first time Preston had Lennon on his own.

Preston had shown up at the bakery to steal a morning squeeze from his "beautiful boy" and walked in to find her in the midst of a mini meltdown. Lennon was going through a stage where he needed to be held constantly. That wouldn't be so bad if she didn't have a million things she had to do and if he didn't weigh so much. Sixteen pounds didn't sound like a lot, but it was when it squirmed and wiggled constantly.

Chelsea was supposed to be creating her list of permanent products, staples they would sell at the bakery daily. Of course, they would have a special of the day, either a cookie or pastry, but for now, she was trying to focus on setting the standards.

Lennon's "carry me" phase was working in direct counterpoint to that goal. Ethan was out today, meeting with a graphic designer to establish their brand. She was glad he was taking care of all that crap because she didn't have a clue what any of the marketing lingo he used meant.

Preston had walked in, sensed her frustration, and immediately taken the squalling sixteen-pound boy into his arms. When she'd unloaded her stress over establishing the menu and Lennon's sudden clinginess, Preston offered to take the baby with him while he ran a few errands. She wasn't sure what she'd projected after the offer, but he'd quickly assured her it was fine if she was uncomfortable with the idea. He'd probably mistaken her delayed response as unease. But that wasn't it.

It was just that a major truth had crashed down on her head and knocked her slightly silly.

She realized in that moment that she trusted Preston with their son.

Completely.

Then, when she told him she would appreciate the help, that gorgeous, sexy-as-fuck smile erupted on his handsome-as-sin face and triggered yet another avalanche.

She was falling in love with Preston.

Nope.

Scratch that.

She *had* fallen in love with Preston.

She'd done the one thing she told herself she couldn't do

because Lennon had to come first. She was determined to protect his happiness and his future and his security. Starting an affair with Preston would be the height of irresponsibility, because if it failed…

Well, she didn't want to think of all the bad shit that could go down because it involved that word *custody*, which never failed to make her want to throw up.

The problem was that, while she thought it was her maturity —ha fucking ha—that kept her from giving in to her and Preston's obvious attraction to each other, that wasn't the whole truth, or even half the truth about what was holding her back.

Tomorrow, it would be one month since Preston had walked into this bakery. One month in the scheme of an entire lifetime was little more than a blink. And yet, this past month had meant more to her than all the other months of her life combined.

So much so, it had reawakened a hard truth she didn't want to acknowledge.

She was scared.

Terrified, actually.

Of being hurt again.

Rick's failure to show up at the church had struck hard and deep, leaving behind one hell of a scar. Losing Preston would feel a million times worse.

Her phone chirped with an incoming text, and she wiped her hands on her apron as she walked over to where she'd left it on the counter. She tried to ignore the fact she was hoping it was a text from Preston, who'd already sent a couple photos of him and Lennon strolling through a toy store. She'd texted back asking if a toy store had really been on his lists of errands. He'd replied with a noncommittal shrug emoji that made her laugh because, knowing him, it probably had been.

Sadly, this text was from Rick. God, it was just like *Beetlejuice*. She thought his name and he appeared.

Apparently, Rick must have viewed her sleepover with

Preston on Christmas night as her waving some sort of red flag in his face, because he'd been quite tenaciousness ever since.

Like an idiot, she thought Rick had given up after she told him she wasn't interested in anything beyond friendship, because he'd gone radio silent. She should have known better.

He'd started reaching out after Christmas, texting every couple of days just to see how she was doing. She'd ignored them all.

Haven't seen you in way too long. Wanna binge Below Deck tonight?

She sighed. Below Deck had been their show when they were engaged, the two of them never missing an episode. Clearly ignoring him wasn't doing the trick.

Can't. Busy.

She didn't add more because what she did was none of his business, and she couldn't help but wonder where the hell all this attentiveness had been when they were engaged. Shit, she would have been grateful for just a third of the dedication he was currently showing her back then. Now, it was just annoying as shit.

Seeing him?

Apparently, Rick assumed her silence was Preston's fault, rather than the result of him crossing the line she'd drawn in the sand regarding their "just friends" status.

She rolled her eyes at Rick's question and the petty way he refused to refer to Preston by name, simply saying *him*, as if that pronoun was a personal affront.

Chelsea leaned against the counter, considering her reply. All her energy and focus the past month had been on Preston and

Lennon, watching the father and son build what was truly a beautiful bond. She'd been so wrapped up in that, she'd shoved Rick out of her mind, hoping he'd simply fade into the distance once and for all.

Clearly, it was time to come clean, to tell Rick she didn't share his feelings and officially rescind the friendship offer. Offering even that much had blurred the lines for him, giving him hope that simply wasn't there. Doing it over text felt shitty, but she refused to let him keep hanging on.

> We need to talk.

She groaned when Rick's response came immediately.

> I'm in the neighborhood. I'll come over now.

Fuck.

While she knew this conversation was past due, she'd hoped to handle it all over the phone.

She put her cell back down and finished the frosting. Chelsea did her best thinking while baking. With the cupcakes cool, she'd just started icing them when she heard the bell over the front door tinkle and noise from the street filter in.

"Chels?" Rick called out.

"In the kitchen," she replied.

He walked in, all charming smiles. Unlike Preston, who sported a sexy five-o'clock shadow half the time, Rick was court ready—clean-shaven, hair combed neatly, expensive suit pressed.

"Something smells good."

"Red velvet cupcakes."

His eyes widened. "My favorite."

She knew for a fact his favorite cupcake was chocolate chip, but clearly he was trying to butter her up.

Chelsea handed him a frosted one, schooling her annoyance when he nodded his thanks, then put it down on the counter without taking a bite. Rick wouldn't dare run the risk of leaving here with food in his pearly white teeth.

"It's been a long time. I've been thinking a lot about you. I was sorry when I didn't get to see you on Christmas. Did you get the gifts I left for you?" he asked.

He'd bought her a sweater—something his mother had obviously picked out—and a pair of fuzzy holiday socks.

"I did. Thank you." She hadn't gotten him anything, seemingly yet another *too subtle* hint.

"I know you've been busy lately. With the bakery and…other things," he said. Obviously *other things* was code for Preston.

"I have," she started. "It's important to me—"

"I'm sure you're exhausted, but it looks like you're really starting to get a handle on the bakery," he interrupted, gesturing around the kitchen, which was nearly fully stocked. "And your mom was showing me some pictures of Lennon over the holidays."

Chelsea made a mental note to kill her mother.

"He's getting so big," Rick continued. "It's been ages since I've seen him."

The fact Rick was mentioning Lennon spoke to his level of desperation, considering he rarely paid attention to her son.

Time to cut him off at the pass.

"Rick, this isn't working for me," she said.

His nod was too relieved for him to have understood where she was heading. "I'm not surprised. You're burning the candle at both ends, and you're never going to get the help you need from a professional athlete who's on the road all the time, doing God knows what…and with who."

Chelsea frowned, shocked that the irony of Rick's statement was completely lost on him. Had he already forgotten that he'd struck up an affair when they were ENGAGED? Did he fail to recall that he was the one who'd skipped out on the wedding because he was doing *God knew what*…with Vanessa?

"Is he being difficult about Lennon? I know your mom is worried about a custody battle, but I've got a friend who's a divorce lawyer, and he says it would be virtually impossible for Preston to take Lennon from you, despite his name and money."

Rick had talked to a lawyer?

"His name isn't on the birth certificate, so it's a simple matter of us getting married and me legally adopting Lennon," Rick added.

What. In. The. Sweet. Mother. Fuck. Was. Going. On?!

"Stop!" Chelsea said, when it was clear slick lawyer Rick was on a roll, and only just getting started. "Preston is a *great* father, and his name *will* be going on the birth certificate." She intended to make a call the second Rick got out of here, in fact.

"Chelsea, that's a mistake."

"No. The only mistake I made was in foolishly thinking you were capable of being just my friend. It's obvious that's not something we can be to each other."

Rick looked her in the eye. "You're right. We can't. I'm in love with you, Chelsea. I always have been. My goal these past seven months has been to win you back." He moved closer as he spoke, forcing Chelsea to step backward to maintain distance. That attempt failed when she ran out of room, her back hitting the counter.

She placed her hand in the center of his chest when he shifted as if to kiss her. "If you try to kiss me, I will kick you in the balls."

Her threat caught him off guard, and he took one step back, though not nearly big enough. "I don't understand."

"You *cannot* be this oblivious. I know you're an only child, and I know you're used to getting your way, typically by steamrolling over all obstacles, but none of that is going to work in this case. Any relationship you and I might have had ended the day you failed to show up at our wedding."

Confusion marred Rick's features. "You said you forgave me for that."

"I did. But I'm never going to *forget*, and I'm never going to trust you again. The most I could offer was a casual, surface-y friendship, and I only did that to appease our mothers, who are driving me up the damn wall!"

Rick scowled. God, he was such a mama's boy. "My mother has been very good to you. She made Lennon's Halloween costume, for Christ's sake."

"She did. And he was a super-cute pumpkin, but that doesn't mean I want her as a mother-in-law. She's my mom's best friend. That's it."

"I helped your dad build Lennon's crib and repaint the nursery."

"And I appreciate that. But to be honest, I thought you did it because you felt fucking guilty and were trying to make amends, not because you were living in some la-la land where we got back together."

"I've been there for you since Lennon was born."

Chelsea wasn't sure what equated to "been there" in Rick's mind—then she realized she did. It meant, he had been there— like, in the room—watching while *she* took care of her son. Apparently, his mere presence was supposed to be some great gift he offered while she fed Lennon, changed his diaper, and rocked him to sleep. Rick had only held Lennon a handful of times, always done at her request—not because he offered— when she needed to go to the bathroom or grab a bottle from the refrigerator.

There was absolutely no comparison between Rick's contributions and Preston's.

Preston was a true partner when it came to caring for their

son. Perhaps the argument could be made that was because Lennon wasn't Rick's son. But she knew her ex well enough to know that even if they'd gotten married and had kids, the majority of the childrearing would have fallen to her, because he made more money and therefore would have considered himself the bread winner.

"Rick, I'm sorry you got the wrong impression about my feelings, but—"

Rick cut her off. "You're saying all of this because of *him*, aren't you?"

"Not at all. I knew we were in two different places the morning you kissed me."

"How convenient that also just happened to be the day he showed up."

"His name is Preston," she said, louder than she intended.

"You're making a mistake, Chelsea. You barely know this guy, and yet you're ready to throw away a lifelong relationship with me in the hopes that what? He'll pick *you*? Just because you had a baby with him? The guy is using you, and he's going to hurt you. The only reason he's hanging around is because you gave him a son. I'm sure that's feeding his overweening ego for now, but something or someone else will come along soon, and you'll be left on your own. I'm offering you a real future. I know you're unhappy living with your parents. Move in with me. Today. Let me prove myself to you. And then…maybe soon, you'll consider marrying me. I'll be a good husband to you and father to Lennon. I'll give you a home and provide for you."

"I seem to recall you making that offer before. You didn't show up."

Rick stilled, and for the first time, she got the sense her words were sinking in. "You're right. I didn't. And it was the biggest mistake of my life."

Preston said Rick would regret letting her go the night they met. He assured her that he'd be sorry one day. It looked like that day had arrived, but it didn't make her as happy as she thought it would.

"I know you don't want to hear it again, but I *am* sorry, Chelsea. More than words can say."

She nodded, her throat tight. "I know that. But you and I are done. And I mean completely. I don't want to see you again. Not for a long, long time."

"That might be tough…our mothers…"

"You managed to avoid me for months after the wedding. I have no doubts about your abilities there."

Guilt suffused his features. "You're right again. I did. Chelsea, I hope, for your sake and Lennon's, that man…" Rick drew in a slow breath. "That Preston sticks around and follows through."

"He will," she said, with a certainty she felt all the way to the core.

Rick leaned forward, attempting another kiss. She pulled away, shaking her head.

A rustling sound captured their attention, and they turned toward the door of the kitchen, spotting Preston standing there, Lennon sleeping soundly in his stroller in front of him. She'd been so distracted by Rick, she hadn't even heard the bell.

Preston didn't say anything, simply looked from her to Rick, then back again. One of these days, she was going to have to ask him for pointers on how he managed that poker face of his because, while she couldn't read a single thing on his face, she feared he was seeing every speck of the panic on hers.

"Uh…Preston Jacobson, this is Rick Dwyer. Rick, this is Preston." While Rick didn't need the introduction, Preston did—and the slight furrowing of his brows told her that he remembered exactly who Rick was. That was when the poker face faltered, just slightly.

Both men nodded by way of greeting, but neither reached out to shake the other's hand. Instead, they looked like kickboxers sizing each other up before the ringing of the bell.

So…this was going well.

Rick cried uncle first on the stare down. "I need to get back to the office." He turned toward Chelsea. "I'll see you…" He paused.

"Goodbye, Rick," she said firmly, reinforcing her stand.

Rick walked away without another word, ignoring Preston—and Lennon—on the way out.

Preston leaned on the doorjamb, clearly waiting for an explanation.

"So…that was my ex," she started lamely.

He nodded. "Yeah, I figured that out on my own."

"I should have told you that he was sort of back in the picture, hanging around since Lennon was born. Actually, before that."

Preston tilted his head. "What does that mean? Hanging around? I thought you said you weren't seeing anyone."

"I'm not," she replied quickly. "Not at all. And definitely not him. It's just…he and Vanessa broke up before I moved back to Baltimore. I told you that his mom and mine have been best friends forever. Rick and I grew up together, so our paths cross from time to time."

Preston nodded, but didn't ask any questions, waiting for her to fill in all the blanks.

"Obviously, when he showed up shortly after my return to apologize, I told him to take a hike. But he kept coming back, trying to make amends. He gave my parents a check to cover all the money they lost on the wedding, and he helped my dad build Lennon's crib and repaint my old bedroom, turning it into a nursery. I didn't speak to him for months, even when he was doing all that, but after a while…"

"He wore you down."

She lifted one shoulder. "Being angry at him all the time was exhausting. So I told him I forgave him and we could be friends," she stressed. "*Only* friends. But a month or so ago—the day you found me, actually—he kissed me, and I realized he wanted more than just friendship. I told him I wasn't interested, but Rick's not the type to give up easily. Apparently, my mom's been telling him about you and your career, and…he showed up today to…" She stopped.

"Warn you about me?" Preston correctly surmised.

"There are a lot of misconceptions about professional athletes out there."

"In some cases, they're not wrong. You haven't met my friend Tank yet."

Chelsea forced a grin, grateful he was giving her a chance to explain without getting angry. "Rick knows I'm going out of my mind living with my mother, so he said I could move in with him. Said he wanted to marry me and adopt Lennon and—"

"Lennon *has* a father," Preston interjected hotly, glancing over his shoulder, as if he was tempted to chase Rick down and make that fact painfully clear.

She raised her hands to calm him down. "I know he does, and I told him that. *You* are Lennon's father. I'll call someone this afternoon, try to figure out how to add your name to the birth certificate—"

"I have a friend who practices family law, Colm Collins. I can call him and see what we need to do…if you're sure you're ready."

"I'm very sure."

"I saw him kiss you the day I found you," Preston confessed. "I saw the bakery on my way to meet Victor for breakfast. Before I could cross the street, you came outside to talk to Rick. When he kissed you, I walked away."

Chelsea was shocked by this information. "Why didn't you say anything before now?"

"You said you weren't seeing anyone, and I knew you wouldn't lie to me."

"I wouldn't," she reassured him. "But if you thought…when you saw us… Why did you come back?"

"Because I couldn't stay away. I thought when I walked in here, you'd tell me that you'd fallen in love with someone else. I needed to hear that, knew it was the only way I'd ever be able to move on. I didn't expect…"

Chelsea looked at Lennon, sleeping in his stroller. "Him."

Preston smiled down at his son. "I expected to have my heart broken, not to find it."

That was the greatest thing Chelsea had ever heard.

"I told Rick I don't want to see him anymore, not even as friends. Our families—especially his mother," she amended, "are just going to have to find a way to deal."

It took a moment, but Preston's troubled expression faded, and that easygoing grin that never failed to excite her returned. "Yeah, I guess they are. But don't worry. I'm great with mothers. I'll find a way to win yours over…somehow."

She laughed. "If anyone can win Ellen Murphy over, it's you."

He checked on Lennon, who was still sound asleep, then approached her. "Now, are those cupcakes for anyone or…"

She gestured at the platter, letting him know he could help himself. He reached for the closest, which was the one she'd offered Rick, and polished it off in two large bites, his closed eyes and moan of delight doing wicked things to her libido.

Everything about this man turned her on, and the crazy part was, most of it wasn't even sexual. She swore she popped out a new egg every time she watched him cuddle Lennon in his arms. Or watched him skate across the ice—she and Dad were officially hockey fanatics these days.

Or even now, as he grabbed another one of her cupcakes, grinning like a kid getting dessert before dinner.

He demolished the second cupcake as quickly as the first. "Holy *shit*, those are good."

She laughed, then reached toward him. "You have a little frosting…right there." She started to wipe it off for him, but Preston grasped her wrist, pulling her closer.

"Might work better if you licked it off," he said, his voice as rich and velvety as her cupcakes.

Chelsea didn't even bother refusing because she really, *really* wanted to taste that frosting from his lips. Lifting on her tiptoes, she moved closer, Preston leaning forward to meet her halfway. Her tongue darted out, swiping away the sweet confectionary sugar and butter, and her moan matched his.

His hand gripped the side of her throat, his intention clear.

He was going to kiss her, and all the common sense in the world wasn't going to stop Chelsea. She was tired of fighting this attraction. And Preston wasn't making it any easier. The man was always touching her. Like when he took her hand to help her out of the car and held fast. Or when his hand rested on the small of her back as they walked beside each other. Or the way he rubbed her shoulders whenever she was tired or tense.

Every little touch had worked its way past her defenses, so much so, she was struggling to recall why kissing him would be a bad idea.

Chelsea waited until his lips were a mere inch from hers before turning her face away so that they landed on her cheek. She felt his sigh, knew he was misinterpreting her actions as rejection.

Which made it even harder for her to keep a straight face when she reached behind her. She felt around until she found another cupcake. Running her finger over the top, she gathered a large dollop of icing, lifting it to her own lips.

Chelsea painted the lower one with the white frosting, grinning at him.

"Oops," she said. "Now I'm a mess too."

Preston's eyes darkened with hunger. "I better clean that up." His tongue tickled as he licked every bit of icing. "You're delicious."

There was something so freeing and fun about flirting with him that she couldn't resist driving the heat even higher. She pushed the finger that was still sticky with frosting into her mouth, sucking it suggestively as Preston watched.

"Dirty girl," he murmured, pushing her against the counter at her back. "You realize you're playing with fire, don't you? That rule of yours…"

She gazed up at him through lowered lashes. Releasing her finger with a pop, she ran her hands down his chest, tightening her fists in his shirt, pulling him closer. "Bend it. Hard."

Preston didn't need to be asked twice. He lowered his head, claiming her lips in a kiss that was incendiary and rough, almost bruising in its intensity. Ever since Christmas, he'd respected her wishes, keeping things between them platonic, never stepping over the line she'd drawn.

All that was out the window now.

He pulled her hair tie out so that her chestnut curls fell loose around her shoulders. Then he ran his fingers through them, gripping her tresses tight enough that her scalp tingled. He made her feel naughty and wicked and wild, and she loved it.

Their tongues danced together as Preston wedged his thick, hard thigh between her legs. Chelsea gave up fighting for control, taking what she needed, what she wanted. Her core rocked back and forth on that thigh as she sought pressure against her clit. Preston grabbed one hip, moving her faster.

Every now and then, her thigh brushed against his crotch, his erection full-blown. She ran her hand over it, applying pressure, wanting to make him feel as good as he was making *her* feel, but Preston pulled her fingers away.

"No. This isn't about me. Right now, all I want is to see you falling apart. You're so fucking beautiful when you come. I've spent too many months imagining it over and over in my memories. I need to see it again."

He placed his lips against hers, devouring her again as she gyrated madly against his leg.

When Chelsea's breathing became labored, she broke the kiss in order to draw in some air. Preston growled—an honest-to-God growl—his lips finding hers again, refusing to let her go.

She felt light-headed and dizzy, but decided breathing was over-fucking-rated. Moving harder against his thigh, Chelsea gasped, her pussy clenching, her clit pulsing.

"I...think..." she breathed against his lips, even though he was still kissing her.

Holy crap. She was going to come. Just from dry-humping his leg.

How was that even possible?

Preston's lips traveled to the side of her neck, his breath hot in her ear. "Come undone for me, Joy."

She loved it when he called her that.

"Please," she gasped, not even sure what she was begging for.

Preston somehow knew. She felt him pop the button on her jeans, sliding down the zipper. His fingers burrowed their way beneath the elastic of her panties, stroking her clit as she continued to ride his thigh.

"God!" she cried out.

A full minute didn't pass before she shattered, the orgasm ripping through her like a tornado. Her body trembled as he drew out the experience, his fingers playing her like a guitar. As far as orgasms went, that one was in her top five. Which wasn't surprising, considering the other four spots were also held by Preston-induced climaxes.

Slipping his hand from her jeans, he wrapped his arms around her, holding her as he lowered his leg. Her thighs instinctively tightened together, hating the loss.

Chelsea sank into his embrace, her right cheek pressed against his broad chest as she tried to recover. She heard the hard, steady thud of his heart, the sound of it calming, relaxing.

Once she found her strength, she lifted her head, looking at him. "I…" She didn't have a clue what to say, because now that reality was returning, so was that inkling of fear she couldn't seem to shake.

Preston cupped her cheek, gazing deeply into her eyes. "Don't regret that, Chelsea. It wasn't wrong."

She bit her lower lip, then realized his words were wasted. She'd yet to regret a single thing she'd done with this man. "I don't regret it," she said, hoping to reassure him.

"I know you're worried, and I understand the reasons behind that anxiety. I intended to give you all the time you needed, but…" Preston shrugged, a small grin tugging at the corners of his lips. "You and your cupcakes are too damn sexy."

She laughed loudly, realizing there hadn't been nearly enough lighthearted fun in her life until this past month. Chelsea had spent the last year working her way through a veritable roll call of emotions. From homesickness after the move to Paris, shock over the pregnancy, grief over Agnes's death, stress over moving back to Baltimore, wonder after Lennon's birth, regret over not knowing how to find Preston, and a whole shit-ton of exhaustion and second-guessing as she tried to work her way through the minefield of first-time motherhood. It had been twelve months of the scariest fucking roller coaster known to man.

With Preston back in her life, peace had returned to her world, and it brought joy and laughter along for the ride.

"My first review," she joked, holding up her hand as if reading it aloud from a sign. "Stingrays left winger, Preston Jacobson, says Sugar and Spice's cupcakes are too damn sexy."

Preston laughed. "Hey, I'll skywrite that if you want, but you don't need my words to sell your cupcakes. One bite of those and you'll have fans for life."

She reached up on tiptoe and kissed him on the cheek. "You make me happy."

"Ditto." His smile in response to her compliment warmed her even more. Before either of them could say more, Lennon's quiet cry distracted them.

Preston beat her to the stroller, lifting him into his arms, cooing softly, and Lennon instantly quieted.

Chelsea was amazed by how quickly Preston and Lennon had bonded. Not even Ethan, who'd been around since Lennon's birth, was able to soothe him so quickly.

"He's probably hungry," Preston said. "It's been a few hours."

Chelsea nodded, walking to the refrigerator to fetch a bottle. Preston claimed one of the new kitchen stools, settling in to feed Lennon so that she could finish frosting the last few cupcakes.

Silence descended for a few minutes, Preston's gaze traveling back and forth between her and Lennon. She got the sense he wanted to say something.

"What is it?" she finally asked.

"You're really unhappy living with your parents?"

Chelsea shrugged. "I wouldn't say I'm completely miserable. It's just…challenging. Mom is very opinionated about childrearing and my personal life."

"Is she Team Rick?"

"No. I wouldn't say that. But…well, she doesn't really know you." Chelsea was aware that was a lame answer. Preston had met her parents, of course, and he'd stopped by the house a few times, usually prior to hitting the road for an away game, but other than that, all their time together was spent at his place.

Which was her fault.

Preston's condo had quickly become her happy place, because she was free to be the mother she wanted to be without dealing with her own mom's scrutiny. Plus, watching Preston with their son was her favorite thing—way better than anything TV offered.

"Your place offers me a respite because I hate confrontation, and my mom is sort of driving me crazy. The reason I try not to push back is because she really does help me a lot, with laundry and babysitting Lennon two days a week. I've been focusing too much on the negative when it comes to her. I know all of her comments and concerns come from a place of love."

"It's been a lot of changes…for both of you," Preston said.

He was sweet to say that.

"Chelsea, I know we said we'd take things slow, and I'm fine with that."

The strain in his face told Chelsea that was a lie.

"But the more I'm with him, the more it hurts when I'm not. Christmas night was…" He ran a hand through his hair. "It was the best night of my life. I'd like…I want more nights with Lennon."

"I get that." She didn't mention that Christmas night was high on her list of perfect nights too.

Today was the first day Preston had taken Lennon on his own. It was obvious things had gone well, judging by the pictures he'd texted and how content their son was with his father.

Preston blew out a long, slow breath, clearly gearing up to ask for what he wanted. She understood why he was so hesitant to start this conversation, but it was time they had it.

"You want to keep him some nights." Her insides quivered at the thought of sleeping away from Lennon.

Preston rose from the stool, approaching her with Lennon still nestled in his arms. "Not alone. I wouldn't ask that of you, because I know you're not ready for that." He lifted one shoulder. "But I've only seen the nighttime routine once, one bath, one midnight feeding. I liked it, liked being a part of that."

"It was nice," she agreed.

"I was thinking…maybe you and Lennon could move in with *me*. You can live in the guest bedroom with him," he hastily added. "I know the two of you share a room at your parents' place. It would add a whole slew of time I get to spend with him. Even if it's just watching him sleep."

It was a fair request, as well as a solution to a problem she hadn't had time to solve. She'd resolved to move out sooner rather than waiting until summer. Preston was offering her not only a place to stay but the same kind of help her parents had been providing. Someone to share the load of caring for Lennon.

Chelsea couldn't think of a single reason why she shouldn't say yes.

Well, that wasn't exactly true. Staying at his place and attempting to sleep across the hall from him was going to be an experiment in torture.

But, from Lennon's perspective, she knew including Preston in all the things he just mentioned would only continue to strengthen the bond between father and son, and she wanted that desperately—for both of them.

"I think we could do that. Maybe a trial run? See how it goes?"

Preston wasn't able to mask his surprise at her unexpected agreement, but he recovered quickly, smiling widely. "Okay."

"Maybe…" She bit her lower lip. "Maybe we shouldn't bend that rule any more just yet, then. It would add an extra wrinkle…if we're going to give this living-together thing a fair shake."

Preston was slower to respond to that request. He made no secret of his hopes for the two of them, and as much as Chelsea wanted to just say fuck it and give in completely, she wasn't quite there yet.

"Okay," he said again. "I'll agree to that—if you'll agree to move in tomorrow."

She laughed. "Tomorrow?" Then she recalled Erika's and Ainsley's remarks about how quickly their Stingrays had moved them in.

"You know what? Sure. Why not?"

Preston raised a fist in victory. "Hell yeah!"

Then he bent down to kiss her on the cheek before snatching yet another cupcake.

CHAPTER THIRTEEN

"EVERYTHING IS FINE. HONEST."

Preston could tell from Chelsea's tired voice that everything was *not* fine, but he didn't call her on it because what the hell could he do to help her, when he was all the way across the country in L.A.?

He'd stepped out into the hotel hallway to call Chelsea, not wanting to disturb Victor, who had fallen asleep three minutes after they'd reached their hotel room.

There hadn't been time to call her before the game, thanks to some last-minute promotional gig the team's social media coordinator, McKenna Bailey, had set up. So, Preston had resigned himself to the fact he wouldn't get to see her and Lennon via FaceTime today, thanks to the damn time difference.

Instead, he texted her just before heading onto the ice to say good night, and to ask her to give Lennon a kiss from him.

She hadn't replied to that text until ten minutes ago…at one a.m. her time. When his phone pinged and he saw her name, he figured she was up for the middle-of-the-night feeding, until she confessed she hadn't gone to bed yet.

That was when he decided to call.

Lennon was running a fever and had been restless all day, crying. It was the first time their son had been sick, and Preston could tell Chelsea was frazzled and stressed out, even though she knew his crankiness and fever were the result of the vaccines he'd gotten earlier in the day. He wished he could be there—to help Chelsea and to comfort his baby boy.

"He's not sleeping at all?"

"Just brief spurts, no more than fifteen minutes at a go. Then he wakes up screaming and I walk the floor with him until he settles back down again. I'm currently on my fortieth trek around your condo."

"*Our* condo," he corrected—also for the fortieth time, since she refused to consider his home theirs.

Chelsea and Lennon had officially moved in a month ago, and as far as he was concerned, they were hitting the trial run out of the park. Chelsea was laid-back and not prone to drama, so he'd known from the get-go she would be an easy roommate. She hadn't proven him wrong. He'd done the cohabitation thing with a couple of his exes, but neither of those experiences had been without more than a few road bumps.

So far, he and Chelsea hadn't hit a single one, their personalities lining up perfectly. He hated doing laundry, which was something she didn't mind at all. So she'd taken over that chore and, in exchange, he did the grocery shopping, something Chelsea couldn't stand.

As far as dinner went, on nights when they were both home, they took turns cooking. Preston had a woman who came in twice a week to do the general cleaning, so the condo maintenance ran like a well-oiled machine.

Just as the childcare duties had. Mrs. Murphy still babysat a couple days a week, the rest of the time divided between him, Allyson, Ethan, and Chelsea. Since the bakery hadn't opened yet, she and Ethan were maintaining workweek hours and taking the weekends off. That would change in a few weeks, when the part-time nanny they'd hired took over caring for Lennon whenever his and Chelsea's schedules overlapped. They'd been fortunate to find a nanny who was willing to work flexible hours, though Preston knew Chelsea was still anxious about leaving Lennon in the care of a stranger.

When it came to Lennon's bath and bedtime routine, he and Chelsea shared the duty, him filling the tub and handing her whatever she needed as she scrubbed their adorable little butterball. Then the three of them would sit together on the bed in the guest room, each of them taking a turn reading him a story. It was Preston's favorite time of the day, one he hated missing whenever he was on the road for an away game.

Chelsea ignored his condo comment. "It's just been a long day. After the doctor's appointment, I had to drop Lennon off with Mom because Ethan and I were meeting with a vendor. The guy showed up late and then the meeting took way longer than I expected. Then when I went to pick up Lennon, Rick's mom, Angie, was visiting my mother. She managed to bring Rick's name up three times in a ten-minute conversation."

"Great," he said sarcastically, his jaw clenched.

Preston had been fighting an uphill battle with Ellen Murphy, trying to prove himself worthy. In addition to visiting with her whenever he picked up Lennon, he'd given her and Mr. Murphy season passes to the Stingrays games, and he and Chelsea had invited them over for dinner on two different occasions. While she'd been polite, there was still a wariness in her expression whenever she looked at him that told him he hadn't passed the test yet.

"And how is dear Rick?" Preston's tone was pure smart-ass.

Chelsea snorted, her reply matching his voice, amusing him. "Oh, he's fantastic. He's just made partner at his law firm and he's taking his parents out to Charleston Restaurant to celebrate."

"Ooo. The Charleston. Fancy," he joked, the two of them

laughing. When Preston had spotted Chelsea with Rick at the bakery last month, and seen the man lean forward to kiss her, his vision had gone green around the edges. He'd nearly been knocked down by the strength of his jealousy.

That emotion faded a bit when she turned her head, refusing to kiss him back, then it vanished completely when Chelsea explained what he saw the day he'd found her in Baltimore, assuring him she had no feelings for her ex.

"Seeing Angie just topped off what had already been a spectacularly shitty day. God, I miss you."

As much as Preston loved hearing those words, he hated that he wasn't there. He'd agreed to her request that they return to platonic hell, but maintaining that distance was easier said than done.

Because...after stealing those forbidden, rule-bending tastes, it was hard to go to sleep, knowing she was in the room right across the hall. His teammates thought the dark circles he'd been wearing lately were the result of midnight feedings, and he hadn't bothered to correct them.

In truth, Lennon only woke once a night, and that time had become Preston's favorite part of the day. The moment he heard Lennon cry, he went to the kitchen to grab a bottle, then, like at Christmas, he and Chelsea tucked their son between them, taking turns feeding him until he fell back to sleep. For the first few nights, Preston returned to his bed, but on the fourth night, Chelsea told him he could sleep with them if wanted to.

As if he'd pass up that invitation.

Chelsea usually drifted back to sleep quickly, but it always took Preston longer. Because the image of her curled up with their son was the sexiest fucking thing he'd ever seen. So he spent at least half an hour willing away his raging hard-on.

"I miss you too, Chels. I'll be back tomorrow afternoon. Maybe the three of us can take a long nap together."

"Sounds like bliss."

Preston heard Lennon start to cry in the background.

"Duty calls," she said wearily. "Time for lap forty-one. Sorry about the game," she quickly added.

"Can't win them all," he replied, aware just how out of character that comment was. Preston used to hate losing, but nowadays...other things felt more important than winning. "Good night, Joy."

"Night, BFG."

Preston hung up the phone and sighed, leaning against the wall, wishing he was back in Baltimore.

"Preston? Everything okay?" Coach Dean Fields stepped off the elevator, heading to his own room. "What are you doing in the hallway?"

Preston lifted his phone. "Called to check on Lennon. He got his vaccines today and he's running a fever."

"Ah. Well, that's a normal thing, right?"

Preston shrugged. "I guess so. At least, Chelsea said it was. Apparently he's fussy, and I can tell she's at the end of her rope. I hate that I'm not there to help out."

"I was just going to say you dodged a bullet," his coach joked.

"Remind me again why you never married, Coach?" Preston asked, grinning widely.

Dean rolled his eyes, ignoring the bachelor jab. "Cut that coach shit out. Don't mind hearing it from the young guys—nice show of respect—but when it comes from you and Victor, I feel a hundred years old."

Dean's last year as a Baltimore Stingray was Preston's first, and the two of them had grown close during that season. Sadly, Dean's hockey career was cut short by a series of knee injuries. Coming back following one or even two ACL tears was possible, but Dean simply couldn't get his knee back into hockey shape following the third, so he'd hung up his skates and become an assistant coach in Vancouver.

Since then, they'd met for drinks whenever their schedules lined up. Then Preston had been thrilled when Dean was announced as the Stingrays' new head coach at the end of last season.

"You're not alone on that feeling-ancient thing," Preston said. "During that interview this afternoon, I mentioned the year I started playing hockey. Fucking Rookie interjected that was the year he'd started school. Asshole was just going into kindergarten, and I was playing professionally. Talk about a kick in the teeth."

Dean chuckled. "So other than the fussy baby, everything else going good with the new roommates?"

Preston's love life had been the hot topic in the locker room since he'd found Chelsea at the beginning of December. Not that he cared. Given how much time he and his teammates spent together—on and off the ice—it wasn't surprising they knew practically everything about each other.

"It's great. Better than great. Which is why it's hard to be here when they're there."

"That's the life of a hockey player," Dean replied.

Preston sighed. "It is. Before this season, I didn't mind the away games."

"And now?"

"Chelsea and I are still trying to find our way, and every time we start to get into a good routine, it's disrupted by me hitting the road again. It's also impacting how quickly I'm able to form a bond with Lennon. When I get back home after being gone a few days, it feels like I'm starting from scratch with him."

"He's only a baby. That'll get easier as he gets older."

"Yeah, I guess." But Preston didn't like the idea of Lennon getting used to him being away.

"Juggling this career and a family is hard work, Preston. The trick is to manage a life/work balance. I never figured that out myself, but if anyone can do it, it's you. You've always been good at prioritizing things in the right way. It might take some time to get there, but you will."

"What if I don't *want* to get there?"

Dean frowned. "What do you mean?"

Preston hadn't broached the subject of him hanging up his skates with anyone on the team except Victor, nearly two months ago. "I'm thirty-five, Dean. You know as well as I do, I'm quickly approaching the sell-by date on this career."

"Plenty of guys play into their forties these days."

"Says my coach."

Dean smirked. "Physically, you're still in top shape, Preston. I wouldn't play you if you weren't keeping up, but the fact is, you are. And more than that, you're a hell of a role model to the young guys just coming up. They look up to you."

Preston appreciated hearing all of that, but his current issues with hockey didn't stem from his abilities. "It's not the body that's struggling. It's this." Preston tapped his temple. "And this." He dropped his hand to his heart. "Because I'm standing in this hallway right now, resenting the fuck out of the fact I'm here instead of with them."

Dean leaned against the opposite wall, grimacing. "Sounds to me like you've made up your mind."

"I haven't," he said quickly, because he hadn't. Not really. Although, it was something he'd been thinking about more and more with each passing day. It was stupid to even bring the subject up to Dean, considering he was Preston's coach. However, the man had been his friend first and he respected his opinion.

Dean rubbed his jaw. "As your coach, I feel compelled to convince you to stick around, to continue playing, but as your friend…"

"As my friend?" Preston prodded.

"I always put hockey first, Preston. Always. And it cost me. When I was younger, all I ever wanted was to be on the ice or living the life of a big-shot athlete—complete with puck bunnies and bad financial decisions. I made all the wrong choices. You love this sport as much as I do…so trust me when I say, you should leave before this resentment you're feeling right now turns into something much worse."

"What's worse than resentment?" Preston asked.

"Regret."

There was no question Dean was speaking from personal experience, but Preston knew his old friend well enough to know that was as much as he was going to say on the subject. Hell, that was more than Preston had ever gotten from him. Dean was tight-lipped when it came to talking about his personal life.

"I need to reiterate that this is just me thinking out loud," Preston reasserted. "I really haven't made any solid decisions."

"I understand. I won't say anything to anyone else. I appreciate you giving me a heads-up, and I hope you'll let me know once you *do* decide."

"I will," Preston vowed.

"Got any idea what you'll do after you retire?"

Preston shook his head, even though that was a lie.

As far as he was concerned, stay-at-home dad sounded like a pretty sweet gig.

"Well, if you find yourself missing the sport too much, let me know. I'm sure I could find a place for you on the coaching staff."

Preston was touched by the offer—but not tempted.

"Alright, then," Dean said, pushing off the wall. "I'm fucking exhausted. Going to bed. Hope Lennon feels better soon."

"Thanks, Coach," Preston said, with a shit-eating grin as Dean flipped him off.

"Good night."

Preston returned to the room, sighing heavily. Sleep was going to elude him, and not just because of Victor's snoring.

Nope. Tonight, he was fighting with himself.

Stay-at-home dad in one corner.

Hockey in the other.

And he didn't have a clue which one was going to win.

* * *

Chelsea sat on the couch, staring at the TV, even though it wasn't turned on. She was exhausted—from the sleepless night and from walking a tightrope she didn't want to walk anymore.

Her love for Preston grew more and more with each passing day, making it impossible to maintain this roommate façade.

She was letting fear hold her back.

If Aunt Agnes was still alive, she would read Chelsea the riot act for being such an idiot about this relationship with Preston. Then she thought about what Agnes had said in her will, suddenly seeing the words in a different light. Chelsea had only considered Agnes's advice from the perspective of opening the bakery, but she could see it applied to much more than that.

Because Agnes was right. The most important decisions were made with the heart.

Chelsea was letting her stupid head run the show, feeding her a bunch of preconceived notions about professional athletes —none of which were true about Preston—and some ridiculous idea that love required years, not minutes. That, combined with her fear of having her heart broken again—thanks to douchebag Rick—was guiding what she thought were smart, well-thought-out choices.

"You have my permission to haunt me," Chelsea directed toward heaven and Aunt Agnes. "I deserve it."

She jumped, her heart spiking, when she heard a knock. For a split second, she thought it was Aunt Agnes's ghost responding to her invitation. She rolled her eyes at herself when she realized someone was at the door.

239

Chelsea peered through the peephole, surprised to find Mom standing in the hallway.

"What are you doing here?" she asked, as she opened the door and Mom walked in.

"I had a few errands to run today, and I thought I'd drop this by." Mom held up Lennon's favorite blanket. "You left it yesterday."

"Oh, thanks. I was looking for that this morning." Chelsea took the blanket, following as Mom crossed the living room, peering into the bassinet to steal a peek at Lennon, who was—finally—sleeping peacefully after their restless night.

"Is he feeling better?"

"Yeah," Chelsea said. "His fever broke around four a.m. and we finally managed to grab a couple hours of sleep. Mercifully, it's the weekend, so I don't have to go to work today."

Mom studied her face, giving her a sympathetic smile. Obviously, Chelsea looked as wrecked as she felt. She hadn't had a chance to shower, so she was pairing the dark circles under her eyes with a spectacular bedhead hairdo.

"When does Preston get home?"

Chelsea glanced toward the kitchen, checking the clock on the oven. She blew out a hard breath. "In two hours." Then she looked around the condo. She'd been on the go since Preston left town the day before yesterday. As such, she'd let the place go to hell. There was a pile of laundry on the dining room table, waiting to be folded and put away. The sink was loaded with dirty dishes and the counter covered with bottles waiting to be sterilized, as well as food she'd failed to put away. The living room was equally cluttered, with toys, shoes, and clothes scattered everywhere.

Ordinarily, the chores wouldn't seem so daunting, but she was coasting on fumes after managing only a few hours of sleep last night.

"You fold the clothes," Mom said. "I'll tackle the kitchen."

"You don't have to—"

"Many hands make light work," Mom interjected, as she walked to the sink.

Chelsea smiled tiredly. "Thanks. I'm usually better at keeping up, but the past couple of days have been nuts."

Mom rinsed the dishes before loading them in the dishwasher. "You're doing just fine, Chelsea. To be honest, I don't know how you manage to do as much as you do."

She looked up from the shirt she was folding, trying to figure out if she'd heard what she thought she had. A compliment? From *Mom*?

Her mother must have caught her confused/amazed expression, because she gave her a rueful smile. "I know I'm not the easiest person to live with."

Chelsea had to bite her lip not to laugh, not that her effort was necessary, since Mom narrowed her eyes, feigning anger. "Okay, Henry. I know you think that's an understatement."

She laughed when Mom called her by Dad's name, something she always did whenever Chelsea did or said something *he* would.

"Did Dad say something to you?" Chelsea wondered if her father had instigated this visit and conversation.

"No, he didn't. It's just…" She paused, and Chelsea could tell whatever she planned to say next would be hard for her mother. "I heard Angie yesterday, singing Rick's praises to you, and I was afraid maybe you thought that I…" Mom sighed, changing directions. "I've been worried about you this past year. I mean, you decided to move to Paris on a whim."

Chelsea wanted to argue that it wasn't a whim, but the truth was, she'd let her broken heart and wounded pride make that decision. Part of her couldn't help but wonder if she'd still be there if she hadn't gotten pregnant. She sort of suspected she wouldn't. Because she'd been terribly homesick her first few months, and that was *before* she knew about Lennon.

"Then you moved back, pregnant after a one-night stand. And you didn't even know the man's last name."

Chelsea winced slightly, because when her mom said it like that, she could see just how bad it all sounded.

"When Rick started showing up again, I was just as annoyed and angry about it as you were, because he hurt you badly. But then...he *kept* coming around and, well...I've known the man since he was born. I could tell he was sorry. Between him helping us set up the nursery and Angie talking in my ear, telling me how Rick admitted leaving you at the altar was the biggest mistake of his life... I guess I started thinking perhaps the two of you could work things out. Especially after you forgave him."

"I forgave him for *me*, Mom. Not him. I was tired of being angry all the time."

Mom nodded. "I get that and I respect it."

Chelsea wasn't sure how to reply to that because...wow.

"When you came home from Paris, seven months pregnant, and decided to open your own business, Chelsea. I was afraid that was another whim."

This time, Chelsea defended herself. "I've dreamed of opening my own bakery since I was a kid. You know that."

"I do, but it still scared me. I was afraid you were taking on too much, and I was worried..."

"I'd fail."

Mom shook her head, then shrugged. "Maybe at the beginning. But I've seen how hard you and Ethan are working, and I'm impressed by everything you've set in motion. Your bakery is going to be wonderful."

Chelsea smiled, blinking rapidly so that she didn't cry. This was the most peaceful conversation she and her mother had had in months. "Thank you."

Mom cleared her throat as she bent to put a pod in the dishwasher before starting it. "And then Preston showed up."

Dammit. She should have known the peace couldn't last.

Chelsea would die on the Preston hill. He'd been nothing but amazing since day one, and if her mother criticized him, she would seriously lose her shit.

"When you came home and said you'd found Lennon's father, and he was a professional hockey player, all the anxiety I'd been feeling for a year was amplified. I was terrified that he'd take Lennon from you."

"He would never—" Chelsea started.

"I know he wouldn't."

Wait. *What?*

"There's nothing worse than seeing your daughter crushed by a broken heart. I was so scared you'd be hurt again, but the more I get to know Preston, the more I can see that he won't. He's a good man, Chelsea, and a good father. I understand why you're in love with him."

Chelsea hadn't said that she loved him. At least not aloud, even though she knew she did. "We're not really a couple."

Mom frowned.

"I sleep in the guest room," she confessed, shocked to the core that she was confiding in her mother. "I told him we should keep things between us platonic."

"Why? It's obvious you're both crazy about each other."

"I'm worried if things fail, it will hurt Lennon."

Mom's shoulders drooped. "*I* made you feel that way, didn't I?"

Chelsea shook her head, then lifted one shoulder, because while her mom had planted the seeds of fear, Chelsea had watered them until they took root.

"Are you sure you're holding back because of Lennon?" Mom was reading her like a book today.

"I'm afraid of getting hurt again too. When Rick didn't show up at the wedding, I was devastated, and it took me a long time to pull myself back together. If Preston broke things off, it would be so much worse, and I don't think I'd ever recover."

Mom wiped her hands on the tea towel, crossing the room to her. Placing her arm around Chelsea's shoulders, she gave her a comforting squeeze. "Of course you would. Because you're one of the strongest women I've ever known. Sweetheart, love always comes with risks, but the rewards make them worth it. Preston loves you and Lennon, and I think the three of you will make a wonderful family. Stop letting your fear hold you back."

It was the exact same thing she'd just decided for herself. Hearing her mother say the same lifted the weight that had been crushing her since she found out she was pregnant.

Chelsea didn't bother stemming the tears, letting them flow down her cheeks as her mom embraced her, softly swaying with her in that way moms did. Chelsea did the same thing whenever she was trying to comfort Lennon.

It took a few minutes, but Chelsea finally managed to pull herself together. Once she did, she and Mom worked together to finish all the chores she'd let slide. Then Mom hung out for a little while, cuddling Lennon.

"Well, I'll get out of your hair now," Mom said, handing Lennon back to her. "I still have those errands to run."

"Thanks for all your help, Mom," Chelsea said. "And for the advice. I needed to hear it."

"No. You need to take it," her mom replied sternly, because Ellen Murphy always thought she knew best.

Of course, in this case, she was right.

CHAPTER FOURTEEN

PRESTON UNLOCKED the door to the condo, smiling when the smell of tomatoes and garlic hit his nose. His flight from L.A. had been delayed due to weather, so his early-afternoon return had turned into an evening one.

Which had driven him crazy, because he'd been chomping at the bit to get back to Chelsea and Lennon.

Just a few months ago, this condo had been too quiet and lonely. Now, it was abuzz with sounds and smells and…family.

Lennon was sitting in his bouncy chair, Miss Rachel singing "The Wheels on the Bus," on the television, while Chelsea was in the kitchen cooking. She was singing along loud enough that she hadn't even heard him open the door.

He took a moment to watch her, amused by the way she wiggled her ass as she stirred the sauce, her ponytail swishing back in forth in time with the music. She was already in what she called her comfy clothes, a soft long-sleeved tee and colorful lounge pants.

Lennon's hands were waving wildly, and he was bouncing so hard in his chair, Preston was surprised he hadn't launched himself off it.

Chelsea startled when he closed the door, her surprise morphing to genuine happiness as he walked in.

"You're home!" she said, rushing over to greet him.

After her sleepless night, he'd expected to find her subdued and exhausted, not hopping around like the Energizer Bunny.

Preston tried to hide his shock when she went up on tiptoe, giving him a kiss. A *real* kiss. A real not-just-friends kiss. His surprise was short-lived as he grasped her waist, holding her close so he could draw the kiss out as long as she'd let him.

Jesus.

She wasn't wearing a bra.

That realization had him pulling back, since she was pushing the envelope as far as his control went. "Chels?"

"I really missed you," she said, her dimples appearing as she grinned at him.

"I missed you too. Like fucking crazy."

She rewarded that confession with another kiss, and while this one didn't linger as long, it still packed a punch, her tongue meeting his, sneaking him a taste of the sauce she'd been sampling. There was something different about her tonight...and he liked it.

"I thought you'd be tired. What's all this?" He gestured toward the stove. When he'd called to say he was going to be late, he told her not to worry about dinner, that he would just heat up some soup.

"Spaghetti," she replied. "I've also got a salad ready to go in the fridge. I was just waiting for you to get here before I cooked the noodles and baked the garlic bread."

"You didn't have to go to all this trouble."

She grabbed his hand, leading him to the island that separated the kitchen and the living room. "It was no trouble. Besides, I wanted to do something nice for you. I know it was a long day of travel."

As she spoke, she poured him a glass of red wine, topping up her own. Lifting the glass, she tapped it against his. "Cheers."

"*Salud,*" he added, before taking a sip. Setting the glass down, he walked over to Lennon, bending over to pick him up. Preston's heart melted every time his sweet son greeted him with a wide, gummy smile. "Somebody looks like they're feeling better."

Chelsea dumped noodles into the boiling pot of water and set a timer. "He turned the corner around four a.m."

"Ouch." Preston sat on one of the stools by the island, bouncing Lennon on his knee.

"When you called to say you'd be late, he and I took a long afternoon nap."

That explained why she wasn't exhausted.

The two of them chatted about the game and his flight and the crappy weather in L.A. while she finished cooking. Once she had their meal plated and on the table, Preston moved to join her, touched when she lit the candle in the middle, trying to make the dinner special. Preston kept Lennon on his lap, quite accomplished at eating with one hand these days.

Chelsea asked about his schedule for the rest of the week, then filled him in on what she and Ethan had accomplished at the bakery. To most people, their conversation topics probably sounded mundane, but Preston loved having her here, being able to share even the smallest tidbits about his life.

After dinner, she cleared the table while he carried Lennon to the bedroom, getting him ready for his bath. He and Chelsea had become quite adept with the nightly routine, their roles well established. After the bath, Preston gave Lennon his bottle as she read *Don't Tickle the Shark.*

Rising slowly, Preston placed Lennon in his bassinet, following Chelsea back to the living room. He expected them to claim what he now considered their spots on the couch, but

Chelsea surprised him once again by sitting right next to him, curling against his side.

The delayed flight had given him a lot of time to think this afternoon, as the question that had kept him awake for hours last night still hovered in the background.

It wasn't until he'd walked into this condo and saw Chelsea singing and dancing to that silly children's song that he realized there was no question after all.

He knew exactly what he wanted his future to look like.

Chelsea bent forward, intent on grabbing the remote from the coffee table, but Preston grasped her wrist, pulling it back.

"I need to talk to you about something," he said, aware his tone sounded too serious when alarm flashed in Chelsea's pretty brown eyes.

"Is everything okay? Is it us living here? If it's not working—"

"Jesus, Chels. It's working great. As far as I'm concerned, this is no longer a trial run. I love having you and Lennon here, and this is our home. *Ours*," he stressed.

Her shoulders relaxed. "Thank God. Because I love being here too. Plus, I think moving out has really helped things with me and my mom. She stopped by today."

Usually after a visit with her mother, Chelsea was tense or upset, which didn't jive with her current good mood at all. "And everything went okay?"

"Better than okay." She leaned closer as if revealing some deep dark secret. "You passed the test. In record time too."

Preston tilted his head, slightly confused. Because while he hoped Ellen was starting to thaw toward him, he hadn't gotten the sense she was anywhere close to accepting him yet. "Seriously?"

"She said you're a good man and a good father. Said I was lucky."

Preston didn't even realize exactly how much he wanted her

parents' blessing until that moment. He'd tried to console himself with the knowledge that her dad liked him, and it wasn't unusual for guys—husbands—to have issues with their mothers-in-law.

Now that he'd made the decision regarding his future, he went ahead and embraced all his hopes and dreams.

Because in addition to being a stay-at-home dad, he also wanted to be Chelsea's husband.

"Told you that I had a way with mothers," he said with a wink, loving the way she giggled. So Chelsea's good mood was driven by her mother's visit. Obviously she'd wanted the approval as well, because even though Chelsea and her mother butted heads a lot, he could also see there was genuine love between them.

"Oh my God. I totally shanghaied the conversation. You had something you wanted to talk to me about," Chelsea said, guiding them back to his original statement.

She twisted to face him, waiting expectantly for him to continue.

"I've been thinking about my future," he started, then he amended his words. "Our future."

"Our future?" she asked, with equal parts hope and hesitance.

"I'm retiring from hockey at the end of this season."

"What?"

"It's time for my next big adventure."

She blinked a few times, shaking her head as if fighting to get his words to sink in. Then she asked, "What's the next adventure?"

Preston drew in a deep breath. Then said, "I want to be a stay-at-home dad."

Chelsea's eyes widened, but before she could reply, he forged on.

"I've lived my childhood dream. For fifteen years. I've loved every second I've spent on the ice, but now, I want to live my *adult* dream. The one I didn't even know existed until that first moment when you put Lennon in my arms."

Tears gathered on Chelsea's lashes, but she didn't speak, so he continued.

"It's your turn to live *your* dream, Chelsea. To open the best damn bakery in Baltimore. Hell, the whole country. And you deserve the chance and time to do it right without worrying about Lennon in the care of strangers. I mean, I think—hope—you'd be more comfortable if he was with me, right?"

"Of course, I would," she said so loudly, there wasn't room for doubt. "He loves you and you're amazing with him. It's just...are you sure? I would hate for you to make this decision, then somewhere down the road regret—"

"I'm not going to regret my choice," he interjected. "Never going to regret spending every moment I possibly can with him." Preston paused, then went for broke. "And our other children."

"Other...children?" she whispered.

"We can debate how many later, but I don't want Lennon to be our only child. Siblings are important."

Chelsea shook her head, but again, he could tell she wasn't saying no. Simply trying to shake the words into her brain. "I... I..."

Preston reached out to take her hand in his. "I know I said I'd take things slow."

"This is the opposite of slow," she pointed out. He thought her inability to formulate her thoughts was based on panic, but there was a twinkle in her eye as she made the joke.

"You can still take all the time you need. I'll wait until you catch up, but I want you to know, right now, where I see this thing going between us. I'm in it for the long haul. Forever."

Chelsea was silent for a moment, and damn if for the first time since he'd met her, she hadn't perfected her poker face. He was accustomed to being able to read her emotions through her expressions. His girl was always so open and honest and transparent. But right now…she might as well be a brick wall.

Finally, after too fucking long, she spoke. "I keep waiting for that word *forever* to freak me out," she confessed. "Because Rick promised me that too, and…" She didn't bother finishing her thought. They both knew what that douchebag had done. "But I'm not freaking out."

He grinned at the look of wonder on her face.

"I've struggled with trust ever since my almost-wedding. And it wasn't just my trust in men that was shaken. It was my trust in myself, in my decisions, that was also ruined. Because I honestly thought Rick was the one."

"Do you think *I* could be the one?"

She shook her head, and this time, the gesture was a resounding *no*.

An immediate crushing weight pressed on his chest.

Until she added, "I don't *think* you are. I *know* you are. I've known it since the night of the Ugly Christmas Sweater party. Preston, I'm so in love with you, it makes me dizzy."

Preston released her hand, cupping her adorably dimpled cheeks. "I feel exactly the same way. You and Lennon are everything in the world to me. My family, my life. And I don't want to spend another day away from you."

Chelsea soaked in every amazing, incredible, perfect word he said, letting them drown all her negative thoughts once and for all.

"Break the rule, Preston," she said, her gaze locked on his, her words steady, confident, demanding. "Right now."

She wanted Preston Jacobson so much it hurt. She'd spent the last year dreaming of him, tossing and turning every single night, wishing he was lying next to her. She'd been an idiot, trying to convince herself that they could maintain a platonic relationship.

Chelsea met him halfway as he tugged her into his arms, his kiss rough, hungry, passionate, but far too short.

Until he grasped her hand and pulled her from the couch, the two of them walking to his bedroom. The fact that he remembered to pick up his phone—the nanny cam app open—to carry with them to the bedroom made her love him even more.

The second they entered his room, he shut the door and tossed the phone on a dresser. The next thing Chelsea knew, she was pushed against the door, Preston's lips back on hers.

"I've wanted you for so long," he murmured, his lips brushing hers.

"So long," she agreed, her fingers slipping through his hair, holding it tight enough that he couldn't stop kissing her until she was good and damn ready. Chelsea's vision went gray around the edges due to lack of air, but she still didn't relent.

Preston grabbed one of her legs, lifting it, encouraging her to wrap it around his waist. She groaned when she felt just how hard he was.

He pressed closer, and her head fell back against the door, her pussy clenching with need.

"Please," she gasped when he continued to press against her, lifting her other leg. Only his strength and the door at her back kept her upright as he dry-humped her into a state of delirium.

"Hold on to me," he demanded, giving her only a split second to do so before turning and carrying her across the room to his bed.

Once there, Preston loosened his grip, and she slid down his body until her unsteady feet hit the floor. Not that she needed to worry about falling. Preston's arms held her tightly, allowing her time to regain her balance.

She looked up at his handsome face and tried to remember why she'd ever thought this was a bad idea. Especially when he cupped her cheek, looking at her as if she was the most special person in the world.

His tender look didn't match his dark tone when he took a single step away and said, "Strip."

Chelsea wanted to demand he do the same, but the wholly dominant look in his eyes sent a shiver through her body, leaving her helpless to do anything but obey.

She tugged her T-shirt over her head. She'd thrown on comfy clothes before starting dinner, and she hadn't bothered with a bra.

Chelsea loved Preston's sharp intake of breath as his gaze drifted lower, taking in what she'd just bared. He never failed to make her feel beautiful.

She closed her eyes as his fingers stroked her stretchmarks tenderly before cupping her breasts in his large, calloused hands. Her breath stuttered when he pinched her nipples, lowering his head to take one in his mouth. Chelsea's back arched when he increased the suction, the pleasure of his touch just barely crossing over into painful. Not in a bad way.

Chelsea got the sense he was trying to maintain control, but she didn't want that. Didn't want him holding back. Because *she* couldn't.

"Harder," she demanded.

Preston's eyes lifted, then narrowed. She laid her desires bare, letting him see exactly what she needed.

"It's been a long time," he reminded her.

"I don't care. I don't want sweet or soft."

Preston released one of her breasts, his fist closing around her ponytail, tugging it until he forced her head back, her face lifted to his. "Be careful what you wish for…"

She gave him a sultry smile. "Give me what I want."

"I don't take commands in the bedroom."

"Do it *now*," she taunted.

"Bad girl," he murmured, his teeth nipping at her throat, his grip on her ponytail tight enough that her scalp stung.

Her hands slipped beneath his shirt, her fingers digging into his waist so that she could pull his body against hers. She parted her legs, riding one of his thick, muscular thighs, seeking some much-needed stimulation.

Before she realized his intent, Preston used her ponytail to twist her away from him. "*Very* bad girl," he growled in her ear.

Holy. Fuck.

So sexy.

Holding her in place with that one hand in her hair, he used the other to roughly shove her lounge pants down. When they dropped to the floor, he said, "Kick them off."

She hadn't bothered with panties either, determined that tonight would end up right here.

Preston ran his fingers through her slit—she was embarrassingly wet—before shoving her forward, facedown over his bed.

Chelsea cried out—more in surprise than pain—when he smacked her ass hard. His hand tightened around her ponytail, holding her upper body to the mattress as he peppered her rear end with his sexy spanking.

Chelsea only resisted through the first half dozen strikes before the heat he produced permeated the skin and drove her arousal to dangerous new heights. "More," she demanded.

"Still trying to tell me what to do." Preston's next spank was harder and lower, hitting her upper thigh rather than the fleshy part of her ass.

It hurt, but she couldn't make herself ask him to stop. Hell, she couldn't stop herself from raising her ass to meet every blow.

By the time he released her ponytail, she was a sweaty, panting mess on the bed. And he hadn't even undressed yet.

Chelsea remained facedown as Preston ran his hands on her ass, the tender skin sensitive to his soft touch.

She glanced over her shoulder as he draped himself over her body, giving her a kiss on the cheek.

"Ready to get serious?"

She laughed breathlessly. "That wasn't serious?"

"Just a warmup."

Chelsea flipped over onto her back as he rose, wincing when her ass hit the mattress. She narrowed her eyes when Preston chuckled, but her annoyance didn't last more than a few seconds when he started to undress.

She remained where she was, enjoying the show, biting her lip when he shoved his jeans and boxers off, his erection knocking against his stomach.

Unable to resist, she sat, ignoring her stinging ass to lean forward. Preston groaned when she took his cock in her hand, stroking it a few times before licking precome from the tip.

Preston reached for her ponytail again, but this time he pulled the hair tie out, running his fingers through her curls as they fell around her shoulders.

Chelsea opened her mouth, taking the head of his dick in, pressing her tongue against the spot just beneath it.

Preston hissed in pleasure, his hands cupping the side of her head, pushing her lower, encouraging her to take more.

She let him guide her, fighting against her gag reflex when his dick brushed the back of her throat. Preston loosened the pressure, allowing her to move back, then forward at her own pace. His cock was too long for her to take it all in, so she gripped the base, her hand moving in time with her mouth and lips.

Preston slid his fingers through her hair, then, with one hand, cupped the back of her neck.

Chelsea's pussy clenched, seeking some sort of stimulation. She'd never been so turned on from a blowjob, never considered this act something that could fuel her own desires.

She increased the pace and depth, only managing a dozen more strokes before Preston took a large step back, his cock falling from her mouth. Chelsea started to chase him, moving toward it, but he placed a firm hand on her shoulder, forcing her to remain seated on the bed, just out of reach of her target.

Her eyes flew up to his. "Preston."

"Not this time, Chels. Lay back." He used that grip on her shoulder to ease her to the bed, her own moan falling from her lips when he dropped to his knees on the floor and pushed her legs apart.

Preston didn't give her a second to brace herself before his lips surrounded her clit, sucking hard enough that she saw stars. Her back arched with delight, even as her pussy demanded more.

"Please," she gasped. "More!"

She hoped he understood what that meant, because she was struggling to form any other words. Mercifully, Preston was well-versed in Chelsea's sex language, because he added two fingers to the dance, pushing them deep inside her.

"God!" she cried, quickly covering her mouth with her own hand, not wanting to wake Lennon.

Preston continued to fuck her with his fingers, his lips, teeth, and tongue laying siege to her clit. Chelsea was helpless to hang on as he drove her straight over the cliff.

She cried out again, the sound muffled by her hand.

Preston gave her no chance to recover, adding a third finger to the first two, keeping that maddening yet beautiful pressure against her clit, until the first orgasm blended with the second without a break between.

Her body trembled, the sensations too good. "Too much…"

Preston raised his head, his lips shiny with her juices. "There's no such thing as too much when it comes to you."

She stretched one limp arm toward him. "Please," she whispered.

Preston took mercy on her, rising and climbing onto the bed, caging her beneath him. She reached between their bodies, guiding his rock-hard cock to her opening.

Before she could line them up, he paused. "Birth control?"

Chelsea couldn't help it. She giggled. "I got the shot. Learned my lesson."

Preston chuckled as well, but the sound was cut short when he completed the trip, sinking his cock into her with one slow, relentless thrust.

Once he was seated to the hilt, they froze, their gazes connected as they savored the moment.

"*Finally,*" he said.

At the same time she said, "At last."

They laughed again, as Chelsea marveled over how utterly perfect this man was for her.

"You were made for me," Preston murmured, as if he'd read her mind.

Cupping his beloved cheek, she stroked her thumb over his lower lip. "Take me, Preston. Make me yours. Forever."

Preston retreated until just the head of his cock remained, then he took her on the ride of a lifetime, pounding into her body and giving her everything she needed, everything she wanted, everything she'd ever dreamed of.

Within minutes, she reached the peak again, tumbling head over ass into a climax so hard, it almost hurt. Preston didn't retreat, didn't give way, thrusting, fucking, claiming.

When she came again, he was right there with her, her name rasping from between gritted teeth as his climax shook his body.

"Chelsea! Joy. My Joy."

Chelsea clung to him, the two of them panting and sweaty, but neither ready to part.

"I love you," she said, certain she'd never felt those words so strongly before.

"Love you," Preston offered back, kissing her cheek, her chin, her forehead, before offering her one of his deliciously long, breath-stealing kisses.

With all the words spoken, the dreams shared, the future opening before them, their kisses were less frantic but no less amazing.

Another five minutes passed before Preston pulled away. "Shower?"

She nodded, accepting the hand he proffered. Once again, he grabbed his phone, taking it into the bathroom with them before turning on the water.

They took turns washing each other, both lingering until the steam in the bathroom was thicker than fog. Once they were clean, he pushed her against the tiled wall and made her very, very dirty again.

Turning off the water, Preston stepped out of the shower, grabbing a towel that he used to dry her. Chelsea returned the favor, then they returned to the bedroom. Walking to his dresser, Preston grabbed one of his T-shirts for her and a pair of boxers for himself and they crawled back under the covers.

Wrapped in each other's arms, they talked for hours, excitedly planning their lives together. Their conversation was eventually interrupted by the soft cry of their son, who was clearly hungry.

"Meet you in his room," Preston whispered as he went to get a bottle.

Chelsea crossed the hall to her room—or, well, she supposed now it was officially the nursery, as Preston's room became theirs.

"Hush, my sweetest little angel," she said, as she lifted him from the bassinet. "Daddy's getting your bottle." She smiled as she said those words, recalling all the father/son plans Preston had just shared with her. "You're so lucky," she murmured as she drew back the duvet, claiming her side of the bed.

"Because he has the best mother in the world," Preston said, joining her in the bed. "His life will be filled with happiness, fun…joy."

"Not to mention a big friendly giant."

EPILOGUE

"STILL THINK WE'RE INSANE?" Ethan asked as he hip-bumped her.

"In general? Hell yeah," she replied, mimicking the response he always gave her. "But about this? No way."

Valentine's Day had arrived. The shop had officially opened at eight a.m., and Chelsea was blown away by how many people had walked in from the street. She'd already had to make two more batches of her special heart-shaped cookies, underestimating how popular they would be. Which was insane, because she was certain she'd made way too many to begin with.

Ethan had planned a Grand Opening event, inviting the press as well as quite a few social media influencers, and he was delighted by how many had shown up. The party had begun an hour ago and the place was still hopping.

Mom and Dad were sitting at one of the window tables with Preston's parents, who had flown in from Seattle for the big day.

Preston stood near the display case, holding Lennon, he and several of his teammates who'd come to support her, and they were all stuffing their faces with cupcakes. She'd been touched by how quickly Preston's friends welcomed her into their group.

She smiled at Ainsley and Erika, who both lifted champagne glasses in her direction from across the shop, offering a silent congratulations toast.

Ethan wrapped his arm around her, leaning close. "I can't believe there are no less than ten Stingrays in our bakery right now. Pinch me, Cupcake, because this can't be real."

Chelsea didn't have to be asked twice, pinching Ethan's arm hard enough he yelped, then laughed.

"Okay, okay," he said, lifting his hands in surrender. "It's real."

They watched as McKenna gestured for all the players to squeeze together for a photo.

"McKenna said she'd post the pics on the team's social media. She likes the idea of showcasing the Stingrays supporting a new local business. How huge is that?" Ethan asked.

"Huge," Chelsea agreed.

Preston gestured for her to come over, so she and Ethan joined the guys, posing in the next few photos with them. Ethan was trying to play it cool, but she knew her best friend well enough to know he was dying inside, thrilled to be standing in his own store with his hockey heroes.

Preston wrapped his arm around her shoulders as she reached for Lennon, snuggling their sweet son, who was taking in all the action with great interest.

"Best fucking cupcake ever," Victor said. "Congratulations, Chelsea."

"Thanks," she said, grinning. Preston had warned her about his teammate's love of the F-word, and he hadn't exaggerated.

Preston shifted her until she and Lennon stood in front of him so that he could wrap his arms around both of them.

Erika and Ainsley joined their group, stepping next to their guys.

Tank put his hands up and took a couple steps back, acting as if they all had cooties. "I gotta keep my distance in case all this falling-in-love shit is contagious."

"What's wrong with falling in love?" Preston asked.

"Nothing. For you guys. But you'll never catching me settling down. There are too many delicious fish in the sea."

Chelsea turned her head toward Preston. "Did he just compare women to fish?" she joked, both of them recalling her asking the same question of Preston the night they met.

Preston chuckled and winked.

"Back me up on this, Rook," Tank insisted.

"I can see the benefits to having a girlfriend…if she's the right one." Rookie stole a glance at Allyson, who was too focused on the huge slice of cheesecake she was shoveling in her face to even notice.

Chelsea and Ethan exchanged a glance, both rolling their eyes in amusement before Preston took Lennon out of her arms, handing him to Ethan.

She gave Preston a curious look but followed his lead when he grasped her hand and pulled her away from the crowd and back into the kitchen.

"I know we're taking things slow," he started.

Chelsea snorted at their now familiar joke. Everything between them had been a whirlwind. An amazing, wonderful, perfect whirlwind.

"But I thought today might be a good day to speed things up."

Before Chelsea could question how, Preston dropped down to one knee, an open ring box—with the biggest, most beautiful diamond ring she'd ever seen—resting on his palm.

"Chelsea, Joy, will you—"

"Yes! Oh my God, yes."

"So much for the speech I prepared." Preston laughed as he slid the ring onto her finger. It was a perfect fit.

"You can say it to me later. In bed." Chelsea stared at the ring on her finger, overcome with happiness. "I can't believe this. The day was already perfect enough, and then you just blew it out of the water!"

While Preston hadn't formally announced his retirement from hockey yet, he'd let his coach and teammates know. In just a few months, he was starting his new gig as full-time dad.

"Felt right to propose to you here," Preston said. "After all, this was where I found you and Lennon."

"Fate led you straight to us," she said, kissing him on the cheek.

He cupped her face, smiling down at her, whispering, "Serendipity."

Be sure to check out the entire Stingrays Hockey series!

Restraint

Resist

Rematch

Release

Reclaim

Remain

Reaction

Return

And meet some former Stingrays players in these books!

Making His Play

Wild and Wicked

ABOUT THE AUTHOR

Virginia native Mari Carr is a New York Times and USA TODAY bestseller of contemporary romance novels. With over three million copies of her books sold, Mari was the winner of the Romance Writers of America's Passionate Plume award for her novella, Erotic Research. She has over a hundred published works, including her popular Wild Irish and Italian Stallions books, along with the Trinity Masters series she writes with Lila Dubois.

Follow Mari:
www.maricarr.com
mari@maricarr.com

Join her newsletter so you don't miss new releases and for exclusive subscriber-only content.